“SO IF BLUE SPRINGS IS A
LITTLE FAR
ELLA SAID,
YOU T

“Ah.” He leaned [illegible] to his lips, whispered, “It’s a sec[illegible]

Ella feigned a look of grave seriousness. “In that case, you’d best not be telling me, or anyone else, your business. Otherwise it won’t be a secret any longer.”

“Quite true. The best way for people to keep a secret is if they don’t know it.”

The dirt path ended, and they were on the main road. Ella stopped walking and glanced both ways to see if anyone was coming. “This is the main road to town.” She pointed to the left. “Walk about a quarter mile or so, past those three houses, and you’ll be in the center of town.” While facing him, she took a few steps backward. Her house was the second house in the other direction, just after the unpaved lane that led away from town. “I wish you success in your business . . .” She paused. He had never properly introduced himself. “I’m sorry, I never did catch your name.”

He gave her a broad grin. “That’s because I didn’t tell you.”

“Is that part of your secret?” she asked.

Also by Sarah Price

Belle: An Amish Retelling of Beauty and the Beast

Published by Kensington Publishing Corporation

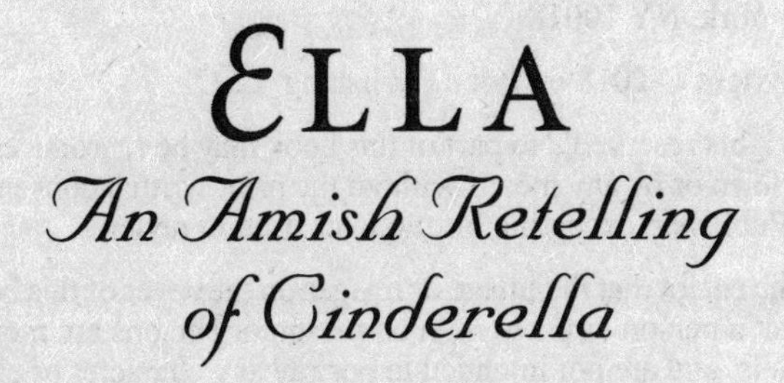
ELLA
An Amish Retelling
of Cinderella

SARAH PRICE

ZEBRA BOOKS
KENSINGTON PUBLISHING CORP.
http://www.kensingtonbooks.com

ZEBRA BOOKS are published by

Kensington Publishing Corp.
119 West 40th Street
New York, NY 10018

First Printing: June 2018
ISBN-13: 978-1-4201-4506-9
ISBN-10: 1-4201-4506-1

eISBN-13: 978-1-4201-4507-6
eISBN-10: 1-4201-4507-X

10 9 8 7 6 5 4 3 2 1

Printed in the United States of America

Prologue

Ella stared out the window, her forehead pressed against the glass as she waited for her father's buggy to pull through the open gate. She wore her favorite blue dress with her freshly washed black apron tied at the waist. In anticipation of meeting her future stepmother, she had even bleached and ironed her prayer *kapp*.

Three years had passed since her mother had died. During that time, Ella and her father had lived alone in the small white house in the center of Echo Creek, just down the road from the general store that her father owned. And while Ella was perfectly content, she had known for a while that her father was lonely.

Only a few days earlier, her father had sat her down for a serious talk. Ella had felt extremely grown up. She could remember when her parents had had serious talks—talks that she was not allowed to hear. Sometimes those talks had been about the general store. Other times, it was about things related to the annual Council Meeting that was held each October.

"Ella, it's been a long time since your *maem* passed

away," her father had started. "And it's well past time that I remarry."

He looked uncomfortable as he spoke, tugging at his beard and avoiding her blue eyes. Ella wondered if *this* serious talk had anything to do with the serious talks her father had recently had with their church district's bishop and deacon.

After clearing his throat and tugging once again at his beard, he finally met her gaze. "I want you to understand, Ella, that no one will ever replace your *maem.* But you'll be finishing school this year, and you need a new *muder* to help you learn things. Woman things."

Ella gave him a soft smile.

"Cooking. Gardening. Canning. Sewing. I can't teach you those things, even if I did have spare time from tending the store."

"It's okay, Daed," Ella said, sounding much older than her thirteen years.

But he wasn't finished.

"Now, Bishop has introduced me to a woman from Liberty Falls." His eyes darted away from hers. "A widow. Linda has two *dochders* just a little older than you. She's agreed to join our family."

For a moment, Ella's heart began to sink. She had always suspected that her father would remarry. Most Amish men did. Yet this news was surprising to her. After all, it was one thing to have a stepmother—but stepsisters, too?

"I've invited them to visit this Sunday after worship. So that you can get to know them."

Ella blinked. "What are they like?" she asked. "My new *schwesters*?"

Her father had merely stared at her with a blank expression. And that was when Ella had realized the visit on Sunday was not just for her to get to know Linda and her daughters, but also for her father to do the same.

Now, as Ella waited for their arrival, she kept repeating the words her mother had told her just before she died: *Be kind and good, no matter what happens, for God has a plan for you.* While Ella didn't quite fancy the idea of sharing her father and their home with three strangers, she certainly would follow her mother's sage advice and make them feel welcome.

She heard the sound of an approaching horse and buggy. Taking a deep breath, Ella moved away from the window and hurried to the front door. *Be kind and good . . .* She said a quick prayer for God to help guide her tongue, and then she stepped outside onto the porch to greet them with a smile and a wave.

The front window of the buggy was open, and Ella saw her father wave back. The woman seated beside him, however, did not. Ella shielded her eyes from the bright September sun. She could barely make out the woman's features. Perhaps Linda *had* waved, and Ella hadn't seen it? Or perhaps Linda was as nervous as Ella?

As her father stopped the horse in the driveway along the side of the house, Ella hurried down the porch steps and followed the gravel path toward them.

Her father slid open the buggy door and bounded out, grinning at Ella with a look of joy on his face that she hadn't seen in years.

"Ella! *Kum* and meet your new *muder.*"

Stepmother, Ella thought before her own mother's words echoed in her head. With a forced smile and determination to make her mother proud, Ella stepped forward as her father helped Linda down from the buggy.

For a moment, Linda stood there with her back to Ella. She seemed to be waiting for her daughters to climb over the folded-down seat, rather than turning to meet her soon-to-be stepdaughter.

Her father didn't appear to notice.

"Hello, Linda," Ella said, hating how small her voice sounded.

When the woman turned around, Ella fought the urge to catch her breath.

Linda was a tall woman; taller than Ella's father. And she was robust in her build. Her dark, steely eyes stared at Ella, narrowing just a little as she studied the young woman standing before her. Her mouth pursed, and little lines creased her lips.

"My goodness, John," she said, her voice almost sounding like a cat purring. "You never mentioned that your *dochder* is so"—her eyes trailed Ella from head to foot—"pretty."

Ella's father gave a nervous laugh. "I suppose I focus more on her inner beauty than her outer."

Ella blushed and stared at the ground.

"Me first!"

"No, Anna! I'm older!"

"I'm closer, Drusilla!"

Linda turned toward the buggy, her movement slow and fluid, as if it were calculated and not in response to her two daughters fighting in the back of the buggy. "Girls. Please," she cooed. "Come and meet your *schwester.*"

The buggy jostled and eventually two young girls emerged. They stood beside their mother, one on either side of her. Ella gave them a quick assessment and smiled.

Neither Drusilla nor Anna returned the gesture.

The first thing Ella observed was that both daughters had inherited their mother's big bones. And while they weren't necessarily obese, they were far too heavy for girls of such a young age. Ella wondered if they ate poorly or simply didn't work around their house.

"I'm Ella," she said at last, breaking the silence.

"She has a prettier dress than I do," said the shorter of the two girls.

"Anna. Please."

"Is this going to be our new home? It's much smaller than where we live now," complained the other girl.

"Drusilla, mind your manners."

Ella glanced at her father, but he was tending to the horse.

"Perhaps you'd like to come inside?" Ella gestured toward the front door. "I've made some meadow tea and cookies."

Linda stared at her as she nudged her daughters toward the house. "Isn't that sweet, girls? Your new sister has made cookies."

Anna glanced up at her mother. "She's not our new *schwester* yet."

Linda gave a light laugh as if to mask her daughter's impertinence. "Well, she *will* be in just a few weeks, so go along, girls. Get to know her and our new home."

Reluctantly, Anna and Drusilla walked past Ella and headed into the house. Ella was about to follow them when she felt a hand on her arm. Surprised, she turned around to face Linda.

"They're nervous," Linda said in a soft voice. "Forgive

their ill manners. A lot has happened in the past year . . . losing their *daed*, and now their home."

Ella digested what Linda had just told her. For a moment, she put herself in Anna and Drusilla's shoes. Oh, she knew the pain of losing a parent. Whether one year or three, the pain never lessened. She could truly empathize with how distressing all of this must be to Linda's daughters.

"I understand," she said at last. "Truly I do. And I promise to do what I can to help make them feel welcome and at home."

Linda reached out to pat Ella's cheek. "Not only pretty, but kind."

To Ella, her words and gesture sounded more patronizing than genuinely sincere. As soon as she thought that, Ella scolded herself, remembering that the loss of Linda's husband and home must be impacting Linda just as much as her daughters.

"Now hurry along, Ella." Linda shooed her away, a forced smile on her lips. She glanced over her shoulder at Ella's father and squared her shoulders. "We've adult matters to discuss, so make certain to keep the girls busy."

It wasn't a request but a directive. No "please." No "thank you." Just a fake smile and marching orders to disappear.

As Ella hurried along the walkway toward the front door, there was one thing she knew for sure and certain. Her father had been correct when he had told her no one would ever replace her mother. And even if someone might come close, Ella knew that "someone" was *not* Linda, for her soon-to-be stepmother was everything that her mother was not.

Chapter One

"Oh, these mice!"

Ella looked up at the sound of her stepmother's voice. Linda had just emerged through the cellar door, her arms laden with a dusty cardboard box of canning jars.

"Honestly, Ella!" Linda scowled at her stepdaughter as she kicked the basement door shut with her foot. "I won't go down there anymore if you cannot get rid of those dirty little creatures!"

Ella lowered her head so her stepmother couldn't see that she smiled to herself. "I'm sorry, Maem." It wasn't a lie, although if her stepmother had inquired as to what, exactly, Ella was sorry about, she'd be surprised to learn that Ella was sorry about having no intentions of getting rid of the mice.

Dropping the box onto the kitchen table, Linda brushed some dust from her sleeves. "You should be! I don't know why you fight me so on mousetraps!"

Ella knew better than to reply. It was an argument that was many years old and not worthy of rehashing. The truth was that Ella thought mousetraps were inhumane. And the sticky pad traps? Even worse. Whenever her stepmother brought home mouse poison, Ella would sneak down in the early morning hours to throw it away. After all, even mice were God's creatures and had a role in the world, even if her stepmother thought otherwise.

"I want that basement cleaned, Ella." Linda frowned, the deep-set wrinkles in her forehead making her look older than her fifty years. "It's full of cobwebs and dirt. I don't know how you can stand it."

It wasn't as though Ella went down there every day, but she didn't want to point that out to her stepmother. Besides, she knew that the basement wasn't half as bad as Linda claimed. Long ago, Ella had learned that sometimes her stepmother just needed something to complain about. Clearly, today was one of those days.

"I'll do it later," she said, even though, deep down, Ella knew that she probably wouldn't be able to get to it. After all, today was Saturday, and she needed to finish the laundry. Tomorrow was a worship Sunday, and she needed to make certain that everyone's worship clothes were clean and pressed. While she always washed the family's Sunday dresses and aprons on the Monday following service, leaving them hanging on a hook in each person's room, Ella never knew what her stepsisters might have done since then: dropped them on the floor, pushed other dresses into them, carelessly spilled something on them . . .

Tending to the clothes worn for worship always took a long time.

And, of course, she needed to finish baking the bread that she had already started. Fifteen loaves of it.

Every day she made bread for her stepmother to sell at the store. Afterward, Ella would clean the bathrooms and kitchen floor, letting the sweet, yeasty smell of the bread fill the house while she worked. And then, of course, she needed to make supper. But, if time permitted, Ella would try to get to cleaning the basement so that her stepmother would have no complaints when she returned from working at the general store that evening.

No evening was enjoyable if Linda had reason to complain, that was for sure and certain.

Linda walked around the kitchen table and quickly washed her hands in the sink. "When Drusilla and Anna awake, make certain they eat breakfast before you send them to the store to help me. Otherwise they'll be snacking on inventory all day!"

Glancing at the clock, Ella saw that it was seven thirty. She had already been up for over an hour and was sorting the laundry by color. Whites would get washed in hot water, and colors in cool. While many Amish women disliked washing clothes in the old diesel-powered machines, Ella didn't mind. There was something relaxing about ridding the clothes of dirt, almost as if fresh clothes gave the wearer a second chance.

And her sisters definitely could benefit from that.

"I will, Maem."

Linda reached up to touch the sides of her graying hair that poked out from beneath her prayer *kapp*. "And send them with a nice dinner meal for the three of us. Something hot today, I think." She leaned down and looked out the window. "*Ja*, perhaps chicken and mashed potatoes."

The request made Ella pause as she mentally added it to her long list of chores. How would she be able to cook that in the short period of time between now and when her stepsisters needed to get to the store?

"And not so much pepper on the chicken," her stepmother scolded. "Why, I near choked to death on your last batch."

Linda smoothed down the front of her dark burgundy dress and reached for her purse. Without so much as a goodbye, she swept from the room, loudly shutting the door behind herself.

Picking up the basket of whites, Ella settled it on her hip and carried it to the back porch, where the washer and wringer dryer were located. She set the basket onto a bench and hurried down the three steps to where the diesel engine was. Within minutes, she had it started and hot water was pouring into the washer.

While she waited for it to fill, Ella glanced over to the bird feeders she kept at the corner of the property near the sunflower patch growing there. She knew the birds loved her sunflowers, which stretched from the end of the house all the way to the white picket fence in front of the house. When people walked to town, they always paused to stare at the giant sunflowers and to admire the collection of birds that lingered nearby to pluck the seeds growing from their big, friendly heads. But September was almost upon them, and with that, the end of summer. Soon the birds would migrate south, the sunflowers would droop and dry up, and the leaves from the trees would flutter to the ground—the end of yet another season in Echo Creek.

It had been a quiet summer, at least for Ella. Between managing the garden and tending to the house, she had more than enough work cut out for her. Her workload was so great that she hadn't even attended many of the youth gatherings or singings.

But that would change once autumn arrived.

At least she hoped so.

"Ella? Ella, where are you?"

She sighed. Drusilla was in the kitchen. "Out here, Dru. Washing clothes."

The door burst open and her oldest sister emerged, her long hair hanging down her back. "I can't find my brush. Where's my brush? Did you put it somewhere?" It wasn't so much a question as an accusation.

"*Ja*, I did," Ella replied, matching Drusilla's harsh tone with a congenial and light one. "In the bathroom drawer, where it belongs."

"Oh! Don't get sassy with me!" Drusilla snapped before promptly disappearing back through the door.

Ella glanced at the washer and decided she had time to investigate why Drusilla was in such a frazzled state. She followed her sister's footsteps and, after her eyes adjusted to the dim light in the kitchen, watched Drusilla fuss with her mousy-colored hair in the downstairs bathroom that everyone shared.

"Something important happening today?" Ella asked.

Tossing a quick look over her shoulder, Drusilla raised an eyebrow. "Why?"

"You seem rather . . ."

Ella searched for the appropriate word. She certainly didn't want to insult Drusilla, who had almost as hot a temper as Linda.

". . . flustered."

"Oh, you silly goose!" Drusilla pursed her lips and frowned. "Mind your own business!" And with that,

Drusilla used her bare foot to kick the bathroom door so that it slammed in Ella's face.

The sound of footsteps on the wooden stairs announced that Anna, too, was awake.

"I'll tell you, Ella," Anna said with a mischievous smile. She was one year younger than Drusilla and always seemed to be cheerleading for her older sister. But there were occasional moments when Drusilla wasn't around that Anna almost behaved like a real sister. Almost. "There's a new vendor coming to the general store today. From Liberty Falls! Drusilla is hoping he will be young and unmarried."

From behind the closed door, the muffled voice of Drusilla could be heard crying out, "Anna! You hush now!"

But Anna paid her no attention. "I'm hoping that, too." She giggled, her shoulders lifting up to her ears as she did.

The bathroom door flew open and Drusilla stood there, hands on her hips, glaring at her sister. "Now, Anna, gossip is akin to sin!"

"Then I'll confess to the bishop," Anna quickly retorted.

Ella knew that this conversation would end up with her two sisters having a heated argument, so she did what she always did: changed the subject. "What does the vendor sell?" She was genuinely curious, as she always liked to know what new products Linda purchased to resell at what used to be her father's store. For, while Troyers' General Store still bore his name, the Troyer in charge was no longer her father but her stepmother.

"What does he sell?" Anna repeated the question and gave her an incredulous look. "How should I know?"

Drusilla marched out of the bathroom, apparently satisfied with her hair. She had placed her prayer *kapp* on the back of her head and secured it with a single straight pin to a thin elastic band that she wore around the top of her head. "Clocks. He makes and distributes clocks."

Anna made a face. "Clocks? How unromantic!"

But Ella was intrigued. "Are they small ones or big ones? Do they sit on tables or hang on the walls?"

"Aren't you the inquisitive one?" Drusilla said hotly. "Perhaps *you* should be working at the store instead of us." She paused and put her finger to her lips, as if thinking. "Oh, wait, you can't because you have too much to do around here." And with that, Drusilla moved her hand and knocked the bowl of flour onto the floor. "Oops. Sorry about that."

Anna laughed.

But Ella reacted with neither a grimace nor a harsh word. Instead, she ignored Drusilla's unkind act and said a quick little prayer for God to forgive her sister. In the past six years, Ella had grown used to her sisters' mean-spirited ways. She forgave them every day at least seven times seventy, just as the Bible told her to do. Sometimes she wondered if she forgave them seven times seventy times seventy-seven, especially now, since her father had passed away unexpectedly the previous year.

"Now, I'd like some eggs for breakfast. Do you think you can manage that without making a mess of your kitchen?" The mocking tone in Drusilla's voice made Ella say the second prayer of the day for her sister.

"Mayhaps one of these days you might get up early enough to cook breakfast yourself."

Drusilla spun around and gave her a stern look.

"My word! It seems you woke up on the sassy side of bed today, Ella."

Ella sighed, her shoulders slumping just a little. She hadn't meant to sound impudent. The truth was that all of the household chores fell on her shoulders, with Drusilla and Anna doing less and less every day. For so many years, it had been Ella doing all of the cooking, all of the cleaning, all of the everything!

While she knew that her two stepsisters worked many hours at the store, especially since Ella's father died, she also knew that their continual shirking of responsibilities in the home was a shortsighted plan. No Amish man would accept a wife who behaved in such a manner. And word traveled fast along the Amish grapevine. Perhaps that was why neither one of them had any serious suitors vying for their attentions. Well, at least not suitors that Drusilla and Anna felt were worthy *of* their attention, anyway—with the exception of Timothy Miller, who had brought Drusilla home from a singing recently, which was all the attention Drusilla needed. For two weeks, she had bragged about that buggy ride, and ever since then, she often disappeared from the store to visit someone—anyone!—who lived near the Miller farm, clearly hoping that Timothy might offer her a ride home.

"What was that sigh for?" Drusilla snapped.

Ella knelt down and began to clean up the flour on the floor. The more she tried to sweep it into a dust pan, the more the white cloud spread on the linoleum. "Oh, Drusilla. How will you ever feed your family if you don't know how to cook or bake? Isn't it time you learned?"

But Drusilla merely laughed at her. "Mayhaps I'll always have *you* around to do it for me, Ella. After all,

I don't see many young men tossing pebbles at *your* window at night."

Ella was thankful that her back was to Drusilla so that her stepsister couldn't see the horrified expression on her face. Ella had several dreams for her future, but not one of them included living with either Drusilla or Anna, that was for sure and certain.

But Anna appeared oblivious to Ella's aversion toward Drusilla's comment and delighted with her sister's announcement about the pebble. "Oh, Dru! Was that the noise I heard on Saturday night?"

Ella looked up, startled at this news. Had someone come calling on Drusilla at last? She hadn't heard a buggy approach, nor had she heard any noises. She couldn't imagine who it might have been, for most of the young men in Echo Creek were already walking out with young women. Unless, of course, it was one of the men who lived farther from town. Despite being curious, Ella refused to ask any questions, for she knew that was exactly what Drusilla wanted her to do.

Anna, however, grabbed her sister's arm and demanded more information. "Who came calling on you?"

"I'll never tell." But the smug look on Drusilla's face said otherwise. Ella had no doubt that Drusilla would share her little secret with Anna the moment they were out of the house.

Sitting back on her heels, Ella placed her hands on her lap, not caring that the flour left white palm prints on the black fabric. "Well, it will be a short-lived romance if he starves to death during the first month of your marriage," she quipped.

Drusilla glared at her one last time, stomped her foot, and promptly turned to leave the kitchen, Anna in tow.

"What about your breakfast?" Ella called out.

"I'd rather starve with my future husband than have *you* cook for me!" Drusilla shouted over her shoulder as she dragged her sister out the door.

"You forgot to take the bread," she called after them, but knew that neither one of them would respond. She sighed, knowing that she'd have to box up the loaves and carry them to the store by herself. Just another chore added to her already long list for the day.

Still, as quiet descended upon the house, Ella tried not to feel pleased with herself. She suspected that, if the church leaders knew about her behavior, they would reprimand her for taunting Drusilla. They'd most likely have her reflect long and hard on her inability to behave prudently and hold her tongue. However, Ella also knew that the church leaders would disapprove even more of how her stepmother and stepsisters treated her.

It had started slowly, shortly after her father had married Linda. Drusilla and Anna were constantly excused from certain chores, due to their delicate nature or tendency toward having headaches. Ironically, after Ella's father died, both of her stepsisters seemed to suddenly have much stronger constitutions, and neither experienced another headache again.

But they refused to work around the house, which meant that Ella was left doing everything. The more chores Ella did, the more they seemed to expect of her. While Ella wasn't one to run to the church leaders, she knew that the time for change was coming. She felt it in her bones and sensed it with each passing day. Simply put, Ella knew she couldn't take much more of it. However, she also knew that her increasing aversion to the unfair treatment was not an excuse for her to behave in less than a perfect Christian spirit.

"Please, Lord," she prayed aloud, "I know that you have plans for me, that there is a time for everything, and that I prove my faith by rejoicing even when distressed by the trials of life set before me. Please forgive me for my sharpness of tongue and lack of patience with my family."

Chapter Two

Later that afternoon, the sun was beating down on Ella's back as she knelt in the dirt, weeding the family's vegetable garden. Nearby was a large basket, filled to the brim with juicy red tomatoes and vibrant green cucumbers. She didn't remember having planted so many cucumbers, but the vines seemed to have multiplied overnight. They were overtaking the rest of the garden, strangling the other plants. Try as she might to keep cutting them back, the cucumbers continued to grow.

At least we'll have plenty of pickles for the winter, she thought.

Just as she was plucking the last of them, she heard the voices of her sisters, and then the creak of the gate, announcing their arrival.

Ella knelt back on her heels and wiped the sweat from her brow, her eyes staring down the gravel driveway as she waited for them to appear on the walkway.

"I can't believe that this is happening!" It was Drusilla's voice.

Anna mirrored her sister's sentiment.

They stomped up the porch steps, ignoring Ella as

they slammed the front door behind them. It was only a few minutes later when Linda appeared.

Ella stood up and wiped her hands on her apron. "Everything going well?"

"*Nee,* Ella!" Linda snapped. "It's not going well at all." She, too, stomped up the porch steps and disappeared into the house.

With a mixture of curiosity and concern, Ella decided to follow them so that she could learn whatever news seemed so upsetting to her family.

Inside the house, all three of them sat at the kitchen table, the two girls slumped over with their heads resting on their hands. They looked miserable. Linda appeared equally distraught, but instead of staring at nothing, she was reviewing some information on a piece of paper and shaking her head.

Something must be troubling them indeed.

Without being asked, Ella hurried to the refrigerator and pulled out a pitcher of fresh mint tea. She poured three glasses and carried them to the table. "Is there anything I can do to help?" She set down the glasses and sat beside Drusilla.

"Not unless you have fifty thousand dollars stashed in your dresser." Drusilla's sharp tone was almost as strong as her sarcasm.

Fifty thousand dollars? Ella wondered what her stepsister was talking about.

"Please, Drusilla." Linda rolled her eyes and shook her head. "Our business need not be aired to everyone!"

Ella frowned. She wasn't "everyone." She was family. Even more importantly, she was the only child of the man who had started that store. If anyone should know what was going on, Ella knew it was she.

Clearly her stepmother felt otherwise.

After so many years, Ella wondered why she hadn't gotten used to the hurtful comments from her stepmother. The truth was that words stung harder than a pinch or a slap. Still, she managed to ignore the slight from her stepmother's comment, and she dared to ask, "Has something happened at the store, then?"

"*Ja*, Ella! If you must know, something *has* happened at the store!" Linda mimicked Ella's concerned tone of voice. "Sales are down for the year, and I've only just learned that we have unpaid taxes! From last year and the year before!" Linda tossed the paper onto the table. It fluttered and landed in the middle, too far away for Ella to reach it without leaning over Drusilla, which, given the current temperature in the room, didn't seem like a good idea.

"Taxes?" she asked instead.

Linda waved her hand at the paper in disgust. "Taxes. You know. As in paying taxes to those *Englischers* and their government!" Clearly she didn't like that idea one bit.

Aha. Now Ella understood. Even without reaching for the letter, she suspected it was from the Internal Revenue Service. "Daed always paid his taxes on time." She paused, realizing that if the unpaid bills were from the previous year, Linda hadn't paid them since her father's passing. And that meant that she was also late on the quarterly taxes for the current year.

"Oh. I see," Ella whispered.

Linda narrowed her eyes and glared at her, which was confirmation enough for Ella that she was correct. Linda had, indeed, neglected to stay on top of paying the government their fair share. And that certainly did not bode well.

"Surely Irvin Landis helped you with the taxes?" Ella asked.

"Who?" Linda, Drusilla, and Anna asked at the same time.

"Irvin Landis, the Mennonite from Liberty Falls," Ella replied. Being much larger than their town, Liberty Falls was where many of the Echo Creek Amish traveled for services and goods that were not sold locally. However, from the blank looks on everyone's face, she quickly realized that they had no idea whom she was talking about "The accountant? He always helped advise Daed about financial matters," she explained. "And prepared his taxes."

Once again, Linda waved her hand, this time at Ella as if she spoke nonsense. "Oh, *that* man."

There was a glimmer of hope. "So you met with him?" Ella asked.

"*Nee*, I did not," Linda said with an air of superiority. "I don't need help from a *Mennonite.* In fact, I don't need help at all." She lifted her hand and brushed her fingers down the side of her cheek, a supercilious gesture. "I happened to be very good with numbers. I was the best math student in my class, I'll have you know."

Oh help, Ella thought, fighting the urge to cover her eyes with her hand and shake her head in disbelief. Was her stepmother truly referencing her education from forty-plus years ago? And, since the Amish did not continue formal education past the eighth grade, Ella suspected that Linda's tax situation wasn't going to end well if she didn't get any help from a professional accountant.

"We've no choice but to raise prices at the store." Linda sighed. "Again."

That made no sense to Ella. And it wasn't the first

time that Linda had raised prices. In fact, Ella had heard grumbles from her friends Belle and Sadie regarding the ever-increasing prices at the Troyers' General Store. The Amish of Echo Creek were not wealthy by any stretch of the imagination. In fact, many of the Amish struggled to make ends meet. They lived off the land as much as they could, but they also had to adhere to strict financial budgets.

"Maem," Ella started slowly, hoping her tone displayed the respect she did not particularly feel. "Mayhaps you should rethink that and consider doing the opposite."

"The opposite?" With a short laugh escaping her lips, she gave Ella an incredulous look. "What little you know of business!"

That comment smarted. But Ella marched forward. "It's supply and demand. That's what Daed always said. When there is a high supply and low demand, you lower prices. And right now that seems to be the case at the store. You raised them just two months ago, *ja*? And sales have declined. Try the opposite and see how it goes."

"Oh, Ella! You know *nothing* about profit margins!" Linda glanced at Drusilla, who snickered as if on cue. "Why, it's simple, really. If you lower prices, you make less profit! Everyone knows that!"

Ella wished that her stepmother would listen to her. Not just let her speak, which was rare enough, but actually stop and hear what she was saying. "But, Maem, if you sell more items because of the lower prices, you make up the profit by moving inventory and satisfying the customers."

"Enough, Ella." The stern tone of her voice made it

clear that Linda was not interested in hearing any more of Ella's ideas.

It was always that way. Linda knew best and did what she wanted. While Ella's father had been alive, Linda had often argued with him about how he ran the store. However, when he disagreed with her suggestions, which was most of the time, he hadn't been one to compromise just to soothe a bruised ego.

And the store had been more than profitable.

Once her father passed away, Linda had wasted no time in reorganizing the store. She shut it down for a week, something that most people thought was due to her husband's death. But Linda had had other plans. After the funeral service and burial, Linda had thrown herself right into the store, implementing idea after idea that seemed to have been fermenting during their marriage.

Ella had worried that her stepmother was attempting to avoid mourning, but she quickly realized that Linda was simply moving on, and a bit too fast, for some people's taste.

A week after Ella's father died, Linda reopened Troyers' General Store. Everything was rearranged and the prices had increased. Everyone in the town mumbled about the change. And then Linda began introducing new inventory—items that weren't normally found in an Amish general store. When that, too, didn't go over very well, Linda began raising prices again.

And she refused to support some of the community members. In fact, just that summer, Linda had refused to carry a new wood-burning grill created by Melvin Beiler, the father of Ella's friend Belle. That was unfortunate for Linda, as the grill had taken off, becoming an amazing success among the *Englischers*, and the Beiler family had seen a change of fortune.

Ella sighed. There was simply no talking sense into her stepmother.

"What happened with that vendor, the clock maker?" Drusilla asked. "Did he stop by today?"

Linda made a scoffing noise in her throat. "Oh, *ja*, sure he did. Just when I received this letter about the taxes. I asked him to come back another day."

Oh help! Ella thought. She could only imagine her stepmother's reaction to the letter—probably ranting and raving!—just as a new potential vendor walked into the store. Surely he had overheard Linda and knew there were money issues.

"So what'll happen when you meet with him, then?" Drusilla asked.

Drusilla's questions caught Ella off guard. Hadn't Drusilla been working at the store all day? Or had she, once again, snuck off to go visit with Timothy Miller?

"I told him to come back next week to discuss the matter further."

Ella wondered what was so difficult to discuss. With only one general store in Echo Creek, it would be wise to offer clocks . . . if they were of good quality, of course. In fact, if her stepmother had asked *her* for advice, she would have recommended keeping a sample of several different models on display and letting people order them, thus eliminating the need to keep an inventory in the storeroom.

But Linda never asked *her* for advice, and Ella knew better than to offer it.

With a heavy sigh, Linda drank her tea and set down the empty glass on the kitchen table. "Reckon I'll retire early tonight," she said, even though the sun had not fully set in the sky and Ella had supper warming on the stove top. "Need to figure out how to pay these taxes. Seems like a bank loan is the only option left."

Ella cringed. Her father had worked so hard to ensure that they lived a life free and clear of debt. The house was paid for, the store building was paid for, and his inventory was paid for. He always claimed that it was better to owe money to no man, even if that meant hard work and sacrifice.

Clearly Linda had never been listening when her father said that.

"A bank loan?" Ella blurted out. "That can't be the answer, Maem!"

"Oh, what would you know of such things?" Linda snapped at her.

The criticism chafed, but Ella persisted. "If you aren't making money now, you'll only owe more money to the banks, that's all. And that's if you can even *get* a loan."

"Of course I can get a loan!" Linda's expression said it all: she thought Ella was speaking absurdities. "Why, I'm the only general store in town. Where else will people purchase their goods? From Liberty Falls?" she asked as she stood up. "No one will travel that far, for sure and certain!"

Ella wished she had the courage to remind Linda that Melvin Beiler had done that very thing: taken his business to Liberty Falls when Linda had refused to sell his newly designed cooking grills. Had she been more forward thinking, she could have been an exclusive distributor of the product and made enough money to cover any losses from the rest of the store.

But she had turned him away.

"Perhaps someone else will open a store."

Linda whirled around and glared at her. "There isn't room in town for two general stores!"

And *that* was exactly Ella's point. The people needed to buy their dry goods from somewhere, and if Linda didn't lower prices, people would go elsewhere. It wouldn't be long before Linda might lose all of her customers to Liberty Falls or, even worse, unconsciously invited competition into the town. "Either way, you will keep losing business if you don't lower prices."

"Why, Ella! You'd have me give half of the store away with little to no profit. Then where would we be?" A noise that sounded like a cackle escaped her thin lips. "Such nonsense, Ella. Really." She started walking to the bedroom door near the staircase that led upstairs. "If I choose to get a partner or even to sell the store, you should mind your own business. The store's mine now, not yours."

Furious, Linda stormed out of the kitchen, making certain to shut her bedroom door just a little too loudly, a further indication of her displeasure.

Ella, too, felt displeasure. The thought of someone else being brought into the store as a partner didn't sit well with her. Her father had started it and had created a wonderful enterprise that benefited the community. Ever since his death, Linda had been slowly destroying it. And if Linda actually sold the business, Ella could only foresee more problems.

"Now look what you've done, Ella!" Drusilla said abruptly as she, too, stood up.

Anna followed her older sister's example. "You've gone and upset Maem!"

Both girls hurried to the first-floor bedroom, knocking once before entering, as if they intended to console their mother. But one look around the kitchen and

Ella knew the truth. While they feigned concern for their mother, it was the evening chores that they were most likely trying to avoid.

Again.

With a little sigh, Ella stood up, gathered the untouched cups of tea, and carried them to the kitchen sink. After turning on the faucet, she stared out the window while waiting for the hot water.

If only her father hadn't passed away. If only Linda would listen to some advice instead of thinking she knew it all. If only . . .

Ella knew better than to keep listing the *if onlys.* The list was endless and only further disheartened her. It was better to push the problems into the back of her mind and focus on the here and now. And *that* was full of a long list of another kind: chores.

At least she had *something* to distract her.

Chapter Three

On Sunday, Ella sat on the hard pine bench listening to Deacon King preach. She always enjoyed when he preached, for his sermons were spirited in nature and always full of good, practical guidance taken right from Scripture. Sometimes the preachers, especially those who occasionally visited their church, were not as eloquent as Deacon King. With his long white beard and shaved upper lip, he was a striking older man. His voice was kind and never condescending, especially when he spoke before the congregation. And he always preached about matters that seemed appropriate to whatever was happening in the community at that moment.

Today, John King was preaching about humility and why it was so important for the congregation to keep modest views of their own importance. For Ella, it was a timely sermon, and she certainly hoped that she was not the only person seated on the hard pine benches who was not just listening to but actually *hearing* the deacon.

On that Sunday, service was held at the Millers' farm. Ella knew at least one person who wasn't listening to the sermon, and that was Drusilla. She was too busy making moon-eyes at Timothy Miller, who sat on the other side of the barn in the back with the rest of the baptized, but unmarried, young men. Though many of the young men in Echo Creek were either already walking out with someone or, according to Linda, beneath her daughters, Drusilla clearly was interested in Timothy.

Ella could understand why.

He was a tall, stocky young man, no more than twenty-two years old. He was fine-looking—not that personal appearances should matter—and hailed from a kindly family; on top of those attractive qualities, he was destined to inherit his father's farm. Most young women would love to have Timothy Miller escort them home from a singing, or even toss a pebble or two at their window, and Drusilla was no different.

But with her tendency to avoid chores, both inside and outside the house, Drusilla would make a poor match for an aspiring farmer who would require a hard-working partner, not *just* a wife.

The other church leaders were now commenting on Deacon King's sermon. Half listening, Ella looked ahead of her and saw the back of her friend Belle's prayer *kapp*. There was a woman who, despite the odds, had found an unusual match in Adam Hershberger. Even though she could not spot Adam on the other side of the barn, Ella was pleased to see Belle attending worship.

Earlier that morning, Ella, Anna Rose Grimm, Sadie Whitaker, and Belle Hershberger had walked down the lane together. They were good friends, although Ella was closest with Belle and Sadie. Usually they all sat together in church, or at least near one another. But not today, for Belle now sat with the married women, and Sadie and Ella sat on the bench in front of Anna Rose, who was younger than they. People sat on the benches according to their marital status and their age.

With the exception of guests.

One of the young men on the other side of the barn stood up and quietly excused himself. Ella watched, her eyes once again scanning the rear of the barn where the men sat. As the departing man moved, Ella noticed a strange face staring in the direction of the deacon. He was a young man with thick, curly, dark hair that hung over his forehead. And Ella knew that she had never seen him before.

Curiosity got the best of her, and she wondered who he was. Perhaps because he was seated in the back, no one else had noticed him. Not yet, anyway. Ella suspected that, upon catching a glimpse of the handsome stranger, the young women would fight over trying to serve him for the fellowship meal. She could only imagine her stepsisters' reaction.

The time came to sing "Das Loblieb," the second hymn of the three-hour worship service.

Oh, how Ella loved to sing!

And the only thing better than singing a hymn to praise God and recognize the sacrifices of those who believed in Jesus was singing with the congregation during worship.

There was something amazing about two hundred or more people singing in unison as they lifted their voices to praise God. It didn't matter if some people were off-key or sang too softly to be heard. Sometimes people forgot the words to a hymn—although no one ever forgot "Das Loblieb," for it was Hymn 131 of the

Ausbund and the second hymn sung at every church service regardless of what church district was meeting.

O Lord Father, we bless thy name,
Thy love and thy goodness praise;
That thou, O Lord, so graciously
Have been to us always.
Thou hast brought us together, O Lord,
To be admonished through thy word.
Bestow on us thy grace.

As she began to sing the second verse, Ella kept her eyes shut, her face lifted just a little toward the ceiling of the barn. She could feel the power of God's love flowing through her as she sang her prayer for God to bestow upon her the wisdom to glorify him through both word and deed, to speak with truth of his power, and to live in submissive righteousness in order to honor God and his glory.

Whenever she sang "Das Loblieb," Ella found herself remembering her mother's last words: *Be kind and good, no matter what happens, for God has a plan for you.* Just singing those beautiful words to Hymn 131 renewed Ella's faith and gave her strength to face another week living with her stepmother and stepsisters. After all, her mother had promised her that God had a plan for her, and surely that plan was more than just slaving away for Linda and her daughters.

When the fourth and final verse of the hymn ended, Ella opened her eyes. But something felt odd, as if someone were watching her. Discreetly, she scanned the room. Most people were quietly waiting for the next preacher to stand up to give his sermon—the shorter of the two for the day.

Well, *almost* everyone was waiting.

One pair of bright blue eyes, so blue that they stood out among the sea of men wearing black who faced the place where the preacher stood in the middle of the room, was focused on her.

It was the stranger.

Quickly, Ella looked away. She pressed her lips together and turned her eyes toward the preacher. But that didn't help, for she could still feel the intensity of those blue eyes on her. She felt heat rise to her cheeks, and she tried to remain focused, even as she wondered if he was still watching her. Curiosity drew her own eyes back to him.

Sure enough, he had not torn away his gaze.

Once again, Ella's eyes flickered away from him, and she forced herself to pay attention to the preacher. She wanted to hear what he said. She also knew that she *needed* to hear him, for *that* particular preacher had a habit of approaching the young people after the service and inquiring about what they had learned from his sermon. Woe to the person who could not answer him correctly! While he had never asked *her*, Ella knew that some young people who hadn't been able to answer him correctly were subjected to lengthy visits at the preacher's house during the week to listen to a long, one-on-one reiteration of the sermon.

Despite knowing this, Ella continued to glance occasionally to where the stranger sat.

Fortunately, the young man was paying attention to the service now.

After the preacher's sermon and lengthy prayer, it was time for the third and final hymn. Ella tried to concentrate on the words that she sang. But it was increasingly difficult, for she felt rather than saw that the stranger was once again watching her. This time, Ella somehow felt the courage to look at him while she sang.

Even as he, too, sang, his eyes were upon her. It was as if he was listening just to her. Was it possible to filter out the voices of over two hundred people? To hear just one voice among the many? If it was possible, Ella would have guessed that was what the young man was doing. The way he watched her made her feel as if he was hearing no other voice but her own.

Feeling uncomfortable, she stopped singing and merely mouthed the words, pretending that she was singing.

Who was he? And, if he was truly a guest, why was he seated in the back with the other unmarried men?

The hymn ended, and it was time for the kneeling prayer. The sound of two hundred people kneeling down and pressing their foreheads against their folded hands as they rested on the pine benches quickly gave way to silence. A long silence. Not even one child fussed during the silent prayer.

Ella took this time to pray for her stepmother and her stepsisters. She also prayed for her friend Sadie, who was going through a rough time with her own stepmother, and for her friend Belle, who had just recently married a man she did not love. With so many people in need of God's love and caring hand, Ella never even stopped once to think about praying for her own needs.

When the prayer ended and she stood up, her back toward the center of the room as she faced the wall, Ella found herself feeling as if God were in the room with everyone. Perhaps her prayers would be answered this week, she thought. Perhaps this week God would help the people in Echo Creek who needed it the most.

She genuflected before turning around. The men were standing now, and it was nearly impossible to locate the stranger. And yet she had hoped to spot him. Perhaps she might see him talking with someone and get a hint as to who, exactly, he knew in Echo Creek.

Try as she might, she could not find him.

"Oh, Ella. There you are!"

She looked up and saw Deacon King's wife, Miriam. A stout but cheerful woman who had always been a take-charge kind of person, Miriam was hurrying toward her. "How are you today, Miriam?" Ella asked with a warm smile on her face. She had always admired Miriam King for her kind heart and quick wit.

Unlike many of the other aging Amish women in Echo Creek, Miriam did not always hold her tongue. If she saw something she didn't quite like, she would not hesitate to point it out. Ella often wished that she could be more like Miriam King.

"I'm in a hurry today, I'm afraid," Miriam replied. Then, as if she noticed Ella's eyes scanning the large area of the barn, she asked, "Are you looking for something in particular, Ella?"

Embarrassed that she had been caught, Ella felt the heat rise to her cheeks. "Not something, but someone." She shook her head, suddenly feeling silly. She redirected all of her attention to the deacon's wife. "I'm sorry, Miriam. You were looking for me?"

Miriam gave her a sideways glance. "Must be someone important, then."

"Oh, no!" Ella was quick to dismiss that idea. "*Nee*, it's not like that at all. Just that I noticed a stranger was among us, and I was curious as to whom he arrived with."

"I see." Despite those two words, it was clear to Ella that the older woman did not see at all.

"It's not important. Honest." Another smile. "What did you need me for?"

"What?" Miriam gave her a quizzical look before the realization seemed to strike her that she had, indeed, been looking for Ella. "Oh help! I reckon I'm getting to be an old, *ferhoodled* woman." She gave a light little laugh. "*Ja,* I was looking for you." She touched Ella's arm and guided her away from the other people, leaning close to her as if telling her a grave secret. "I usually help in the kitchens, but I must leave before the fellowship meal to go visit some family. I was wondering if you might take my place in the kitchen? You always seem much more attentive than some of the others." As she said that, Miriam glanced in the direction of Drusilla and Anna.

Ella suppressed a smile. "*Ja,* of course, Miriam."

The older woman gave a sigh as if relieved that Ella had agreed. She patted the younger woman's arm. "Such a good girl. You always have been." Then, lowering her voice, Miriam added, "Some day you'll make a *wunderbarr gut fraa* to a very special young man."

The compliment caught Ella off guard. She wasn't used to flattering remarks. It just wasn't the way of the Amish. Coming from Miriam King, it felt extra special. Still, to acknowledge the praise would be to sound prideful. "Oh, Miriam, no more so than any other, I reckon."

At that comment, Miriam chuckled and gave her arm one last pat. "We'll see about that, Ella Troyer." And then she hurried away to gather her things and join her husband, who was waiting near the door.

Ella puzzled over Miriam's strange behavior for only

a few seconds. Then she hurried toward the house, where she knew that the other older women were preparing the platters of food in the kitchen. Outside the barn, the men were busy carrying the worship benches to a shaded area, quickly converting them into long tables for the dinner meal.

On her way to the house, as Ella passed through the different clusters of waiting people, she looked for the stranger who had attended the worship service. But he was nowhere to be found. He wasn't among the young men who were standing around catching up on the latest news and probably talking about the youth gathering that evening. Nor was he among the older men.

"Where are you going, Ella?" Sadie called out as Ella passed a group of young women.

"Going to lend a hand to the women. Want to come with me?"

Without even hesitating, Sadie nodded and joined her. Ella noticed that none of the other young women offered to help. Miriam's words echoed in her mind.

As they approached the porch, Ella paused and cast one more glance at the sea of men standing near the tables. "Sadie," Ella asked cautiously, "did you happen to see someone new seated with the young men in the back of the barn today?"

Her friend frowned and gave her a quizzical look. "*Nee*, I did not. Why?"

"No reason," Ella said with a slight shrug. She felt foolish just for having asked the question. "Just thought I saw a newcomer. Was wondering who he might be."

As she held the door open for her friend, Ella sighed. Was it possible that he had slipped away, along with the other members of the church who couldn't stay for the fellowship hour, such as Miriam King and Belle Hershberger, or had she merely imagined the young man? She slipped inside the door, realizing that she probably would never know.

Chapter Four

The water on the pond barely rippled in the soft breeze as Ella sat on the edge of the bank, her toes buried in the wet soil. Surrounded by trees, Ella listened to the symphony of birds singing in the branches. Their songs filled her with joy, and she leaned back against her hands and shut her eyes, enjoying the warmth of the sun on her face.

The pond was a place she had often escaped to when she was younger and her father was still alive—when Linda spent more time at the house. As the least domesticated woman Ella had ever known, Linda often created more of a mess than Ella could bear watching. It was easier for her to quietly leave the house rather than witness the demolition of the kitchen as Linda attempted to cook or bake.

But that had been before Linda recruited Ella to take over the kitchen duties. And now, with her father gone, Ella rarely had time to herself. On the infrequent occasions when she had caught up on her chores and knew that no one would be home for another hour or so, Ella loved to sneak away to sit by the edge of the pond and talk to God.

Today was one of those days.

And Ella was grateful for the respite from the confines of the house.

Ever since Monday, Linda and her daughters had been caught up in the turmoil of the store's future, and no one seemed to pay any attention to Ella. And that was fine with her. Between washing clothes, cleaning the house, and weeding the garden—never mind cooking for such finicky eaters!—Ella welcomed the unexpected time alone on this lovely Friday afternoon.

For a long moment, she sat there, just watching the water. She loved how the sun reflected off the shimmering top of the pond. With the trees overhead bending, just slightly, in the cool breeze, it was the perfect August day.

It was also a perfect day to converse with God.

If there was ever a time when she needed to speak with God, it was now. Ella often had private conversations with him, asking him for help or, if that was not part of the plan, the strength to get through troubled times. She had leaned heavily on her faith ever since her father had passed away. But now was one of those times when she knew she needed to lean on God a little more than usual. There was so much as stake, and if Linda made the wrong decision, their lives would certainly change, and Ella suspected it would not be for the better.

Please God, she prayed, *help my family through these troubled times. Let Linda get her bank loan so that the store remains solvent and we don't need a partner in the business or, even worse, to sell it.*

Oh, if only Linda would let Ella help at the store.

Not just on the few occasions when she worked there because Drusilla or Anna needed to go somewhere or wanted a day off. If she could assist Linda with managing the finances, balancing the books, and controlling the inventory, perhaps there would be no problems at the store. After all, her father had taught her so much about running the store. She knew—just knew!—that her father had intended to leave the business to her. But no one, especially her father, had thought that he would die at such a young age. Without a will, or even a letter expressing his wishes, everything automatically transferred to his wife, and that, unfortunately, was Linda.

Her stepmother could do what she wanted with the business, and that was the root of the problem.

To begin with, Ella could not understand why the business was in trouble. Her father hadn't left the business in the negative. In fact, her father had always managed to balance the books and had never once needed to seek out a loan from the bank. The people of Echo Creek always frequented the store and purchased all of their goods from him. Now sales were down, inventory was a mess, and things were clearly not financially stable.

What on earth was Linda doing?

Even more concerning to Ella was that the problems at Troyers' General Store might impact the town. How many people living in Echo Creek depended on the store to purchase their goods? Where would the Amish shop if the store was shut down? Certainly not in Liberty Falls, for that was too far away for most people to shop there on a regular basis. And yet there were grumbles among the Amish community regarding the excessive prices Linda charged on some goods. Still, the people of Echo Creek had few, if any, options.

Ella knew that her father would be most unhappy with the way that Linda was managing—or mismanaging—the store. And that broke her heart.

She shut her eyes and began to sing one of her favorite hymns.

When she had finished the song, she exhaled. How difficult life could be! Sighing, she saw a stone in the dirt and dug at it with her fingers. Once she freed it, she threw it into the pond, sending ripples through the glassy surface.

"That was a good strong throw!"

Startled, Ella turned in the direction of the voice. A man was standing thirty feet behind her. He was leaning against a tree, his dark hair swooping over his forehead. His straw hat, which looked brand-new, cast a shadow across his face. He was definitely Amish—his clothes told her that much.

Clearing his throat, he took a step forward, giving her a broad smile as he removed his hat. "Bet you played a lot of baseball when you were at school, *ja*? Probably the first one picked when the teams were sorted."

He looked familiar but she couldn't place him. She eyed him suspiciously. "I'm not so certain about that."

"Surely you remember?" His blue eyes twinkled at her. "You can't be so old that you'd forget."

And that was when she recognized him. He had been the young man seated in the back of the barn during the worship service just last Sunday. Despite his rather rapid disappearance after the service had ended, there was something about the stranger that did not frighten Ella. His face was open and jovial, with a sparkle of mischief in his expression, but nothing that spoke of harm.

Even though she was usually shy around strangers, Ella felt unthreatened, and his teasing tone put her at ease. "*Ja, vell,* memory *is* the first thing to go with old age," she quipped back.

He raised an eyebrow. "Oh, *ja*? I thought it was eyesight." He paused, glancing toward the sky as if trying to remember something. "Or mayhaps it's hearing?"

"I'm sorry. What was that? I couldn't hear you."

The man laughed at her joke. With those pretty blue eyes and a broad white smile, the man definitely was not intimidating. Ella didn't even mind when he knelt down beside her. His eyes appeared to scan the surface of the pond, which had already returned to mirror smoothness.

"I recognized you from worship the other week," he said in a soft voice. "Or rather, I recognized your voice as I was passing by."

She gave a nervous laugh. "Out of two hundred people? You recognized my voice?"

He turned his head and gave her a long look. His eyes flickered back and forth as if he was studying her face. "Kind of hard not to recognize the prettiest voice in the congregation."

"Oh!" The word came out as a breathless whisper. She wasn't even certain how to respond to such praise.

The young man chuckled and looked back at the pond. In the trees, the birds called out to one another, one swooping down to fly across the surface before disappearing into a tree on the other side. Nearby, a frog jumped from a rock into the water, its splash sending a small ripple across the otherwise glassy surface.

"Sure is a pretty spot," he said, breaking the silence at last. "You come here often?"

Ella sighed. "*Nee.*" If it were up to her, she'd be at the pond every day. "Not as often as I'd like, anyway."

He returned his gaze to her. "And why's that, little water nymph?"

Water nymph? She tried to hide her smile. No one had ever called her such a pretty name. "One must always finish one's work before it is time to play, *ja*?"

He nodded his head and fixed his eyes on the surface of the water. "That's wise advice there . . . ?" He dragged out the last word as if waiting for her to fill in the blank with her name.

Embarrassed—where *were* her manners?—she quickly introduced herself. "Ella."

"Ella." He said her name as if he savored each syllable. "Seeing that you're so old you can't remember whether or not you were a baseball star at school," he said, a light tone to his voice, "it's no wonder you have such sage advice stored up in that aging brain of yours."

This time, she couldn't hold back her delight at his teasing banter. "With age comes wisdom . . . if we can only remember what it is."

He laughed.

"You're not from around here, are you?" Ella asked. She already knew the answer, for she knew all of the people who lived in Echo Creek.

He shook his head. "Nope. If I were, you'd surely recognize me from church and youth singings."

She waited, wondering if he was going to introduce himself. He didn't. When the silence between them began to grow uncomfortable, Ella leaned forward and started to get up. "I'd best get going. Too much idleness on anyone's hands surely opens a door for sin."

He stood up and reached out his hand to assist her. Ella glanced at him as she stood without any assistance.

"You headed back to Echo Creek?" he asked as he slid his hat onto his head. The brim shielded his eyes, and Ella couldn't quite see where he was looking.

She nodded, wondering how he knew she was from Echo Creek. "I am."

"Mayhaps you'd show me the way. I have an appointment in town."

She wanted to ask him about his appointment. There were only a few stores in Echo Creek, and strangers didn't happen by the town too often. She imagined he must be visiting with the leather maker, perhaps to purchase a new harness for his horse. And yet, as they walked up the path toward the main road, she saw neither a horse nor a buggy nearby.

The road toward town took them past the Beilers' farm. No one was outside, although Melvin's new buggy was parked in the driveway.

"You're from Echo Creek." It wasn't so much a question as a statement.

Ella glanced at him. "*Ja,* I am. Where're you from?"

He walked with his hands behind his back and kept a respectful distance from her. But he glanced at her whenever he spoke to her. "Blue Springs."

She frowned. She had never heard of Blue Springs before. "Where's that?"

"About thirty miles south of here. Just outside of Liberty Falls. Pretty little town with old white farmhouses and rolling fields. Most everyone there's a farmer, which makes for a nice, quiet community."

"Amish?"

He laughed and gestured toward his clothing. "*Ja*, of course."

She blushed. How silly she must have sounded, asking whether or not he was Amish. From his plain black pants to his straw hat, he was the picture-perfect Amish man. The only thing missing was the mustacheless beard that was worn by the married men.

"And I reckon you, too, are"—he paused—"Mennonite?"

His teasing made her smile. "*Ja*, Mennonite," she said lightly. "Because Echo Creek has such a big Mennonite community."

For a moment, he looked as if he believed her. "Truly?"

"No!" She laughed, feeling a bit of freedom in doing so. It wasn't often that she was given the opportunity to joke with anyone, and she certainly did not laugh very often. "Not one bit."

"Ah. I see." He gave her a sidewise glance. "So you're . . . Amish?"

Ella laughed, especially when she saw the playful twinkle in his eyes. "Echo Creek's almost all Amish folk. Mostly elderly people live in the town center, and the Amish farmers live on the outskirts."

"Sounds like Blue Springs."

"I can assure you it's not always nice or quiet," she quipped, using the words he had just spoken to describe his hometown.

Why, just a few weeks before, the town had been in an uproar over the very unexpected wedding of Ella's friend, Belle, to the reclusive Adam Hershberger. But Ella knew better than to say such a thing. Gossiping about others was sinful and something she tried to avoid, even if her stepmother and her daughters did not.

"There's something to be said for a community that isn't always a hundred percent quiet." He glanced at her. "Too much quiet would make it rather dull, don't you think?"

"Mayhaps. But it sure would be interesting if it was a hundred percent nice, *ja*?"

There was a wise look on his face. He tilted his head as if pondering what she had said. She liked that. No one paid much attention to anything she said. Not at home, anyway. And she had little reason to interact with many people other than family, except during the fellowship hour after worship or whenever she worked the front counter at the store.

"Well, Jesus came for the sinners now, didn't he?" The young man from Blue Springs made a whimsical face. "And I reckon it's just too hard for *everyone* to be nice *all* of the time."

She couldn't stop herself from smiling at the truth of his statement. While Ella always remembered her mother's last words of advice, she knew that, try as she might, she, too, was a sinner and wasn't always a hundred percent kind—*or* good, for that matter. Just that past Saturday she had goaded Drusilla and had prayed for forgiveness from God.

"So if Blue Springs is a quiet little farming community," Ella said, "then what brings you to Echo Creek?"

"Ah." He leaned over and, with a finger to his lips, whispered, "It's a secret."

Ella feigned a look of grave seriousness. "In that

case, you'd best not be telling me, or anyone else, your business. Otherwise it won't be a secret any longer."

"Quite true. The best way for people to keep a secret is if they don't know it."

The dirt path ended, and they were on the main road. Ella stopped walking and glanced both ways to see if anyone was coming. "This is the main road to town." She pointed to the left. "Walk about a quarter mile or so, past those three houses, and you'll be in the center of town." While facing him, she took a few steps backward. Her house was the second house in the other direction, just after the unpaved lane that led away from town. "I wish you success in your business . . ." She paused. He had never properly introduced himself. "I'm sorry, I never did catch your name."

He gave her a broad grin. "That's because I didn't tell you."

"Is that part of your secret?" she asked.

He seemed delighted with her playful retort. "My *daed* calls me Hannes. So do my friends." He narrowed her eyes and studied her for a long, drawn-out moment. "I reckon I'll put you in that category so you can call me Hannes, too."

She smiled at his playful comment. "Hannes?" *What a strange name,* she thought. "Well, one can never have too many friends. Have a great day, Hannes." She wondered if he was the new vendor her stepsisters had mentioned, the one who made and distributed clocks. The one they had sent away and told to return another day because of the situation with the IRS. If so, Ella felt sorry for him, because she knew that Linda was still in a tizzy trying to figure out what, exactly, she was to do about the fifty thousand dollars owed to the government.

Ella turned around and continued walking down the road, sensing that Hannes had not yet started walking toward town. She suspected that he was watching her, and for that reason, she continued walking past her house, feeling intrigued by the stranger but not confident enough for him to know where she lived. It wasn't until she reached a safe distance that she turned around. Seeing that he was long gone, she retraced her steps until she reached the safety of her home, still puzzling over the strange yet lively encounter with that handsome outsider who had happened upon her at the small pond outside of Echo Creek.

Chapter Five

"Oh, such news!" Anna rushed into the house, her round face flushed with excitement.

Behind her, Drusilla carried a large box and dropped it onto the counter, not caring that Ella had just cleaned the kitchen. The box left a poof of white powder that coated the area, something else that Drusilla didn't care about. "You'll never believe what happened," Drusilla said as she stood there, a bag hanging over her arm.

Getting up from the chair where she had been hemming her stepmother's dress, Ella set down the dress and crossed the kitchen floor to peek into the box. Flour. Sugar. Other goods from the store. Drusilla always brought groceries home on Mondays.

Without being asked and certainly without expecting any assistance from her stepsisters, Ella began to put the items away in the cabinets. "Something exciting, I imagine."

Drusilla removed the bag from her arm and dropped it on the floor at Ella's feet. "Oh, absolutely! Why, it's the most exciting thing that I can remember in all our years living in Echo Creek!"

Suddenly, Ella tensed up, wondering if it had to do with Hannes, the mysterious young man she had met the previous Friday afternoon at the pond. She had been pondering their encounter ever since, smiling at the memory of their conversation. How rare, indeed, it had been to share her sense of humor with someone. Years ago, she had realized that her new family members didn't share her sense of the absurd, so she kept a running commentary in her head, amusing herself, if no one else. It had been refreshing to share her humor with someone who could—and did!—appreciate it.

Now the thought that Hannes might still be in Echo Creek and might, perhaps, have stopped at the store and met her stepmother and stepsisters didn't sit well with Ella. Surely they wouldn't have understood his wit, and if they did laugh at his pithy comments, they would have been pretending just for the sake of getting his business. Or, in the case of Drusilla and Anna, a beau.

Ella hadn't confided to anyone about her unexpected meeting on Friday with the handsome stranger. She wasn't certain why. Perhaps it was because nothing exciting ever happened to Ella. Or maybe it was because she remembered those blue eyes watching her when she had been singing at church. From what he had said, it seemed he had been listening to just her voice as she'd sung her worship to God. And, if so, that made Hannes very special indeed. Or it could have been that he had called her a water nymph when he approached her at the pond and talked with her as she imagined a young man would talk to a woman on a buggy ride home from a youth singing.

No, she didn't want to share anything about Hannes

with anyone, least of all her stepsisters. And while she didn't believe in secrets, she knew that sometimes there were things that were best kept to oneself.

As expected, Drusilla didn't bother to help with the box. Instead, she practically skipped across the floor to the table and sank into the chair at its head. "Deacon King met with Maem today."

Immediately, Ella relaxed. A meeting with Deacon King would have nothing to do with the stranger named Hannes. Her stepmother, who made it a point to be front and center as the female voice of the Amish community, often had meetings with the church leaders. Since the store was in town, the bishop or deacon often went there to talk with her. Still, Drusilla's reaction surprised her. Whatever could be so exciting about Deacon King visiting Linda at the store?

However, Ella remained mildly curious if for no other reason than her stepsisters were rarely excited about *anything* unless it had something to do with them.

"So what was the meeting about?" Ella asked. "The situation at the store?"

As soon as she asked that last question, Ella realized how much she truly hoped that was the case. Perhaps the community had come together to help Linda, as they often helped others in need. Why, just a few weeks ago, after a terrible accident on the road to Liberty Falls, Melvin Beiler needed a new horse and buggy. The bishop had asked the community to help. Unfortunately, as it turned out, few people had actually chipped in to help Melvin, mostly because Linda herself had made a big fuss about supporting a man who dabbled with inventions instead of doing what she considered real work. Fortunately, someone had been kind enough to donate enough money so that Melvin could buy his new horse and buggy.

Still, Ella could only hope that, perhaps, her stepmother had reached out to the bishop for advice and the town would help Linda with that unpaid tax bill. And, of course, the bishop would certainly discuss the matter of the ever-increasing prices of the items at Troyers' General Store. Potentially it could be a win-win for both Linda and the town.

But Ella's hopes were quickly dashed.

"*Nee,* goose. It's nothing to do with the store." Drusilla rolled her eyes as if Ella should have already guessed that. "Why would I care about *that*?"

Ella could think of a dozen reasons, but she voiced none of them. Instead, she chided herself for having held any expectation that her stepsisters would spend even a moment's concern over Linda's financial situation. Clearly they had no idea how owing so much money for unpaid taxes impacted all of them.

It was Anna who finally told her what the big news was.

"The town is holding a bake sale!" Anna practically spun around, her dress billowing slightly about her and exposing her dirty, bare feet. "For charity."

A bake sale? Ella frowned. Now it was Ella's turn to wonder why her stepsisters would think *that* was so special. Their church district frequently held charity auctions to raise money for people in need. And bake sales were equally common, especially in the late summer and early autumn, when fresh fruits were abundant. Ella usually donated her favorite apple crisp pie, the one with the secret recipe that her own mother had written down on an index card and kept with her other recipes.

Ella had hidden that recipe in her Bible and shared it with no one.

"It's always nice to raise money for charity," Ella said at last, still wondering why Anna was so excited about a simple bake sale. "What charity is it for?"

Ignoring Ella's question, Anna slid onto the bench by the table and reached into the fruit bowl for an apple. Wiping it on the front of her dress, she gave her sister a stern look. "Tell Ella the best part of it, Dru!"

Ah! So there's more! Ella leaned against the counter and, smiling, waited for her stepsister to divulge what she had not shared.

"It's going to be a *secret* auction!" Drusilla said, lowering her voice.

"Secret?" Ella had never heard of such a thing.

"*Ja*, secret." Drusilla looked rather smug as she explained. "The baked goods will be on display and people will bid on them. But the bidders won't know *who* baked them until after they win the item!"

Anna bit into the apple, and some of the juice ran down her chin. "And the bishop has extended invitations to neighboring church districts."

Ella didn't have to guess why *that* excited Anna. If families from other towns came to the event, that meant young men would come, too. While Ella appreciated the bishop's initiative in expanding the social circles for both the families and the unmarried youth of Echo Creek, she felt unsettled by Anna's fervor to meet new prospective husbands. Eagerness for courting had been the destruction of many a young woman's reputation. It was always best to let God handle such matters.

Anna, however, was oblivious to Ella's thoughts.

Anna sighed, a dreamy look on her face. "How much

fun it'll be to try to guess who made which pie or cake!" She leaned toward Drusilla and lowered her voice as if sharing a big conspiracy. "I just know Jenny Esh will make that pecan pie like she always does."

Drusilla snorted. "And burn it as usual."

Anna laughed out loud.

"That's not very nice," Ella scolded, returning her attention to the box, which was filled with dry goods from the store. Flour, sugar, salt, yeast. Everything she needed to make her daily bread except butter and milk, which she always got fresh from their own two cows. "Jenny has many talents—"

"Just not baking," Drusilla interrupted.

Hoping to change the direction of the conversation, Ella started putting away the supplies. Long ago, she had stopped being surprised at how judgmental her stepsisters were toward others. She suspected that others had noticed, too. Perhaps *that* was one of the reasons neither of them had been seriously courted by any of the young men who lived in Echo Creek.

And, of course, there was their far-too-obvious eagerness to marry, which was surely a turnoff for possible suitors.

Ella opened one of the cabinets and began putting away the clear plastic bags of flour, sugar, and salt. "And what pie will *you* make, Anna?"

At this question, Drusilla coughed into her hand as if masking a stifled laugh.

Ella turned around in time to witness Anna shooting an angry look at her older sister. "Why did you laugh?"

"I didn't laugh," Drusilla claimed. "I coughed."

Anna rolled her eyes.

"Besides, I can't imagine you baking a pie. It would be as burned as Jenny Esh's!" Drusilla practically cackled.

Frowning, Anna pursed her lips and glared. "As if *you* can bake any better!"

"You know Maem depends on me at the store! I don't have time to bake!"

"As if I *do* have time, Drusilla? Why, I reckon that I work there just as much as you do!"

"But not as hard, that's for sure and certain!" Drusilla's face was twisted into a mask of fury. To say that there was a competition between the two sisters was an understatement. However, Ella knew that the competition was weak on both sides, for whatever the one blamed the other of doing (or not doing) was equally applicable to the accuser as the accused.

"Oh, I wouldn't say that, Drusilla!" Anna retorted. "Why, you've been sneaking off an awful lot of late."

"Have not!"

Anna put her hands on her hips and, with a self-satisfied look on her face, said two words: "Timothy Miller."

Drusilla gasped. "Have you been spying on me?"

Ella sighed. It was always like this with her stepsisters. The rivalry between the two of them always led to arguing and bickering. Neither one ever won. Instead, the quarrels always ended with loud voices, shouting, and then one of them storming upstairs while the other left the house altogether. It was enough to drive her mad. Ella was in the habit of counting to ten, hoping that she could be the calming presence between the two of them. But she usually failed.

Today was no different.

Taking a deep breath, she exhaled slowly, knowing what she had to do in order to distract and redirect the ensuing quarrel. "Why don't I bake something for you?" Ella offered. It was a half-hearted offer, made only because she knew that, sooner or later, they would ask her anyway. At least this way, by proactively presenting a solution, she could avoid listening to the developing squabble.

As she had suspected it would, her strategy worked. Immediately upon making the offer, Ella saw the irritability vanish from Anna and Drusilla's faces, replaced with a look of relief.

Drusilla clasped her hands and pressed them against her chest, the overly dramatic gesture almost causing Ella to roll her eyes. "Oh, would you?"

Anna gave a small sigh of relief and smiled. "*Ja*, Ella. Would you do that for us?"

Sometimes Ella wondered if *that* was why they argued so much. Most of their quarrels centered on doing chores at home. Over the years, even when her father had been alive, Ella had found it easier to just volunteer to do whatever they were arguing over. She had been taught to please others, to put their needs before her own. Even when she didn't want to. That was, after all, the final blessing her mother had shared with Ella before passing.

Unfortunately, Ella knew that her stepsisters had clearly picked up on that tendency, using it to their own advantage.

In some ways, Ella didn't mind. She hoped that, deep down, her efforts were appreciated by Drusilla and Anna, even if they never expressed their gratitude. And, even if that was not the case, at least when the arguments centered around weekend chores, Ella's offers to help meant there would be peace and quiet in the house, for she often did her stepsisters' work so that they could socialize with their friends.

Unlike her stepsisters, Ella rarely had time for youth

gatherings, and she had never attended a social event in another church district. Linda always had a long list of chores for her to do. By the time Ella finished, it was either too late or she was simply too exhausted to attend.

Sometimes she managed to join a Sunday evening youth singing. Most recently, Ella had managed to attend a youth picnic just the other month with her friend Sadie Whitaker. And the previous Friday, Ella and Sadie had walked to the Hershbergers' farm to visit with Belle. But that was the extent of Ella's most recent social life.

To make matters even worse, because her attendance was so infrequent, she had never been asked by a young man to ride home in his buggy. Usually the young men had already asked someone to ride home with them before the singing, and because Ella usually didn't attend, no one ever thought to ask *her.*

"So when is this surprise charity event to take place?" Ella asked, returning her attention to putting away the dry goods.

"In two weeks!" Drusilla stood up and brushed some imaginary dirt from her skirt. "On Saturday evening at seven."

"They're holding it at the schoolhouse," Anna added. "We must let Bishop know as soon as possible that we'll be donating an item." She, too, got up and joined her sister, who had moved toward the kitchen door. "What type of dessert will you make, Ella?"

Surprised, Ella paused. They never asked about her, so she felt a glimmer of astonishment that Anna had thought to inquire. It was one of those rare moments that gave Ella hope that, deep down, her stepsisters actually cared for her. "You mean what will I bake for my donation?"

Drusilla made a face and frowned. "No, Ella. For us!"

I should've known better. "Oh." Ella shut the cabinet door, her hand resting on the polished wood. "Let's see . . ." She tried to think of what she could make to represent their individual personalities.

It was easy enough to think of the dessert she would make for Drusilla: a lazy-daisy oatmeal cake. Ella almost giggled at the thought. As for Anna, that was a bit more difficult. Unlike Drusilla, who was more vocal with her complaints, Anna was more of a cheerleader, chiming in with her support of her older sister's grievances against Ella. It was as if she felt the need to compete with her older sister, even if it was only to prove that she, not Drusilla, was the more miserable of the two. Ella often found herself feeling sorry for Anna, the poor thing, striving so hard to find her place within the family.

Aha, Ella thought. *A poor man's cake for Anna!*

She suppressed a smile. "I'll have to give it some thought, but I assure you, they will be absolutely *wunderbarr*!"

Both of her stepsisters appeared satisfied and, without another word, headed upstairs to their rooms. And Ella, feeling quite pleased with herself, was left alone to continue her household chores in peace.

Chapter Six

On Thursday, Ella was working at the store. Both Drusilla and Anna were too overcome with grief to work.

Or so they said.

If anyone should have been upset, it was Ella. But here she was, working at the store, covering both of her stepsisters' shifts.

As she stood in the back of the store, unpacking boxes that needed to be inventoried and placed on the shelves or in storage, Ella still could not believe the news.

Just the previous evening, Linda had returned from the store, a somber look upon her face. At first, Ella had thought that her stepmother was distraught about the store. Surely something had happened. News, perhaps, that did not please her stepmother. Perhaps about the loan.

Ella had known better than to inquire. If Linda wanted to share the news, she would. Still, all during the supper meal, Ella waited and watched, her anxiety increasing when she realized that Linda had barely touched a morsel of food.

Her mood was contagious—Drusilla and Anna had clearly been infected by it. For once, they both remained silent. Ella could hardly understand the morose atmosphere, but she preferred the quiet over her stepsisters' usual conversation, which either contained gossip or constant bickering.

After clearing the plates, Ella had brought over dessert plates and a fresh peach pie. But Linda waved it away. Neither of her daughters took a piece, either. Now Ella knew that something serious was afoot.

Pushing aside her empty plate, Linda took a deep breath and exhaled. The wrinkles around the edges of her eyes seemed deeper than usual. "I suppose I should just say it."

"Say what, Maem?" Drusilla asked.

Linda shut her eyes and shook her head. For a long moment, she sat there, her hands covering her mouth. "Oh, such terrible, horrible news. Most upsetting, I fear." She sighed and dropped her hands. "I have been trying to think of a way to tell you. But there is no easy way."

Ella froze in place, her hands laden with dirty plates that she had been carrying over to the sink. Now Ella knew that her worse fears must surely be before them. A dozen different scenarios flooded through her mind. Linda was ill. The store was bankrupt. The bank had foreclosed. Each scenario increased Ella's panic.

And then, finally, Linda shared her news.

"Sadie Whitaker." She raised her eyes and stared at Ella. "She's missing."

Ella gasped and almost dropped the plates. "Sadie?" Shocked, Ella took a step backward and leaned against the counter for support.

She had just talked with Sadie after the worship

service on Sunday. They had spent the fellowship hour ensuring that everyone had plenty of food. Afterward, they had enjoyed their own meal with the other people who had helped serve the rest of the congregation. And Sadie had even mentioned that she wanted to go to the youth singing that evening, asking Ella if she might be able to attend, too.

"Missing?"

"*Ja*, missing," Linda confirmed.

Ella felt as if something heavy was pressing against her chest. She could barely breathe. Oh, how she prayed that nothing bad had happened to Sadie. "When?" she managed to ask.

"Monday night, it appears. No one knows where or how. She's just"—she paused and averted her eyes—"gone."

For the rest of the evening, Ella had been in complete shock. Besides Belle, Sadie was one of her very best friends. She had known that things were not good in the Whitaker household, at least not for Sadie, especially when it came to Rachel, her stepmother. But unlike in Ella's case, Sadie's father was still alive to act as a buffer.

Now, with Drusilla and Anna having cried their way out of working, Ella had been enlisted to help at the store. Perhaps the distraction would be good for her, she thought. Throughout most of the morning, everyone who entered seemed to have more news about Sadie. Unfortunately, none of it contributed information about her whereabouts; it was instead merely speculation as to why she had disappeared. Ella tried not to listen, but she began to be more and more convinced that Sadie had run away. And while that, too, broke her heart, at least no one was speculating that something sinister had happened to her.

"Oh, you should see her father," Esther Kauffman said, clucking her tongue as she gossiped with Linda at the counter. "So distraught."

"I can only imagine," Linda responded, which made Ella look up, wondering if her stepmother would feel distraught if *she* went missing. "And poor Rachel. After all she's done to raise his daughter." Linda gave a long, drawn-out sigh. "It's so hard being a mother to another woman's child," she said, sorrow in her voice. "You give so much, and then"—she made a gesture with her hands as if holding nothing within them—"they just run off."

"Oh, and Rachel did so much for Sadie. Such a sorrowful state of affairs, that she would hurt her father and Rachel in this way."

Ella was glad when Esther finally left, taking her wagging tongue with her. She could have shared a different perspective with both Linda and Esther about how Rachel Whitaker truly treated Sadie. Though she was not as harsh as Linda, Rachel's envy of Sadie was known by everyone.

Just before noon, Ella was in the back of the store, where she was unpacking a box of yarn. The bell over the door jingled and, to her delight, she saw Belle walk into the store.

"Belle Hershberger!" she called out as she quickly left the box of yarn in the aisle and hurried around the front counter. She gave Belle a quick embrace, feeling a sense of relief at finally seeing her friend.

"*Gut morgan,*" Belle said, a slight smile on her face. "How are you, Ella?"

"Why, I'm just fine today," Ella said as cheerfully as

she could. She didn't want to burden Belle with her own woes, for her friend was clearly not her regular, cheerful self. She hadn't been that way in a long time, ever since her father had that accident on the road to Liberty Falls a month before. Ella could understand the change in her friend, given that Belle had demonstrated the true meaning of being a dutiful daughter by marrying Adam Hershberger to help save her father's farm.

"And you?"

Belle shrugged. "As well as can be expected, I reckon."

Ella felt as if the weight of the world were on her friend's shoulders. She would have done anything to have been able to help Belle with that burden. "I'm sorry, Belle. I wish things would get better for you and Adam."

Belle quickly changed the subject. "How is life in Echo Creek? I feel so out of it, living so far away."

After checking that her stepmother wasn't watching, Ella grabbed Belle's hand and led her in between two rows of shelves far away from the front counter. "Oh, Belle. The craziest thing has happened!"

"What is it?"

"Sadie," Ella whispered. "She's disappeared."

Gasping, Belle covered her mouth with her hand. "Oh help!"

Ella nodded. "*Ja*, missing. No one knows where she's gone. Her *daed*'s distraught as all get-out."

"I imagine so!"

And then Ella narrowed her eyes as she leaned closer so that she could whisper into Belle's ear. "Last Sunday Sadie had told me that her stepmother was up to something. I don't think Sadie has met with foul play but has run away."

Another gasp. "I will pray for her."

"That's all we can do, I fear. Pray."

They visited for a few more minutes, Ella soaking up as much of Belle as she could. Now that her dear friend lived north of Echo Creek, some distance outside of town, they didn't get to see much of each other. And without Sadie around to accompany her, Ella didn't think she would be walking all the way out to the Hershbergers' farm too often.

It was later in the afternoon, after Belle had left, that Ella noticed the clocks on the shelves. She paused and studied them, each one more beautiful than the next. She remembered that someone had been coming to meet with Linda about clocks, and for a moment, she wondered if that had been Hannes, the stranger she had met at the pond. Was he the clock vendor?

"Maem?" she said when she returned to the back of the store.

Linda sounded vexed when she asked, "What is it, Ella?"

"I just noticed those clocks." She glanced over her shoulder in the direction of the aisle.

"The wedding clocks?"

"*Ja*, those. When did they arrive?" she asked.

"Oh, just the other week. Someone arranged for a vendor to come, and he left some for display."

Ella couldn't help but wonder why her stepmother had the wedding clocks in the same aisle as the kerosene lanterns. That didn't seem like the proper placement for such an expensive product, one that was intended to be a gift from a man to his new bride.

The bell over the door jingled, and Linda looked

up. "Go see who that is and if you can help." It wasn't a request but a demand.

Obediently, Ella hurried to position herself behind the counter.

Miriam King wandered down the aisle, and upon seeing Ella, she smiled. "Well look who is here today!" She set her empty basket onto the counter. "It's always so *wunderbarr* to walk in here and see you."

Ella blushed. "*Danke*, Miriam. It's always *gut* to see you, too. Did you have a nice visit with your family the other week?"

"How kind of you to ask! John and I had a delightful visit with my *bruder* and his family, *danke* for asking." She leaned over the counter and craned her neck to peek into the office where Linda sat. "Awfully busy, I see. That's *gut*, I suppose."

"Might I help you with something, then?" Ella asked.

"Indeed. We're hosting church this week, you know. I'll be needing some flour to make extra bread."

Without hesitating, Ella immediately offered her help. "Oh, Miriam, please do let me make the bread for worship. You've enough to do to prepare for so many people coming to worship in your *haus*." She didn't want to add that Miriam had no daughters still living at home to help her.

"Well!" Miriam appeared taken aback by Ella's kind offer. "Aren't you just so thoughtful, Ella Troyer!" She glanced in the direction of Linda's office. "I'll take you up on that, Ella, but only if your stepmother agrees." Without waiting for Ella to respond, Miriam called out for Linda to join them.

"Good day, Miriam!" Linda said, a smile glued to her face. "How are you?"

"Why, I'm right as rain!" Miriam gushed. "Especially

since your Ella just offered to help me by baking bread for the worship service this Sunday. It's being held at our place this week, you know. I came in to buy the flour and yeast to make it all myself, but, as always, kind Ella was good enough to volunteer to help me."

Linda winced. It was barely noticeable, but Ella saw it right away. "Of course we know. We're looking forward to it, as usual."

"But I told Ella that I would not agree to her baking the bread without your permission." Miriam leaned closer to Ella and gave her a friendly nudge with her arm. "You're always such a busy young woman. I'd hate to add to your workload."

For a moment, no one spoke. Miriam waited expectantly for Linda to grant her permission while Ella braced herself for the backlash she would undoubtedly incur afterward. She could tell Linda was angry that she had made such an offer. But for the life of her, Ella could not imagine why!

"Of course," Linda said at last, her voice strained. "I'm sure that would be just fine."

Miriam clapped her hands together, delighted. "*Wunderbarr!*"

After a few more minutes of visiting, Miriam finally left the store, her basket as empty as when she had arrived.

The door had barely shut when Linda whirled around and, with her hands on her hips and a dark scowl upon her face, glared at Ella. "You foolish girl! How dare you!" she hissed. "Not only could you have sold her the flour and yeast! But now it will cost me the same for you to make all of that bread, plus your time spent baking and not doing other things!"

Ella shrank away from her stepmother. "I'm sorry, Maem. I . . . I thought it was the right thing to do."

"The right thing? The *right* thing?" Linda yelled, her voice rising with each word. "What would you know about doing the right thing?" She squared her shoulders and stared down her nose at Ella. "Not only will you make that bread, Ella Troyer, but you will pay for those ingredients, and don't you think for one minute that I will let you forego any other chore. Honestly, Ella, sometimes you just speak without thinking."

Lifting her chin, Linda turned on her heel and stormed into her office, stopping only long enough to slam the door behind her.

Ella stood near the counter, confused by her stepmother's reaction. There was no sense arguing with her, that much she knew. If she had to pay for the ingredients, so be it. She knew she had done the right thing, whether or not Linda agreed. And she did not regret making the offer.

Still, she could only wonder what terrible list of chores Linda would give her now in order to punish her for having volunteered to help the deacon's wife.

Chapter Seven

To Ella's surprise, when the young men walked into the Kings' house to take their seats for Sunday worship, the mysterious Hannes was among them once again.

Over the course of the past week, Ella had repeatedly scolded herself for mulling over her encounter with the intriguing young man with the dazzling blue eyes and a strange business secret. After all, she wasn't likely to encounter him again. People passed through Echo Creek all the time to do business at the general store, the feed store, or the hardware store. She had not expected that the man from Blue Springs would stick around long enough to join their worship service not once, but twice!

But there he was.

And it became more than apparent that, this time, Ella wasn't the only person who noticed the handsome stranger. Out of the corner of her eye, she saw a few of the other unmarried women seated near her nudging one another and gesturing with their heads toward Hannes. Even Drusilla and Anna seemed interested in knowing who he was.

Hannes had entered the house through the kitchen door with the other unmarried men, which was unusual in itself. Guests usually sat in the front row behind the church leaders. But not Hannes. For the second time now, he sat on the hard pine benches in the back of the room with the other unmarried Amish men.

On cue—a silent cue, at that!—the men simultaneously removed their hats and placed them beneath their seats. Without moving her head, Ella managed to glance to her side. Sure enough, the other women were watching Hannes, some of them openly gawking at him.

She shook her head, and while the church leaders stood up and left the room, she tried to focus on the singing of the first hymn. She knew that it would be anywhere from twenty to thirty minutes before the leaders returned. During that time, the rest of the congregation would sing one hymn, each syllable of every word sung a cappella in a drawn-out, singsong manner. Sometimes it took up to four minutes to sing just one line of a hymn! And rarely did they ever finish the entire song.

Twice during that hymn, Ella snuck a peek at Hannes. Who *was* he? Why was he still in Echo Creek? She suspected he hadn't been *staying* in Echo Creek, for surely the Amish grapevine would have been in full bloom if someone like Hannes was a guest in town. Even if he had been visiting with friends or family farther outside of town, people would surely have heard about it.

From where she sat observing him, Hannes seemed quite at ease, with no appearance of discomfort at joining worship with complete strangers. Just like the last time. And she noticed that Hannes never once glanced down at the chunky black book of hymns he held in his hand. He knew all of the words by heart.

Surely he's a good Christian man, she thought.

By the time the second sermon was just about over, Ella had caught herself gazing in his direction more than a few times. One glance at the other young women seated near her and Ella knew that she was not the only one intrigued by the handsome young Amish man seated on the other side of the room.

Service ended just before noon. Where the room had been still only moments before, it suddenly burst into activity. The men began reorganizing the benches for the noon meal, putting the legs of the benches into a wooden trestle to create long tables, while the little boys collected the black hymn books. Simultaneously, the older women began bustling about the kitchen, trying their best to avoid colliding with each other in the tight space. Ella headed in that direction, knowing they'd need volunteers to carry the food to the tables.

Several young women stood clustered together, whispering and looking toward the spot where Hannes stood talking with the bishop. Among those women were her two stepsisters.

Each time she walked by them, her hands laden with plates to set the table, Ella could hear snippets of their conversation.

"Do you think he'll attend the singing tonight?"

"Where's he from?"

"Wonder if he's walking out with anyone?"

Ella shook her head. They sounded like a little flock of clucking chickens. Even more surprising was that they were talking about Hannes instead of discussing any news about Sadie!

No, Ella had no time for such idle chitchat. She had more important things to do, such as helping the others who were focused on preparing the fellowship meal. As usual, the men would sit at one table and the women at the other. In order to accommodate the worshippers, there were always two seatings, the second one usually for the women who worked in the kitchen or served those who ate at the first seating.

While the young women were often recruited to help serve the others, a task that some avoided by making themselves scarce after worship ended, Ella suspected that the presence of Hannes and the young women's apparent interest in him would translate into there being no shortage of volunteers to serve the men on this fine Sunday.

"There you are, Ella!"

She barely had time to look up before she felt two large plates thrust into her hands.

"Would you mind carrying these platters of cold cuts to the men's table?" Miriam asked.

"*Ja*, sure, Miriam."

Miriam King pointed toward the men's table. "There, *ja*?" As both the wife of the deacon and hostess of that particular Sunday's worship service, she was even more on-the-go than usual, hustling to make certain everything was in order. "Then hurry back." She eyed the group of gossiping women and frowned. "We're a bit shorthanded today, it seems."

"Of course, Miriam."

Before Ella stepped away, Miriam patted her arm. "I cannot thank you enough for baking all of that delicious bread. Your willingness to always help is appreciated," she said. "Unlike some of the others. I hope it was not too much of a bother." And then, without waiting for a reply, Miriam hustled away to oversee the rest of the logistics for the fellowship meal.

The compliment from Miriam warmed Ella's heart. If only Miriam could know how much it meant to Ella to be recognized, especially after Linda had given her list after list of chores for the past two days, ensuring that she had hardly any free time to make the bread she had promised to give Miriam.

But Ella had managed anyway. She had slept very little in order to make good on her promise. She knew that giving one's word was as good as a contract. To break it was almost like lying. Besides, it wasn't Miriam's fault that Linda was so strict with Ella.

Unfortunately, Ella knew that no one was aware that her days were spent laboring at home for Linda and her daughters. And they certainly didn't know kind words of any sort were rare in the Troyers' house. Why, the only time anyone ever spoke their gratitude or showed any appreciation for her efforts was when she helped people at the store or during the preparation for the fellowship meals, where she was always helping even if others weren't.

Like the group of young women still hovering together and gossiping about Hannes.

As Ella walked by, she overheard Drusilla boasting. "I'll be riding home in his buggy tonight, for sure and certain!"

Such bravado brought an immediate frown of disapproval to Anna's face—but not for the reasons that Ella would have thought.

Anna put her hands on her hips and squared off with her sister. "Surely Timothy Miller wouldn't be too happy about that."

Drusilla swatted her sister's arm. "Oh, hush now!"

but not before two of the other young women nodded their heads in agreement with Anna.

Such silliness, Ella thought as she walked past them. Not one of those girls knew anything about Hannes. Despite having walked with him from the pond to town, even Ella knew very little about him. And while she admitted to being curious, she felt no need to make a public spectacle of herself. These women were practically fawning over him. From what little Ella knew, Hannes was merely passing through Echo Creek on business and, afterward, would continue back to Blue Springs. There would be no surprise romances along the way. *That* was something of which Ella was certain.

After setting the platters onto the men's table, she had started walking back toward the kitchen when she felt a hand on her arm. Startled, she turned around and, to her surprise, found herself staring into Hannes's blue eyes.

"Ella."

That one word, spoken from his lips in such a quiet, husky manner, made her catch her breath. Ella felt the heat rise to her cheeks as his hand lingered on her arm. Behind her, she knew that the group of young women was watching, and that only made her feel even more conscious of Hannes having approached her so publicly.

Apparently unaware of the scrutiny they were under, he gave her a warm smile. "I was hoping to see you during fellowship."

She managed to take a step backward so that they were not standing so close together. "Here I am," she managed to say.

Softly, he laughed. "*Ja,* indeed. Here you are."

For a long moment, he said nothing. Instead, his blue eyes searched her face as if studying every freckle that dotted her cheeks. The silence felt heavy, and Ella waited for what seemed like an eternity. Still, he simply stared at her.

"I . . . I must return to the kitchen," she mumbled, glancing over her shoulder in that direction.

Sure enough, the young women who had been bantering back and forth about Hannes stood there, mouths hanging agape, as they watched Ella conversing with the subject of their affections. Drusilla and Anna's eyes narrowed and their lips pursed, their faces etched with displeasure that Ella should be the recipient of the stranger's attention.

Quickly, Ella turned back to Hannes and lowered her eyes. Her heart began to beat rapidly. She wanted nothing more than to escape the scrutiny of her stepsisters. "Is . . . is there something you needed?"

"*Ja.* There is." Hannes hesitated. He tilted his head, his gaze flickering over her shoulder and, most likely, noticing the other women staring. He frowned, just for a second, and then took a step closer to her again. His dipped his head down and lowered his voice. "I was wondering if you might be attending the singing tonight. I understand it's to be held at the Grimms' farm."

The singing?

Ella's heart fluttered. Why would he want to know if she was going to attend the singing? Curious, she couldn't help but lift her gaze to stare at him. "Oh." She breathed the word, a little whoosh of air escaping her lips. If only she *could* attend the singing! Would her stepmother permit her to go? "I'm not certain."

His expression darkened, a look of disappointment on his face. "I see." He dropped his hand from her arm.

Immediately, Ella realized that he misunderstood her response. Could he have thought she was not interested in him or that she was walking out with another fellow? "I mean . . . I'd like to go, but my *maem* doesn't often let me attend." She hoped that her words, spoken guardedly but truthfully, told him what she couldn't say: yes, she was interested in him, even if he was from another town and wouldn't be staying long in Echo Creek.

Immediately, the disappointment vanished from his face. "*Vell*, if you do attend," he whispered, "I'd like to see you home in my buggy."

Once again, she felt her heart flutter. No young man had ever asked her to ride home from a singing in his buggy. She didn't take it personally. Most of the men in Echo Creek knew that her stepmother forced her to work so much that she couldn't attend singings or other youth functions. But now, standing before her with a look of hope in his eyes was Hannes, asking her to ride home with him.

"I . . . I'd like that very much," she heard herself whisper back. She looked up at him. "I'll try to get there tonight."

His smile lit up his face, and he stood up just a little straighter as he beamed at her. "I'll be looking for you, Ella." He took a step backward, still staring at her. Those blue eyes danced with joy, and Ella felt a wave of warmth course through her body.

Perhaps she was wrong. Perhaps there might be a romance in Echo Creek after all with the handsome Amish man from Blue Springs. But what surprised her even more was that it might just include her.

No sooner had she returned to the kitchen than her stepsisters cornered her.

"Who was that man you were just talking to?" Drusilla demanded in a hoarse whisper.

Anna chimed in with her own question. "What was he saying to you?"

Ella looked over their shoulders, her gaze wandering to where Hannes now stood with Deacon King. They were talking as if they had known each other for years.

"I'm not quite certain," she admitted, returning her attention to her stepsisters. "Just someone I met the other afternoon by happenstance."

The cool look Drusilla gave her indicated her clear condemnation. "You met a man? Alone?"

The insinuation irritated Ella. She fought the urge to roll her eyes as she responded, "We met on the road, Drusilla."

"Hmph." Drusilla pursed her lips and narrowed her eyes. "If Maem finds out . . ."

Ella tried to hide her exasperation. It wasn't as if Ella were so overly social that she needed to fear for her reputation. However, she didn't particularly care for the accusatory tone of her stepsister's voice.

"He asked for *directions*, Drusilla. Nothing more." After she said that, Ella immediately wondered if her response constituted a lie. While they *had* talked, it was truly about nothing in particular, or at least about something that would be of little interest to other people. And yet Ella simply could not refrain from thinking about him. "You make it sound so sinister. Why, I don't even know his last name," she added.

Anna gasped and reached eagerly to clasp Ella's hand. "But you know his *first* name? What is it?"

Suddenly feeling protective of Hannes, Ella pressed her lips together. She wanted to share no more information with either Drusilla or Anna about Hannes. While Drusilla was more discreet in her desire to land a husband, Anna was much more overt. The last thing Ella wanted was to turn either of them loose on the unsuspecting Hannes.

Fortunately, before Ella was forced to decide between answering or ignoring Anna's question, Miriam walked up to her once again.

"There you are, Ella! Have you finished setting out all of the food, then?" The older woman glanced at the tables and, from her expression, it was obvious she saw that people were beginning to sit, even though platters of cold cuts, pickles, chow chow, and sliced bread were only set at one table. "Heavens to Betsy, child! Don't get distracted now! There're hungry people waiting." Gently, she pushed Ella toward the kitchen counter. "Get on now. You best finish before the bishop sits. And then I'd like you to pour water for the men after everyone's seated and the prayer is said."

Thankful for the interruption, Ella hurried to get another two platters and began carrying them to the tables, but not before she heard Miriam scold her stepsisters.

"And you two." Her voice didn't sound half as cheerful as it had when she'd spoken to Ella. "Why, it wouldn't hurt either of you girls to help! Now, you go carry those bowls of applesauce and pretzels over to the women's table." As she walked away, she mumbled, "How you'll ever think to get married . . ." and clucked her tongue disapprovingly.

Chapter Eight

"Absolutely not!"

Linda stood in the center of the kitchen, her arms crossed over the front of her olive-green dress as she practically blocked Ella from walking toward the door. Behind her, Drusilla and Anna watched the exchange between their mother and stepsister, both of them wearing a smug expression.

Oh, how Ella wished that both of them were not standing there behind their mother. Their airs of superiority and self-satisfaction made her feel even more nervous as she tried to convince Linda that she should be permitted to go with the others to the gathering. "But—"

Ella didn't have a chance to finish. Linda held up her hand to stop her from speaking. "You've too much work to do in the morning."

Not for the first time that day, Ella bit her tongue. She wanted to respond, to defend herself. After all, she *always* finished her chores. She also *always* finished Drusilla and Anna's chores, too. Today was no different from any other day, and tomorrow, no doubt, would be just the same. Her stepmother's claim that there was too much work for Ella to do the following day was just another way to hinder her from socializing with the other youth. A way to control her. Again.

Despite thinking this, Ella remained quiet. Inside, she seethed. What did her stepmother have to gain from forcing Ella to stay home? To prohibit her from having some occasional fun? But she said none of this, for Ella realized that it would be a losing battle. There would be no winning against Linda's barring her from attending the youth gathering that evening.

With a satisfied expression on her face, Linda unfolded her arms and reached up to touch the sides of her hair as if checking to make certain it was still properly tucked under her prayer *kapp*. "Besides, Miriam King and her *muder* are coming to visit later and play Scrabble. We need a fourth person, and you know how much Miriam enjoys your company."

And so it was settled.

With a heavy heart, Ella watched as Drusilla and Anna practically pranced out of the house as they headed to the Grimms' farm. She moved over to the window and watched as they walked down the street, laughing as they talked. Ella wondered if they were laughing about her.

She sighed and turned away from the window. It wouldn't do her any good to feel sorry for herself. It wasn't as though anything would have come from the buggy ride with Hannes. At some point, he'd finish whatever business he had in Echo Creek, he'd return to Blue Springs, and that would be the end of that. It wasn't as if a true romance could blossom in just one buggy ride anyway.

Still, the idea of having been asked to ride home

with *someone* had made her feel so hopeful. It was a rare feeling for Ella to feel hopeful about anything.

And now, those hopes were dashed.

Again.

After Drusilla and Anna left, Ella went down to the basement, the small beam from her flashlight illuminating the darkness. She walked around several empty boxes and found the square folding table leaning against the wall. As she reached for it, two little mice ran out and scurried over her foot.

Startled, Ella jumped. But she followed the mice with the light and saw that they stopped running just long enough to sit on their haunches and stare at her.

Bending down, Ella lowered her voice. "Hello there," she whispered.

One of the mice twitched its nose and started to sit up, its paws in the air like a trained dog. Ella laughed. "So adorable."

She stood up and reached onto a nearby shelf for a jar of corn kernels.

"Ella? Have you found the table yet?" her stepmother called from upstairs.

"*Ja*, Maem. I'm just dusting off the cobwebs before I bring it up."

Quickly, Ella scattered some of the kernels onto the dirt floor before turning her attention to the table. Within minutes, she was dragging it upstairs, glad that Linda hadn't ventured down the creaky steps. She'd have seen those mice and insisted, yet again, that Ella sprinkle poison in the corners.

Thankfully, when Ella finally reached the top of the stairs, Linda was nowhere to be seen. Most likely, she had retreated to her bedroom, probably to lay down for a nap before her guests arrived.

Of course, Ella thought as she began to set up the table. Whenever there was work to be done, everyone scattered faster than those kernels on the basement floor.

After setting the Scrabble board onto the table, Ella placed two bowls on top of it, one filled with pretzels and the other with popcorn. She had already made a fresh batch of meadow tea, and there was nothing left to do. Satisfied that everything was ready and her stepmother could find no fault with her, Ella wandered over to the small sofa near the back wall and sat down. At least she could take advantage of the peace and quiet to read the Bible.

Her favorite book was Ecclesiastes, and she often turned to the third chapter when she was feeling down. Oh, she knew that there would be a time for her to laugh. She just wondered when that time would come.

Ever since her father had passed away, she felt as if the only season in her life was winter . . . dark, dreary winter. She tried to pretend that every day was spring or summer, but when she truly had a moment alone to sit and reflect, the truth was that there was little sunshine or brightness in her life.

Even when her father had been alive, Linda had been harder on her than on her own two daughters. Ella's father had done what he could to keep everything equitable among the three but sometimes, Ella had thought, being fair to all was not fair at all. Especially when Linda always favored her daughters over Ella, while her father had never favored Ella over his stepdaughters.

And now that he was gone, things had only gotten worse.

Ella set aside the Bible and leaned back against the

sofa. No, Ecclesiastes was not making her feel better today.

"Ella!"

She took a deep breath at the sound of Linda calling for her from the first-floor bedroom. "*Ja*?"

"How many times have I told you about those mice?" Linda appeared in the doorway, an angry scowl on her face. "I just saw two mice in my bedroom. Haven't you set out those traps in the basement yet?"

Ella bit her lower lip. The truth was that she had put out the traps, but she had purposely not set them. She simply couldn't stomach trying to kill the mice. "The traps are out, *ja*," she said, knowing that her vague answer bordered on deceit. Surely God would forgive her.

"Then go outside to cut some fresh flowers," Linda demanded. "Those old ones can go to compost."

Sighing, Ella started to walk toward the back door, pausing only to grab the vase of black-eyed Susans that were only four days old. Some of them did look a little the worse for wear, but Linda always insisted on fresh flowers when company was coming.

She stepped outside and looked into the sky. It was blue and still bright from the sun, which had yet to begin its descent for the evening. To the right, she saw the cows and horse grazing outside of the whitewashed barn, a reminder that she still needed to tend to them.

The compost pile was along the side of the property, just over a barbed wire fence that bordered a dusty country lane. Ella headed in that direction, her heart heavy as she watched a courting buggy pass by with a young man driving, his special friend seated beside him. They were smiling and talking as if they'd known each other for a long time. Ella didn't recognize the man, but she knew that the woman was none other than Anna Rose Grimm's cousin Elizabeth, who was also the schoolteacher in Echo Creek. From the looks of Elizabeth's smile and her companion's laughter, the school board might be forced to look for another teacher come springtime.

"Why, hello there, Ella!"

Startled, Ella dropped the flower vase and spun around to see who had called out to her. "Hannes!" She placed her hand over her heart and gave a weary smile. "You frightened me!"

"Well now, I didn't mean to do that!" But he gave her a broad grin as he approached her.

With the sun shining through the tops of the trees, Ella caught a good look at him. He still wore his Sunday suit, which, she noticed, had not one speck of dust on it. She wondered what he had been doing all afternoon in Echo Creek that he hadn't changed from his worship clothes.

As he neared her, he removed his sunglasses and, as usual, those blue eyes lit up his face. She found herself mesmerized by how handsome he was. Even more importantly, he was clearly a good-hearted man with a kind disposition. She could hardly believe that someone like Hannes had noticed *her* above all the other unmarried women in Echo Creek.

"Fetching flowers?" Hannes leaned against the wooden post, careful not to get pricked by the barbed wire fencing. "Shouldn't you be getting ready for the singing, then?"

She liked how he spoke, his words almost musical. Like many other Amish people, he ended the last word of his sentences on a higher note. It was singsong speaking, she always thought. And while it was a happy sound, her mood was anything but joyful. His question had reminded her of why, exactly, she was outside gathering flowers instead of doing as he suggested: preparing for a night with her peers.

With a heavy heart, she took a deep breath. "It appears that I won't be attending the singing after all," she admitted slowly. She lowered her eyes when she spoke, praying that he couldn't see her hurt.

His response was silence.

When a few long seconds had passed and he still remained quiet, Ella finally looked up. She was surprised to see a frown etched across his face.

Oh, how she hated to disappoint people. And from the way he looked, he was, indeed, terribly disappointed.

"I'm very sorry, Hannes," she said in a soft, apologetic voice. When he didn't say anything, she added, "Maem has company coming over. The deacon's wife. And my *maem* told me that I must stay to play Scrabble."

He raised an eyebrow, a curious response to what she had just said. Still, he said nothing.

"I . . . I truly was looking forward to . . ."

She wanted to tell him that she had thought of nothing else but the proposed buggy ride home with him. Her first. But she didn't want to sound too forward.

". . . the singing."

Hannes reached up, removed his hat, and wiped his brow with the back of his wrist. While he looked less cheerful than when he had arrived, he clearly was not holding it against her. "Reckon a singing is just that . . . a singing." He sounded as disappointed as she felt. "Suppose there's no sense in my going, then."

On the one hand, Ella felt a little bit of joy that

Hannes would forego the singing because she wasn't permitted to attend. She could only imagine how Drusilla and Anna would have behaved as they tried to capture his attention. Hadn't it been Drusilla who had been so boastful after worship that day, vowing that she would drive home from the singing in his buggy?

However, Ella also felt guilty that her inability to attend the singing was causing him distress. What would he do now? Clearly he knew no one else in the town. She hadn't seen him converse with anyone during fellowship, not in a way that indicated he had friends or family there. In fact, when she had served the platters to the tables during the first sitting, Hannes had been seated with the church leaders, not the other young men.

Suddenly, a wave of panic washed over her. If he knew no one, perhaps he had stayed in Echo Creek because of her! Maybe he had stayed just to take her home from the singing! That thought caused her even more anguish. Certainly he would be disenchanted with her now!

Hannes gazed in the direction where the courting buggy with Elizabeth Grimm and her suitor had disappeared just moments ago. As if reading her mind, he said, "Mayhaps I'll go wander to that pond later this evening, though."

She caught him peering at her from the corner of his eye.

"Sit a spell and try to double-skip some rocks, listen to the cicadas and owls . . ."

She could barely breathe. Why was he telling her this? Was he suggesting something? "That . . . that sounds lovely."

Hannes faced her. "The sun sets at eight tonight. Mayhaps you'd find your way to the pond just before then. We could watch it set together and I could walk you home by nine?"

Quickly, Ella did some calculations. The singing wouldn't end until about that time, so she wouldn't run any risk of Drusilla or Anna seeing her. And surely Miriam and her mother would be gone by then. If not, Ella could excuse herself to take a brisk walk. If she just happened to walk to the pond and happened to run into Hannes, no one could fault her, could they?

Ella bit her lower lip and nodded. "*Ja*, I think I could manage that." She could only pray that Linda wouldn't ask too many questions if she left while Miriam and her mother were still at the house.

Hannes leaned forward and plucked the late-opening blue bloom of a morning glory that had climbed over part of the fence, the ever-twisting vines woven throughout the wire. He handed the flower to her, his fingers just lightly brushing against her hand.

The gesture startled her, especially when she felt as if an electric current raced through her veins. She took the flower and looked up at him, equally startled to see him studying her face, with the hint of a smile on his lips. Transfixed, Ella held his gaze, too aware of the fluttery feeling in her stomach.

Without turning, Hannes began to back away, his eyes still holding her gaze. "I'll see you then, Ella."

Nodding her head, she watched as he turned and hurried back down the lane toward town, a bit of a spring to his step. Only before he disappeared did he turn around and lift his hand in the air to wave good-bye. When he turned the corner, she noticed he had not headed in the direction of the singing.

Was it possible that he truly meant it? That he wouldn't go to the singing? And was that because she wouldn't be there?

Smiling to herself, Ella cradled the morning glory in her hand. She'd have to hurry if she wanted to press it so that she could keep the flower forever, a reminder of this special moment when Hannes's intentions seemed clearer than ever: he may have come to Echo Creek on business, but Hannes appeared to have stayed for the pleasure of getting to know her.

Chapter Nine

"Now, Maem," Miriam said slowly to her elderly mother, pointing at the tiles on the Scrabble board. "That's not a word."

The wrinkles in Mary's forehead creased together, forming several deep lines as she scowled at her daughter. "I can't hear you."

Dismissively, Miriam waved her hand. "Oh, you can hear me just fine!"

"Cannot!"

Ella laughed at the playful exchange between mother and daughter. It was bittersweet to watch them, for she knew that she'd never have that type of relationship with Linda. However, she also knew that Linda would never have that relationship with *anyone*, not even her own daughters.

Miriam leaned forward and patted Ella's hand. "What do you say, Ella? Is 'accentor' a word?"

Ella had never before heard the word, but she didn't want to challenge Miriam's mother. The woman was almost eighty-five years old and, despite her age, was known to be rather sharp. Besides, challenging an elderly woman seemed downright disrespectful to Ella.

With a gentle shrug, Ella replied, "I really couldn't say."

"*Ach*!" Dramatically, Miriam threw her hands in the air. "You've always been too kindhearted to stand up for your Scrabble rights!"

Ella laughed.

"Maem!" Miriam returned her attention to her mother. "You can't play that word. It's made up."

"Is not." Mary crossed her arms over her chest, the pale, thin skin on her hands sharply contrasting with the dark navy blue fabric of her dress. Defiantly, she pursed her lips. "Look it up."

Linda clicked her tongue. "Ladies, please! It's just a word."

But Miriam persisted. "It's on a triple-score space, Linda. That's thirty-six points. Plus the fact that she'll get fifty points for using all her tiles."

Ella tried to hide a smile. She knew that Linda would not argue with the deacon's wife, but the irritated look on her stepmother's face was priceless.

Miriam nudged Ella's arm. "Go fetch me the dictionary."

Obediently, Ella pushed back from the kitchen table and hurried to the bookshelf, where the dictionary was set among the other books. She walked back to the table and handed it to Miriam, who proceeded to quickly flip through the book.

Her mouth opened and her eyes widened. "Well! I'll be."

Mary gave a partially toothless grin. "Told you so."

"It's a type of bird!" Miriam shut the dictionary and stared incredulously at her mother. "How on earth . . . ?"

"I know my birds, Dochder!" She couldn't look much more smug. "Now I'm waiting to hear something from you . . ."

Miriam rolled her eyes. "I'm sorry I doubted you."

Ella laughed, enjoying herself much more than she had thought possible. Surely this *was* more fun than a singing, after all.

No sooner had she thought that than the clock on the wall began to chime. It was seven thirty.

"Oh help!" She glanced at the tiles. She couldn't start a new game if she wanted to get to the pond in time for meeting Hannes.

"Something amiss, Ella?"

Looking up at Miriam, Ella realized that she had spoken aloud. For a second, she stammered, trying to find the right words so that her stepmother wouldn't be suspicious. "I . . . uh . . . I forgot that I haven't turned out the cows and horse," she finally said, which was true. She had purposely kept them inside so that she'd have an excuse to leave the house.

"Uh-huh." Miriam gave her a sideways glance, a hint of mischievousness lurking in her gray eyes. "I reckon you'll be wanting to beg off the rest of the game, then?"

Linda made a face and glowered at her stepdaughter. "Absolutely not! You can set them out later, Ella."

"Oh, Linda! It's a Sunday evening, *ja*? You were young once, too, weren't you?"

Linda pressed her lips together.

"I thought so." Miriam winked at Ella. "Ella was more than kind to stay and play Scrabble with us old birds when all the other young folk are out socializing. Such kindness for humoring us should be repaid, don't you think?" And then, as her mother reached for her replacement tiles, Miriam glanced around the room quizzically. "Speaking of which, where are your *dochders*, anyway?" Without waiting for an answer, she continued, "Out gallivanting, I suppose. Surprised neither of them saw fit to spend a Sunday with us."

Oh, how Ella wanted to smile at Miriam's comment. Clearly Linda's plan had backfired; by keeping Ella home from the singing, her own two daughters looked poorly in the guests' eyes.

Leaning over, Miriam placed her hand on Ella's. "You run along, Ella. You work so hard all the time anyway. It's right *gut* for you to have some fun for a bit."

Grateful, Ella mouthed the word "*danke*" at Miriam before she swept her tiles into the little bag and excused herself from the table, but not before she caught the disapproving scowl worn by Linda. She'd have to deal with her stepmother later. For now, she couldn't wait to run to the pond so that she could spend a few stolen moments with Hannes.

It only took her fifteen minutes to get to the very place they had met just a few days before. The entire time she walked there, she fretted that she'd be too late, and then she worried that she was too early. The last thing she wanted was to appear overly eager. After all, Hannes didn't know her very well . . . not many people did. She'd hate for him to think that she was a fast girl on *rumschpringe*!

As she walked down the path that led to the pond, she worried that he might have left already. Even worse, what if he hadn't shown up at all? Upon seeing Hannes standing at the edge, skimming rocks along the top of the water, she felt immediate relief.

Just a few yards away from him, she stopped walking. Her heart pounded, and she realized that this was both the most exciting and the scariest thing she had ever done, sneaking out of the house to meet up with a young man. Her hands shook and she felt shy, standing there, so uncertain what to do.

"Hello," she called out at last, not wanting to startle him.

He glanced over his shoulder, and when he saw her there, he broke into a broad smile. "I wasn't certain you'd make it." He took a step toward her. "Thought your Scrabble game might be a bit too exciting to leave!"

She liked how he teased her. "Oh, it was getting fairly intense, let me tell you. Why, when I left, there was a major battle over the word 'accentor.'"

"Accentor." His eyebrows knit together. "That's a bird, *ja*?"

Stunned, Ella stared at him with an open mouth. "How on earth did you know that?"

He gave her a playful wink. "I know my birds."

"Funny. That's what Miriam's *maem* said just this evening!"

He chuckled, his lips pursed as if enjoying a little secret. "*Ja*, well, my family always liked to bird-watch," Hannes said before, standing upon a rock, he reached for her hand. "*Kum*, Ella. I've gathered some rocks here. We can have a skimming contest."

"A contest?"

He wiggled his fingers, encouraging her to take his hand. "*Ja*, who can get the most skips."

She eyed his proffered hand. Surely he didn't think that she couldn't walk without his help. Over the past year, she had come to this pond more times than she could remember. It was the only place she could escape and think, pray to God and reflect on how much her life had changed since her father had passed away. Oh, she had climbed over that rock many times.

However, he was watching her with such an earnest

look upon his face that she felt compelled to take his hand. *What harm,* she thought, *in letting him assist me?*

Slowly, she placed her hand in his, almost jumping when she felt his fingers embrace hers. She had never held a man's hand before . . . not even her father's! It felt warm and wonderful. The color rose to her cheeks, and she averted her gaze.

Carefully, Hannes guided her over the rock and down the narrow path alongside the pond, where, true to his word, he had gathered several small piles of rocks. Ella couldn't help but wonder how long he had been there, for each pile was large enough to keep them occupied well past sunset.

"My word!" she exclaimed. "You must think an awful lot of my stone-skipping skills!" With wide eyes, she looked up at him. "And after seeing only one throw, at that!"

"Sometimes, Ella, that's all it takes to make a strong first impression."

More heat rose to her cheeks, and she heard him chuckle.

"Now, let's get started with that contest, *ja*?" He pointed to a pile to the left. "Those are yours. I put the flattest rocks there."

She eyed the rock pile and frowned. "And in the other pile?"

With a quick glance over his shoulder, he gave a little shrug. "All the rest."

"Hannes?"

He met her gaze. "*Ja*?"

"You know that flat rocks skip the best, don't you?"

He nodded.

"Then why would you take the pile filled with all the round rocks?"

At that question, he gave her a sheepish grin. "Aw, Ella. You caught me." He held up his hands as if he were giving up. "I figured I'd give you the better rocks and kept the round ones for myself." The expression on his face, complete with his blue eyes flashing at her in a mischievous way, made her laugh.

For the first few minutes, they focused their conversation on the art of rock skimming. Ella wondered if Hannes felt half as awkward as she did. But each time she glanced at him, he seemed poised and collected, completely at ease conversing with her.

"You're quite good at this," he complimented her. "But can you do this?" He reached down for one of her flat rocks and angled his throw in such a way that the rock skimmed not once or twice, but five times across the shimmering top of the water.

When the rock finally sank into the depths of the pond, Ella gasped. "I've never seen a rock skip that many times!"

"Want me to show you how to do it?"

Eagerly, she nodded. "*Ja*, of course."

To her surprise, he walked around behind her and, after stooping to pick up another rock, he stood with his chest practically pressed against her back. His nearness made her nervous, especially when he reached for her hand, his arm pressed lightly against hers. He stood so close that she could smell the lingering scent of lavender on his clothes.

"Now, you hold the rock the regular way . . ." he said, molding her fingers around the rock. "*Ja*, that's right. Just like that. But when you pull back to throw it"—he moved her arm backward and she felt his fingers press against her wrist—"you need to angle it like so." Tilting her hand backward, he pulled her arm farther back and lightly pushed it forward. "See? Like that?"

She held her breath, feeling light-headed.

Hannes took a step away from her and motioned toward the pond. "Now you try it, only with speed this time, of course."

Forcing herself to return her attention to the rock in her hand, and not the man standing behind her, Ella swallowed. If nothing else magical ever happened in her life, Ella would forever remember this very moment as being the most enchanting.

"Ella?"

She cleared her throat, concentrating on the task at hand. She followed his instructions, bringing her arm back and angling her wrist before sliding the rock through the air. One. Two. Three. Four. Five. It skipped five times.

"Good job, Ella!" he shouted good-naturedly. "What an astute learner you are!"

She felt the heat on her cheeks and lowered her eyes. "Perhaps it was the teacher."

He gave a little laugh. "A blending of the two, I think. Just like at school. No pupil can take all the credit, nor can the teacher. It requires both of them to give their best in order to get good results." He glanced at Ella. "I imagine you were a strong student, *ja*?"

His attention on her made Ella feel nervous. She wasn't used to people asking her personal questions. "I reckon no more so than any other student."

He gave her a cheeky grin. "And modest, too. I like that."

Personal questions and sweet compliments made her far too uncomfortable. "What about you?" Ella asked, hoping to deflect the conversation away from her.

"Me? Oh, I was a right *gut* student. My older *bruders* made certain of that. And then, just as they stopped attending, one of my *schwesters* became the teacher." He laughed. "Oh, I didn't dare step out of line with her standing at the front of the school."

"You've lots of siblings, then?"

He gave a firm and serious nod. "*Ja,* I do. Two older *bruders* and two younger ones. Same with the *schwesters.* But the older girls have moved to their husbands' towns and one of my *bruder*'s farms."

"And the other *bruder*?"

"Works with my *daed.*"

He didn't offer any more information, and the way he said that sounded rather flat. So Ella remained quiet. It wasn't her place to pry into other people's business. But she certainly had a lot of questions she would have liked to ask, including why, exactly, he was in Echo Creek to begin with.

"Let me show you something," he said at last, breaking the silence that had fallen between them. Stooping down, he grabbed a round rock from his own pile, trying to skip it, but it just sank to the bottom. "See what happens when you choose the wrong type of stone? When you make bad choices, the stone sinks and the ripples spread far and wide."

Standing up straight, he stared at the pond. "It's like life, I suppose," he said thoughtfully, his gaze still on the water. "Bad stones sink; good stones soar. It's all in the choice."

Ella watched him, taking in his broad shoulders and determined stance. She wondered why he had suddenly grown so serious. Rather than ask, however, she waited patiently for Hannes to finish his reflective moment.

"I try to make good choices, to follow God's Word, and to be fair to others." With a quick glance over his shoulder, he took a deep breath and sighed. "It's hard to watch other people who do not walk the same path."

Ella tilted her head, studying his expression. Gone was the jovial, teasing Hannes, replaced with this more serious, contemplative man. There was another side to Hannes, and Ella found her curiosity piqued. She replied slowly, echoing his serious tone, "The choices we make, Hannes, are the one thing we truly own. If some people choose poorly, we can only pray for them, *ja*? We cannot be responsible for others' poor decisions."

He nodded his head, approving her words. "Well put, Ella."

He said nothing more, but Ella found herself wondering what situation in his life had prompted the observation. Did he, like her, have to put up with disagreeable relatives? Had someone's poor choices made his own life difficult?

She dared not pry, but found herself hoping that he might understand—and feel compassion for—her less-than-happy life.

Chapter Ten

On Monday morning, Ella woke up earlier than usual. It wasn't hard to do, since she had barely slept at all. Her mind kept replaying every conversation, every glance, every moment she had spent with Hannes the previous evening.

While she knew that he would return to Blue Springs soon, she also knew that she would treasure that time spent in his company. How could she not? He had been attentive and kind, funny and charming. And when he had stood behind her, his hand upon her wrist, his chest pressed against her back . . .

Well, she could barely forget *that* moment. It had been as if there was no one else on the planet. Just her and Hannes.

Without doubt, Ella knew he was unlike any other man in Echo Creek.

Knowing that she needed to arise and greet the day, Ella tossed back the covers, sat up, and stretched. The air in her bedroom felt cool that morning, which did not displease her. As usual, she needed to bake bread for the store and tend to the weeds in the garden. The early coolness was perfect for doing both chores.

When Ella walked down the staircase, the dark and quiet kitchen greeted her. Outside the window, she could hear the faint sound of some birds chirping. The sky was just beginning to shed its darkness and morph into a lighter, steely gray color. This was her favorite time of the day, the time she could pray without interruption. Every morning she talked with God, sharing her desire to be righteous and kind, just as her mother had instructed her. And when there were challenges, she asked God to guide her.

He never failed.

Today, however, her conversation with God was different. She thanked him for bringing Hannes into her life, even if it was just a chance meeting. Hannes had taught her something that she needed to learn: other people struggled with goodness just as much as she did. And she had also learned that there were people in the world who were interested in *her* as a person, not just as a servant, the way Linda and her daughters treated her.

While Ella held no misplaced fantasies that Hannes wanted to court her, she was truly thankful for having the chance to get to know him and to feel special, even if only for a short few hours. Her entire demeanor felt recharged and ready for almost anything that her stepmother might throw at her.

By the time the wall clock chimed six times, Ella had been awake for almost two hours. Her dough rested in large bowls, rising beneath clean kitchen towels. Ella had already fed the livestock in the barn. Before she could focus on the garden, she needed to punch down the dough one more time, make the loaves, and let them rise once more before baking them.

Just as she started to do that, she heard the sound of footsteps at the top of the staircase.

"Ella, where's my pink dress?"

With her hands full of dried flour, Ella switched on the faucet and called out, "Hanging on the back of your bedroom door." She could hear Drusilla's heavy footsteps as she stomped back to her room.

"It's not there!" She sounded angry, and that could mean only one thing: recharged or not, Ella's morning was about to go downhill.

"Look behind your Sunday dress," she called out, knowing full well that was where the pink dress hung. Yesterday, Drusilla had changed after worship, leaving her dress in a puddle on the floor. Ella had been the one to pick up the dress and apron, shake off the dust, and hang both items on the hook on the door.

A few minutes of silence followed, and Ella knew that her stepsister had found what she sought.

The door to the first-floor bedroom, the one that Ella's father used to share with her mother and then, years later, with Linda, opened.

"What's all this ruckus about?" Linda shuffled into the kitchen. Her eyes were still puffy from sleep. "Honestly, Ella, don't you ever think about anybody besides yourself?" She headed toward the table, still trying to pin the front of her dress shut. "I had another fifteen minutes before I needed to get up."

Ella rubbed soap on her hands, trying to remove the remnants of sticky dough. "Sorry, Maem." And she was. That would have been an extra fifteen minutes without having to deal with her stepmother.

"Fetch me some coffee. It's the least you could do," Linda mumbled. She sank into the chair at the head of the table and sighed.

After drying her hands on a dish towel, Ella reached for a mug and poured some steaming coffee into it. Carefully, she carried it to the table and set it before her stepmother. "There you go. Mayhaps this'll help shake away the sleep."

"Another fifteen minutes would've done that just as well!" Linda snapped, but she took the mug anyway and lifted it to her lips.

Footsteps on the bottom steps announced Drusilla's appearance in the kitchen. "Ella, did you even wash this?" Angrily, she stormed across the floor and stood in between her mother and Ella, holding the edge of her dress. "Look! It's got a stain on it!" she said accusingly. "Don't tell me you, too, started hanging out dirty laundry just to look like you're working hard."

Linda raised an eyebrow. "Who's been doing that?"

"Susie Lapp. You know. That woman with all the *kinner* across the way." Drusilla gave a delighted laugh. If one thing could switch Drusilla into a good mood, it was gossip. "Why, I saw her the other morning hanging perfectly dry clothing on the line when I woke early."

Ella highly doubted that. It was more likely that she had been arriving home in the early morning hours.

"Well, I never!" Linda gasped.

"She didn't notice me, but those clothes were as dry as a field that had no rain for two weeks in the summer!"

Linda clicked her tongue in disapproval. "I sure do

wonder if the bishop knows about that. Seems rather deceitful."

Ella had no doubt that Linda would be the first to inform the bishop. Hoping to divert their attention, Ella reached for the dress and studied the fabric, squinting as she did so. "Where's the stain?"

"Right here!" Drusilla pointed her finger at the edge. "Are you blind, Ella? Can't you see that?"

With a soft sigh of exasperation, Ella reached forward and plucked a small piece of black fuzz from the dress. She remained silent as she walked over to the garbage can near the refrigerator and threw it out. She didn't expect Drusilla to apologize, but it would have been appreciated.

Instead, Drusilla tossed the dress over the back of another chair and sat down next to her mother, the dress all but forgotten. "I need to visit the Whitakers this afternoon, Maem." She reached for her mother's mug of coffee, but Linda slapped away her hand.

"Fetch your own coffee!"

Drusilla glanced over her shoulder at Ella. "Coffee." It wasn't a question, but a demand. Then she returned her attention to her mother. "The Whitakers? May I?"

"What's going on at the Whitakers' *haus*?" Linda asked, her tone more curious than concerned.

That was always the way it was with Linda and her daughters, Ella thought as she set a mug of coffee before Drusilla. They were the eyes and ears of Echo Creek, spreading tidbits of hearsay and gossip as fast as people could gather it in. *Just once,* Ella thought, *it would be interesting to see how they would respond if the gossip were about them!*

"Well, ever since that Sadie disappeared . . ."

At the mention of Sadie Whitaker, Ella's ears perked up. It had been almost a week since Sadie had vanished. Even though no one had heard anything of her whereabouts, the majority of the Amish community at Echo Creek had not been terribly alarmed. Apparently more people knew that Sadie's stepmother behaved poorly to the young woman. In fact, the suspicion was that Sadie had run away after her stepmother tried to convince her husband that Sadie should marry an old, cantankerous widower with six young children.

While this had been news to Ella, she didn't blame her friend. There were days that she, too, thought about leaving. The idea of running away was much more appealing than continuing to live with her stepmother and stepsisters. The only problem was that she had nowhere to run to. Still, she wondered why Sadie hadn't said anything to her about her stepmother's plans.

". . . Rachel Whitaker's been terribly upset. I promised to go sit with her awhile."

Linda made a soft noise that almost sounded like a cat purring. "What a good girl you are," she said, clearly approving of Drusilla's plans. "So kind and compassionate."

With her back turned, Ella rolled her eyes. Oh, she had no doubt that Drusilla was going to visit Rachel Whitaker. But her certainty wasn't due to Drusilla being overly kind or compassionate to the Whitakers. It was more likely because the Whitakers conveniently lived next to the Miller family. No doubt the real reason for visiting the Whitakers was not to console Rachel over her missing stepdaughter—for *she* hadn't seemed very distraught about Sadie's disappearance to begin with!—but to stop in to the Millers' house and see if Timothy was there.

"Of course you may take off for the afternoon," Linda cooed, reaching out to pat Drusilla's hand in a loving gesture of pride. Then, with a sharper tone, she turned to look at Ella. "You'll have to cover for her at the store."

Ella's mouth opened, just a little. There was no way she could weed the garden, clean the house, and finish baking the bread in such a short period of time. "But I was . . ."

Interrupting her by holding up her hand, Linda narrowed her eyes. "How many times have I told you, Ella, that I do not appreciate your back talk?"

For the second time that morning, Ella found herself apologizing to her stepmother.

Linda scanned the room with an eagle eye. "So finish up your chores here, Ella, then come to the store. And be quick about it. No lollygagging today."

As if I ever do, Ella wanted to say, but she bit her tongue and held back the words. There was no sense in inviting more ire from her stepmother. She knew that would only make for more unpleasantness, something Ella knew was best avoided, especially given Linda's bad temper that morning.

"New inventory arrived on Saturday, and I'll need you there to unpack it, tag it, and stock the shelves. And then the front window needs to be cleaned." She glanced around the kitchen. "I think the floor in here needs to be re-waxed, too. It's not shiny enough for my liking."

Ella wanted to comment that the floor was not only spotless, shiny, and clean, but she had waxed it just two weeks earlier! If it were any shinier, the sunlight would reflect so bright that it would be blinding.

"Of course, Maem," she heard herself say, dreading the thought of having to do that particular chore once again.

Linda walked over to the small mirror that hung near the door. Gazing at her reflection, she lifted her hand and began to pull her hair away from her face, twisting it into a tight bun. As usual, she pulled it back so tight that the part in the middle of her head looked even balder than before.

"And, of course, we'll need those loaves of bread. They always sell quickly on Mondays."

"They're almost ready to be baked."

Linda's eyes traveled to the counter. Silently, Ella watched as Linda counted them and shook her head. "That won't do, Ella. You only made fifteen! I'll need at least ten more. Weren't you listening to me? It's Monday. People buy the most bread on Monday."

Despite knowing that, on the contrary, five of the loaves went unpurchased the previous Monday, Ella found herself agreeing to her stepmother's senseless demand. Often it was just easier to do so and figure out later how to accommodate whatever was requested. On rare occasions, Linda forgot. Perhaps today would be one of those days.

Linda reached for her prayer *kapp* and placed it upon her head, taking a straight pin from the front of her dress. Reaching up, she stuck the pin through the white head covering so that it was attached to her hair. "Now, how about some breakfast, Ella, unless you have some more dirty laundry to hang outside on the line?"

And so Ella's week began. With a tightness forming in her chest, Ella moved over to the kitchen counter.

She wasn't necessarily surprised by how unreasonable Linda was on this beautiful Monday morning. What she was surprised about was how she felt. Though she usually just complied with Linda's orders—for what else could she possibly do?—today she had to fight the urge to bark back at her stepmother.

Be kind and good, no matter what happens, for God has a plan for you.

Her mother's words rang in her ears, like a whisper from the past. Ella paused in what she was doing and placed her hands on the counter. For a long moment, she gazed out the window and looked across the front yard. A patch of morning glory bloomed in the early morning sunlight, a reminder of the wisdom once spoken to her by her dying mother.

Her mother had planted those vines, and every year, Ella made certain to take the seeds so that she could replant them the following spring. She planted them all around the property, including the shaded area along the side fencing so that, even in the afternoons, there were always blooms.

Be kind and good, no matter what happens, for God has a plan for you.

I will, Maem, Ella said to herself. *For you and for God, I will try to do just that.*

Turning to Linda, Ella forced a smile. "Would you prefer eggs for breakfast, or pancakes?" She didn't need to ask, however, for the answer was always the same: both.

Chapter Eleven

Around two o'clock in the afternoon, the store was empty. Ella carried her bucket of cleaning supplies toward the front of the building, passing the table where she had put out the new inventory of fabric earlier. Her eyes caught on the two bolts that had nearly taken away her breath.

What on earth was Linda thinking? No one would buy those fabrics, not with the price tag so dear! Echo Creek was a small, simple town. Young women did not purchase fancy fabrics, and certainly not at the price that Linda had set.

She shook her head, disapproving Linda's choices in inventory. Just another reason the store was in such bad financial shape.

At the front of the store, Ella set about dusting the display window, hoping not to hear any more of Anna's complaining to her mother about why *she* didn't get an afternoon off like Drusilla. It dawned on Ella that if Anna put as much energy into working as she did into complaining, Linda wouldn't need both of her daughters to work at the store every day.

Outside the open window, she could hear the sound of an approaching horse and buggy. It stopped in front of the store. Even though the buggy was so close, Ella couldn't see who it was. Quickly, she shoved the cleaning rag into her apron pocket and hurried to the back of the store so that she could assist the customer, if needed. Clearly, Linda and Anna were too engrossed in their argument to be interrupted.

The bell over the door tinkled, and Ella heard heavy footsteps crossing the floor. But a tall shelving unit blocked the doorway from her view.

"Ella, take care of that customer," Linda hissed from the back room.

"*Ja*, I will," she responded, glancing in the direction of her stepmother's voice. Only when she returned her attention to the store did she catch her breath. A man stood before her, the counter acting as a barrier, as he stared at her with a look of surprise on his face.

Ella, too, was equally surprised. "Oh!" she gasped. "It's you!"

Hannes smiled at her, his eyes lighting up his face. "Startle you, then?"

Ella placed her hand on her chest near her heart and nodded. "*Ja*, you did."

"I'm terribly sorry."

Shaking her head, Ella was quick to dismiss his apology. "*Nee*, there's no reason to apologize." She felt foolish. The truth was that she had started because she recognized him, not just because he had suddenly appeared at the counter. She had never considered that she might run into him again, and it certainly hadn't crossed her mind that he might show up at the store. "I . . . I just didn't hear you come to the counter."

Hannes glanced over her shoulder at the open door

to the room where Anna was pleading her case, one more time, to her mother.

Biting her lip, Ella took a moment to reach behind herself, and, embarrassed for both Linda and Anna, she quietly shut the door. "How may I help you, Hannes?"

"So professional and businesslike," he teased. Then, leaning against the counter, he studied her intently. "I didn't realize you work here."

They had only met those two times—three, if she counted their brief talk after worship. Why would he have given any thought to where she worked at all? Still, there was something about the way he said it, the way his eyes widened, that made her wonder if her working there was a good thing or a bad thing in his eyes.

"*Nee.* I'm just covering for one of Linda's *dochders,*" she responded at last.

He raised an eyebrow as if he found that to be rather curious. "I see." He paused. "Then you don't normally work here?"

She shook her head, the intensity of his gaze making her feel nervous. Why was he asking her these questions? And hadn't she already answered that question anyway?

He straightened up and placed his hand on the counter. "I'm glad to hear that," he said in a strained voice.

Ella frowned, wondering what *that* was supposed to mean, when the door behind her swung open, the edge of it grazing her hip.

Linda stomped out, Anna following with red cheeks. Both of them stopped abruptly when they noticed Hannes standing there.

"Oh, my!" Linda's expression softened at once. "Henry Clemens!" She seemed almost as startled as Ella had been to see Hannes standing there. "Were we supposed to meet today, then?"

Ella's frown deepened. Henry? Meet? She looked from Hannes to her stepmother and then back to Hannes. What on earth was going on here? How would her stepmother know Hannes, and what could they possibly have to meet about? And why had she called him Henry? Ella supposed that Hannes was a nickname and Henry his more formal given name, one that he would use for business.

Clearing his throat, Hannes straightened and shifted his eyes from Ella to Linda. "That's what you said last week."

Now Ella was truly confused. Last week? Hannes had met with her stepmother the previous week? Who *was* this man?

To her further humiliation, Linda looked at her, and something dark shifted over her eyes. "Don't just stand there lollygagging again, Ella!" she snapped. "Get back to work!"

Ella felt the heat rise to her cheeks, mortified that her stepmother would talk to her in such a sharp manner in front of the handsome stranger. What would he think of her? Linda had made it sound like Ella was lazy, someone who spent her time aimlessly, perhaps following idle pursuits. Despite such ideas being the furthest thing from the truth, Ella realized that she didn't want Hannes to think she was negligent when working.

Immediately, Ella longed for her father and wondered why God had taken him so soon. When he had been alive, Linda had treated her better. Not well—just better. But all of that had changed when her father had passed away and the ownership of the store had passed to his wife. Now, Ella was nothing more than an insignificant servant in her stepmother's eyes.

With a downcast gaze, Ella returned to the display window and continued cleaning it. Her heart beat rapidly, and she knew that her cheeks were still red from embarrassment. Fortunately, neither Linda nor Hannes could see her. But Ella made certain to position herself so that she could overhear Hannes talking to Linda.

"Henry!" Linda's voice sounded chipper and more pleasant now, something else that caused Ella to frown. "How good to see you again!" A slight laugh escaped Linda's throat. "I'm terribly sorry I couldn't spend more time with you last week. Something"—she paused—"came up unexpectedly."

Ella knew that eavesdropping was not polite, but in the empty store, it was impossible to not hear them. Besides, Linda had no more ability to speak softly than she had to behave kindly. Curiosity got the best of her, however, and Ella leaned over so that she could peek around the corner of the aisle. She noticed that Hannes straightened his shoulders and pressed his hands on the counter. The way he stood made him seem more authoritative.

"So I overheard," he said drily.

Linda mirrored his stance as if trying to dominate him. "To be honest, I was expecting your father to come, seeing that my intention is to do business with him."

Do business with Hannes's father? Ella's eyes widened. What business could Hannes and his father possibly have with Linda?

"*Ja, vell,* after our first meeting two weeks ago, my

daed asked me to return to town and spend a few days," Hannes said in a short, crisp tone. "You know, to see what I could learn about the store."

"Oh!" Another laugh from Linda, this one sounding just as forced as the first one, but also a bit nervous. "*Ja*, of course."

Two weeks ago? That was when Ella had first observed him watching her at the worship service. And then they had met at the pond. She felt a wave of disappointment. Clearly Hannes hadn't returned to Echo Creek just to see her! He truly did have business.

The shuffling of papers caught her attention, and once again, Ella peered around the shelves to see what Linda was looking for.

"And . . . well, what have you learned?"

"Quite a bit. Seems that prices keep increasing, and the inventory does not vary." Hannes stepped away from the counter and gestured for Linda to follow him. Conveniently for Ella, he led her stepmother to an aisle near where she was working.

"And I understand that you met with the clock maker that my *daed* sent to you and you offered to take six clocks, but only on consignment, *ja*?"

Linda puffed her chest. "Better than pouring out cash for items we've never carried before. After all, our folks in Echo Creek are not familiar with that line of products. Surely you cannot expect me to outright *pay* for such an extravagant inventory item without testing the market first." She smiled at him. Ella could tell that, yet again, it was forced. "Good business practice, don't you think?"

Ella returned her attention to the display, dusting the glass shelves and waiting to hear Hannes's reply.

But she heard only a low mumble and couldn't make out his words.

Consignment? she thought. When had her father ever taken anything on consignment? Undoubtedly, Linda was asking for such an arrangement because there was a cash flow problem, and from the sounds of it, Linda didn't want Hannes to know that. While Ella could understand her reasons, she could not understand why she would outright lie. Nor could she understand what Hannes was doing there, talking business with Linda, in the first place.

Shaking her head, Ella said a quick prayer, asking God to forgive her stepmother, yet again, for deceiving the young man.

"Good business practice for you is not good business practice for the vendor. It signals financial issues, which, I'm sure you will agree, is also not a good practice for investors." Another long pause. "Like us. If you are truly interested in partnering with us, you need to be more up-front about the cash flow situation at the store."

Ella stopped working and quietly stood up. Investors? Partners? Were things so bad that Linda was looking to sell part of the business? Her heart sank, and she felt as if a shallow pit had formed in her stomach. Oh, how heartsick her father would be if he were alive!

Linda appeared panicked. "I can assure you that cash flow is not a problem. Why, ask anyone in town. We *are* the only store in Echo Creek, after all."

"Still, I'll have to discuss this matter with my *daed*," Hannes said, taking a step back toward the counter. "And I wonder about your inventory . . ."

His voice trailed away, and Linda must have followed

him. Ella could no longer see her stepmother, nor could she hear whatever was said next. They both disappeared. Linda must have escorted Hannes behind the counter and into the inventory room, perhaps to talk privately or to show him something in the back.

Trying to calm herself, Ella glanced around the store. So much of it still showed her father's hand. He had taken such care of the store, building the shelves himself, studying how to lay out the goods in order to appeal to the shoppers. And yet, there were small changes that no longer represented her father's practices, but Linda's.

The books that Ella's friend Belle loved so much were now in the back of the last aisle, rather than near the front of the store, where the sewing goods had been moved. Ella had tried to tell her stepmother that moving the sewing goods to the front was a mistake. Women who came for fabrics, needles, and thread lingered. Wouldn't it be better to have them walk through the store so that they could see other items and, mayhaps, make additional purchases instead of just browsing fabrics near the front door without venturing farther inside?

Ten minutes passed before Linda led Hannes back into the store. She swept her hand toward a back aisle and pointed to a top shelf. "There," she said. "That is where we've put the clocks."

Ella watched as Hannes looked where Linda had pointed to the shelf near the kerosene lanterns. Knowing better than to speak up, Ella kept her thoughts to herself. However, if she had felt free to say what was on her mind, she would have told Linda that clocks would not sell in the kerosene lantern section. Perhaps near the aisle with the dish sets would be a better place.

To Ella's surprise, Hannes must have thought the same thing, for he shook his head. "*Nee*, not there."

Linda made a stern face. She wasn't used to having her suggestions turned down. "And why ever not? That's a perfectly fine place to display clocks, I'll have you know."

Hannes appeared as if he were forcing himself to remain calm and patient. It was a look that Ella knew well from her own experience. "Clocks are something young men purchase for their intended bride. They would not be looking for such a purchase in the section stocked with kerosene lanterns." He took a few steps toward another aisle and gestured toward the dishware. "Here. Most young men will also consider purchasing a set of dishes or glassware. Wouldn't it be best to display the clocks here? Surely it is a better place to catch his eye and change his mind on the best engagement gift for his future wife."

"There's no room in that aisle," Linda protested, her tone sounding testy, most likely at having been challenged by the young man.

Ella spoke up. "I . . . I could rearrange the shelves."

Hannes glanced at her, and for a brief moment, a look of confusion crossed his face. Ella wondered if he had forgotten that she was there at all.

Linda, too, looked at her, but *her* expression was of irritation. "I thought I told you to clean the window displays!"

Immediately, the color rose to Ella's cheeks again, and she turned around, hoping that Hannes did not see her embarrassment at that second rebuke from her stepmother.

Ten minutes later, Hannes left the store in a hurry, the placement of the clocks not having been settled and Linda clearly none too happy about it. She marched over to where Ella was and put both of her hands on her hips.

"If I need your help," Linda snapped, "I will ask for it."

Ella lowered her eyes. "I'm sorry, Maem."

"Indeed you should be!" Turning her head, Linda looked outside the window as Hannes untied his horse from the hitching post. "Now we've lost a possible partner, too! Finish up here and go reorganize the stockroom. I've had enough of your interference in how I run my store."

Daed's *store,* Ella thought as she gathered her cleaning supplies and carried them to the back of the building. If only her stepmother would permit her to be more involved, things might actually start turning around for the Troyer family. With Linda as the head of the family, however, it was clear that such change was not something to expect in the foreseeable future.

Chapter Twelve

On Tuesday, Ella stood on the front porch, hanging the wet clothes on the line to dry in the morning sun. Her arms ached from lifting the heavy dresses and pinning them to the line. She usually washed clothes on Mondays, saving the linens for Friday afternoons. But since she had worked at the store, Ella hadn't had time to do the laundry the previous day.

And, as usual, Linda had left her a long list of chores that she wanted finished by suppertime. Some of the chores were ridiculous, such her request to have Ella wax the kitchen floor—and all of the rest of the hardwood floors, too! Why, Ella had just done that over the winter. Twice! Linda had also put on the list another reminder to kill the mice in the basement. *As if Linda has actually gone into the basement since last week,* Ella thought.

Sometimes Ella wondered if her stepmother just made up chores to keep her busy.

The house was quiet. Both Drusilla and Anna had left already to help their mother at the store. The only noise was the little blue birds that sang and fluttered around the different bird feeders that Ella kept filled. The solitude, broken only by their cheerful song, was welcome, as Ella needed time to think about what had transpired the day before.

The previous evening, she had hoped to learn more about why Henry "Hannes" Clemens had visited the store. She had wanted to understand what was happening in regard to the bank loan, the unpaid taxes, and now this partnership with the Clemens family. During supper, however, no one spoke about the visit, Linda being unusually silent as if deep in thought, while the two girls had focused their attention on matters more important to them: the charity auction coming up the following week.

Without any clues to go on, Ella had tried to make sense of why Hannes would be discussing partnering with her stepmother. Hadn't Linda wanted to get a loan? When had she decided it was better to invite a stranger to partner with her? And how, exactly, would such an arrangement work?

Now, as Ella stood on the porch, clipping the last apron to the clothesline, she was no closer to understanding any of this.

Just as she was about to bend down to pick up the basket, she had the strange sensation that someone was watching her. One glance over her shoulder, and Ella saw the very subject of her morning musings observing her from the edge of the street on the other side of the picket fence.

At first, Ella didn't speak. She remembered how Linda had treated her in front of Hannes, and she felt a new wave of shame. What must he think of her now? Dropping her hands, she stood there, waiting for Hannes to say something.

But he remained silent. He appeared to be studying

her, perhaps even unaware that she had straightened and taken notice of him. His blue eyes, normally so bright and full of joviality, appeared much more solemn and contemplative. She wondered what he was thinking, and then realized that she truly didn't want to know. Surely he must have lost respect for her, and that was a realization that made her heart feel heavy.

The silence became awkward, and Ella took a deep breath. *Fine,* she thought. *I'll start the conversation.* "How long have you been standing there?" she asked.

Hannes gave a little shake of his head as if returning to the moment. Then, with a shrug of his shoulders, he took a step toward the gate. "There's something interesting about how a woman hangs clothes on the line," he said in a soft but thoughtful voice. "You can tell a lot about her personality."

Her heart lightened. Perhaps she had misread him and he hadn't been thinking about the exchange with Linda. "Oh?" She felt a smile on her lips. "And how's that?"

Placing his hand on the gate, Hannes pushed it open, and even though she hadn't invited him, he stepped onto the property. "Take a look at how the clothes are hung." He pointed to the clothesline as he walked toward her. "You arranged them by color and created a rainbow."

Ella blushed. True, to amuse herself, she often hung the dresses from light to dark, with the black aprons at the very end, closest to the porch. She had, indeed, created a rainbow. "I suppose I like to make patterns."

Hannes stopped just shy of the porch steps. He gestured toward a neighboring house. "Now, look at that line. There's no thought to how the clothes are pinned.

Trousers are hung in between dresses, shirts among the aprons. There is no pattern or thought to how the clothes are hung. I imagine that woman is very busy and a bit overwhelmed. Her attention to her family is limited, because she has so much to do."

While she listened to him, Ella realized that Hannes's observation was truly quite accurate. Ella laughed. "Susie Lapp lives there. She has eight children, so *ja*, she has a lot to do. I imagine being creative with hanging clothes isn't a big priority for her."

"Exactly!"

"Well, then," she started slowly, "what does my rainbow say about me?"

Hannes raised an eyebrow, clearly amused by her question. "Ah! You? Hmm, let me think."

For a long moment, he appeared to be deep in thought, taking his time to consider the question before responding. That was one of the things that Ella liked about Hannes. He was never in a rush to speak. He protected his tongue—a true man of understanding who had learned that there were times to speak and times to remain silent. Even though she had had few interactions with him, she knew that he was prudent with his words and even-tempered with his speech. A godly man, indeed.

At last, he spoke. "Let's see, Ella," he said carefully. "What does your rainbow clothesline say about you? Well, I suspect that you are both creative and methodical, and organized in how you tackle your chores, even though your efforts are hardly, if at all, recognized."

The accuracy of his description startled her. How could someone learn so much about a person just from how they hung their clothes on the line? In her mind, she tried to envision several other people's clotheslines and match their patterns to the hangers' personality. She felt a smile on her lips.

True to Hannes's description, the few people that she knew who organized their laundry in such a methodical way, such as her friend Belle, enjoyed structure, never shunned hard work, and often sacrificed for their families without being appreciated.

And those who did not care about the order of the laundry, such as Belle's sisters or Susie Lapp, were disorganized and unorganized, whether from laziness, as was the case of the former, or from a general sense of feeling overwhelmed, as in the case of the latter.

"My word!" she whispered to herself.

Hannes grinned. "I'm guessing that's close to the truth, eh?" Before she could respond, Hannes placed a foot on the porch step and leaned forward. "I thought so. Which was why I was hoping to find you."

"You wanted to discuss how I hang my clothes on the line?"

He gave a small laugh and shook his head. "*Nee*, Ella. I was hoping to catch you alone to talk about yesterday."

Inwardly, she cringed. *That* was the last thing she wanted to talk about. She had hoped that he had forgotten about the episode at the store. Averting her eyes, which still stung from humiliation at how Linda had treated her, she managed to respond with a soft "Oh."

"I was surprised to see you at the store yesterday."

Nervously, she swallowed. "Did you get anywhere in your business dealings with Linda?"

A dark cloud passed over his face. "You mean that woman at Troyers' General Store?" He shook his head. "*Nee*, and I'm not so certain I want to do business with such a woman."

Suddenly, it dawned on Ella that Hannes didn't know he was talking about her stepmother. She froze, wondering how to broach the subject. She felt awkward mentioning it, worried that he would think she had purposefully misled him—but she hadn't. She just had never mentioned her last name. In that moment, she knew that she must disclose this information to him, for surely he'd find out sooner or later. If she didn't tell him now, then he would be correct in thinking she had intentionally withheld the truth.

"Oh help," she muttered. "Hannes, I need to—"

But he continued talking as if he hadn't heard her. "Any woman, or man, in business should treat their employees with respect. That is one of the valuable lessons that my *daed* has taught me. While it's not my business, of course, I was not impressed with her lack of"—he hesitated as if searching for the proper word—"esteem for your hard work."

"Hannes, I—"

Once again, he continued talking. "I might not know you very well, Ella, but I certainly suspect that you are a righteous young woman who works hard. I don't believe that anyone should be treated so coarsely, least of all you." He reached down and plucked a weed that grew alongside the porch step. "It's a wonder that your parents permit you to work there at all. I was not impressed with her—"

"Hannes," Ella managed to interrupt him in a soft, but firm, voice. "That's my family's business."

He froze. Something changed in his expression. Was it compassion? Or perhaps pity? Whatever it was, he remained silent for far too long. Her heart began to palpitate, and her palms grew sweaty. Surely he didn't think that *she* was like Linda?

Finally, he cast aside the weed and turned his gaze onto her. "I see, Ella." He paused. "Ella Troyer." The way he said her name sounded as if he were trying it out, tasting the words to see how they complemented each other. She wondered what he decided. "I hadn't realized you were a Troyer."

"So I presumed."

He coughed into his hand. "I'm sorry I said those things about . . . your mother."

"Stepmother."

A look of relief washed over him.

"My *maem* died when I was younger," she heard herself say. Suddenly, she felt protective of her father and thought it was necessary to explain how Linda had become part of her life. "Daed remarried so that I wouldn't have to grow up without a mother."

Hannes remained silent.

"I . . . I guess I'm fortunate that he did remarry. Otherwise, I'd be alone now," she added.

"Fortunate." There was an unusual dryness to his tone. "Indeed."

Ella nodded. "*Ja*, my *daed* started the store, and when he passed away, my stepmother took over running it." She bit her lower lip, wondering what he was thinking. There was only a momentary silence before she found out.

"Let me ask you a question, Ella." He took off his hat and twirled it in his hands. "If *you* were running the general store, what would you do differently from what is being done now?"

The change in subject surprised her, but she was happy to answer the question. Oh! How many nights had she lain awake, thinking of how many changes could be made at the store to improve profitability while addressing the needs of the community?

"Well now, where do I start?" She gave a nervous laugh. It wasn't often that people asked her for her opinion. "I'd start by lowering prices and rethinking some of the inventory. Echo Creek is a small town, and most folks are farmers. It's easy to figure out that fancy fabrics and expensive shoes won't sell."

He nodded, encouraging her to continue sharing her ideas.

"And I'd have seasonal specials to encourage people to buy more of a certain item so that I could get a better wholesale rate. While the prices would be lower, I'd make a higher profit margin."

"Go on."

Ella glanced toward the sky, searching her memory for some of her more recent ideas. "I'd study sales reports and track trends in buying to improve inventory circulation. For example, women don't normally quilt or crochet in the warmer months, so why stock yarn and quilting squares during that time? That's money just sitting on the shelves, *ja*?"

He smiled. "Indeed it is. What else, Ella?"

How she was enjoying herself! The ideas kept coming, and she could hardly sort through them fast enough. "Orders could be taken for something expensive and large, like a quilting frame. Why keep so many in the stockroom, taking up space? Instead, I'd push for people to put down a small deposit during the summer months so that we could place a single order for all of the customers' frames. And all of those items would already be sold. Inventory in and out makes for higher profits, don't you think?"

At this, he laughed. "Indeed I do. Why, I think you

have quite the head for business, Ella Troyer. It's a wonder you aren't running that place."

She wished that she could join him in laughing, but his comment reminded her that she *didn't* run the store, and never would. "I had thought I might run it one day. But Daed's passing ended that dream." She sighed. "He didn't have a will, you see? So everything passed down to his wife. And she doesn't include me in much more than helping out when one of her *dochders* doesn't feel like working."

It was as close to complaining as Ella would ever get. She hoped that she hadn't said too much. She'd hate to have Hannes think she was one of those women who groused all the time.

Forcing a smile, she gestured toward the clothesline. "But that's okay," she said, hoping she sounded convincing. "It's just as important to take care of your family, *ja*?"

He appeared to contemplate what she had said. His eyes flickered back and forth as he studied her. The attention made her feel uncomfortable, and she leaned over to pick up the empty laundry basket, eager to have something in her hands to occupy them.

"I'm sure that you do a *wunderbarr gut* job of that, too, Ella." He took a step away from the porch. "Now, I've a meeting at the store with your"—he paused, his expression changing to one filled with distaste—"stepmother." Just the way he said that word made it sound vile. "So I must say farewell to you." He plopped his hat back onto his head. "For now, anyway."

As he started to walk away, Ella took a deep breath. Her heart always seemed to flutter whenever Hannes was near. She wished she understood why, for she hardly knew him at all. And yet, there was something

about him that simply made her feel light-headed and dizzy. *Ferhoodled.* Yes, that was the word. She felt *ferhoodled* whenever he talked to her.

From the street behind the fence, a buggy rattled by. Ella glanced up in time to see Belle wave at her. Ever since her friend's marriage to Adam Hershberger, Ella barely saw Belle, for their farm was far enough from town to make walking there take too long away from chores, in Linda's opinion. But oh! How Ella could have used a friend right about now.

Chapter Thirteen

"I can scarce believe it!"

It was Thursday evening, and Linda had just arrived home. From the moment she had walked in, she had been in a tizzy. After pacing the floor in the kitchen, she retreated outside, where she had paced some more. Fortunately, all of her walking back and forth must have tired her out, for now she was seated on the front porch with Drusilla and Anna. Both of her daughters leaned forward in their chairs, anticipating more information about whatever was troubling their mother.

Carrying a large tray that held a pitcher of fresh meadow tea and four glasses, Ella walked out the screen door. The sun lingered over the buildings on the other side of the street, and a fresh breeze blew through the air. It was a pleasant evening with hardly a cloud in the sky. And yet Linda's mood was a dark storm that ruined what could have been a lovely ending to the day.

After setting the pitcher onto a small table, Ella handed everyone a glass and began to pour their tea. She wondered what she had missed in the conversation, for Linda looked beyond distressed and extremely unhappy.

Drusilla, however, did not mirror her mother's sentiment. Instead, she leaned forward, her hands clutched together. Unlike Linda, Drusilla appeared excited as she asked, "What did the bishop say, Maem?" Eagerly, she peered into her mother's face. "Exactly," she stressed.

Ignoring her daughter's question, Linda shook her head and clicked her tongue disapprovingly. "It's outrageous! Why, he's just about making the charity auction into a competition!"

Now Ella's curiosity was piqued. How could an auction be a competition?

Anna couldn't keep herself from showing her curiosity. "*Ja*, Maem. What were his exact words?"

Linda cast a scowl in her direction. "Honestly, Anna. I already told you. Must I repeat everything because you never listen the first time?"

Anna looked completely unfazed by her mother's reprimand.

Ella cleared her throat. "Have I missed something?"

Both Linda and Drusilla ignored her. Anna, however, leaned over and whispered, "The bishop told Maem that the deacon had an idea for the charity auction. They want a separate table for all of the baked goods donated by the congregation's unmarried women."

"What's so terrible about that?" Ella asked. It sounded innocent enough to her. And knowing Deacon King, the rest of the church leaders had agreed to his idea.

Unfortunately, Ella's question set off Linda once again. "I'll tell you what's wrong with that! The deacon suggested that only the *unmarried* men can bid on those pies!" She scowled, her lips pressed together in a firm, straight line that emphasized the little wrinkles and deep lines around her mouth. "The young men who win the bids on *those* treats get to sit with the single women after the auction and eat some of the pie!"

Ella didn't think that sounded as awful as her stepmother made it sound, but she knew better than to voice her opinion.

"Why, I've never heard of such a crazy notion!" Linda continued. "He's practically auctioning off the young women! It's just sinful!" She shook her head and clucked her tongue disapprovingly. "It's a wonder that Miriam King is supporting her husband's idea! I never took her to be such a liberal-minded person."

Ignoring her mother's tirade, Drusilla lit up, her face suddenly aglow. She clutched her hands together and pressed them against her chest. There was a dreamy, faraway expression on her face. "*Ach*! I wonder if that Henry Clemens will be there!"

At the mention of Henry Clemens, Anna scowled at her sister. "Why would you ask such a thing?"

Drusilla shot a dirty look at her sister. "Why wouldn't I?"

"Uh . . . Timothy Miller?" Anna's eyes narrowed in a rare moment of standing up to her older sister. "Remember him? You know, *ratta-tat-tat.*" She mimicked the sound of pebbles against the window.

Drusilla kicked Anna's shin. "Oh, hush, you!"

Linda's eyebrows knit together, unquestionably unhappy with her daughter's question. "*Ja,* Drusilla. Why *would* you care if that Clemens boy was at the auction?"

Drusilla gave her mother a blank stare.

Linda wasn't about to drop the conversation. "Surely you aren't interested in the likes of him."

Ella caught her breath at the way Linda said that, as if Hannes were anything other than a right proper young man. She could hardly fathom what Hannes had done to Linda for her to have such a poor opinion of him. If anything, Hannes had the right to think poorly of *her.*

This time, it was Anna who spoke up. "What's wrong with Henry Clemens?" she asked, her voice exposing her dismay at her mother's comment.

"Really, Maem. What faults could you *possibly* find in him?" Drusilla added, a dreamy expression on her face. "Personally, I think he's rather attractive."

Linda, however, merely scoffed at her daughter's remark. "I hardly think appearances matter, Drusilla. Not in business, anyway. What matters the most is whether or not his *daed* invests in our store. After meeting with that Henry, I doubt that will happen. On my part, anyway." She gave a little shake of her head. "Frankly, I haven't been impressed with his son, that's for sure and certain."

"Why not?" Ella managed to ask, hoping that she had properly masked her curiosity. After having talked with Hannes earlier, she was more than impressed with him and couldn't help but wonder why Linda wasn't. And she continued to speak poorly of the young man. Was her stepmother questioning his character? Or was she merely threatened by his business acumen? "He certainly made a good point about the location of the clocks you have for sale on consignment." She couldn't help but stress the word "consignment" and hoped that her stepmother didn't pick up on it.

This time, Linda turned her attention to Ella. "What

would *you* know about such things, Ella? But since you asked, I'll tell you. If the father's so interested in partnering with us, why would he send his *son*?" There was a sharpness to her voice, as if telling Ella that she should have known better than to ask. "I suspect the father must be a poor businessman, that's for sure and certain! And his son?" She made a dismissive noise. "Instead of discussing the partnership arrangement, he hasn't done more than walk around the store and talk about pricing and placement of the items on the shelves. Now, if that doesn't show poor business skills, then I don't know what else does!"

Ella wanted to point out that, just the other day, Linda had been complaining about declining sales and her unpaid tax bill. If Linda wanted to accuse someone of poor business skills, she only had to look in the mirror. Her own lack of business acumen was what had gotten her into such dire straits in the first place. But Ella knew better than to say something so cutting, so she held her tongue.

Besides, she didn't think Hannes's inquiring about pricing and product placement was such a bad idea. After all, any person considering a business venture with someone else needed to understand what they were getting into. Asking questions was the fastest way to learn about how another person operated. And he had learned an awful lot about Linda Troyer from just that one meeting, that was for sure and certain.

"Henry can't be that poor, Maem," Anna said, her face alight with excitement. "I just saw him the other day, and he drives a new courting buggy with a Dutch Harness horse!"

Her remark surprised Ella. Not because Anna was focusing on the material things that Hannes had—no, that was to be expected from her two stepsisters—but because Ella hadn't been aware that Anna knew *that* much *about* Hannes. Or even *cared*, for that matter. While Drusilla had made her interest in the young man more than obvious, especially after the last worship service, clearly Anna, too, was pining for him, even if only in secret.

"Well, after our meeting this morning at the store, I suspect he's driven that new buggy and fancy horse right out of town," Linda said, waving her hand toward the road.

Ella's heart felt as if it dropped to the bottom of her stomach. Had her stepmother truly run Hannes from Echo Creek? And, if so, why on earth would she sound so pleased? Clearly Linda did not understand the ramifications of what she had done. The Clemens' interest in the store had been a miracle in and of itself. If Linda had truly chased away Hannes, what were the chances that another interested party might approach them?

Apparently Ella wasn't the only one who realized that turning off Hannes was a mistake.

Drusilla's face fell as her mouth opened. "Maem! Why would you do that?"

Quickly, Anna chimed in with her own commentary. "I thought you wanted to partner with them, especially after you were denied the bank loan."

Ella's eyes widened, and the color drained from her face. No one had told her that the loan request had been turned down! She turned toward Linda, who appeared completely unperturbed.

While it was clear that Linda truly had no concept of what dire straits the family was now in, Ella did. She stared at her stepmother, shocked at how calm the woman remained. "The bank rejected your loan application?"

"Oh, Ella!" Linda rolled her eyes, demonstrating her contempt for the bank. "It's not a big deal. Who wants to pay such high interest to the bank anyway?"

Someone who wants to keep their business, Ella thought. "And now you've driven off a potential partner?" Ella felt her heart begin to race. Without the loan and without a partner, they were worse off than before. There was one, and only one, thing that could possibly happen, and Ella didn't want to think about foreclosure.

"What will we do now?" she asked. "How will you pay those back taxes?"

"Why, Ella, must you always be so melodramatic?"

"But, Maem," she started, "without the loan, how will you pay the tax bill?"

"I'll just find another person interested in partnering with me."

The solution sounded so simple, but Ella knew otherwise. Anyone from Echo Creek who knew Linda would *not* want to partner with her. They would be too aware of her poor business acumen and difficult personality. And the likelihood that another outsider would come to Echo Creek and be interested was highly unlikely.

"But you *had* someone interested in doing just that," Ella said, struggling with keeping her voice calm. "What happened?"

"Well, Ella, not that it's any of your concern, but I'll tell you." Linda wore an expression of superiority as she answered. "That Henry tried to negotiate with me. He wanted to own fifty-one percent of the business. I had to set him straight as to who runs the show! I'm not about to let someone tell me how to run *my* business."

"That's the whole idea behind a partnership." Ella could tell that she was treading a fine line. However, she simply could not believe that Linda had chased Hannes away. Perhaps it was the fact that Hannes had left Echo Creek, or maybe it was the fact that Linda was a terrible businessperson, but Ella couldn't sit there quietly for one more moment. "Sharing ideas and trying new things in order to improve the business. If what you were doing was working, you wouldn't *need* a partner."

And with that, the line was clearly crossed.

"Enough!" Linda's voice boomed, her irritation more than clear. "I've heard enough from you, Ella. Isn't it time for you to do your barn chores?"

Despite having already finished her chores in the barn, Ella took the opening to escape Linda's increasingly foul mood. She hurried through the kitchen and out the back door, practically running toward the barn.

She sank into a pile of loose hay and covered her face in her arms while she allowed herself a rare moment to cry. If only Linda would let her help run the store, Ella knew things would improve. And as far as the money owed to the IRS, Ella also knew *that* needed to be paid. She was smart enough to have learned from her father about the importance of paying taxes. If the government put a lien on the store, how on earth would the Troyer family survive?

"Oh, Daed," Ella cried. "Why did you get called to heaven so soon?"

She knew crying about her father wasn't a strong testament to her faith. With each tear that fell, she felt shame. But try as she might, she simply could not stop sobbing. She missed him more than she let on, and she thought about him every day. It was hard not to. After all, her life had been one continuous descent into a dark abyss ever since he died.

Gone were kind smiles and kind words. They were replaced with harsh glares and even harsher criticism. Never mind the fact that her days were basically spent serving Linda and her two ungrateful daughters. Yes, she missed her father every single day. Today, however, she felt his absence especially sharply.

Out of the corner of her eye, Ella saw something move. She lifted her head and was surprised to see two little mice darting along the barn wall. As if they knew that they were being watched, they paused and turned in her direction. One of the mice, a silvery gray field mouse, twitched its nose and sat on its haunches, its little paws curled underneath its chest. The other mouse, a darker-colored one, took a step toward her, paused, and then licked a paw before swiping it over its ear.

Ella couldn't help but smile.

"You're so adorable," she whispered and, on a whim, stretched out a hand in their direction, her fingers grazing the dirt floor.

To her surprise, the darker mouse slowly moved toward her hand. It sniffed at her fingertips, its whiskers brushing against her skin and causing her to giggle.

The mouse stopped and sat up once again. It looked toward the other mouse, and that was when Ella noticed the little white spot behind its left ear.

"Simply adorable," she repeated, wishing that she could actually hold it.

But that was not meant to be.

Immediately, the mouse bounded away, the other one on its heels.

"Wait!" Ella cried out. "I won't hurt you."

The mice were gone.

Still, the amount of trust the mouse had shown in approaching her warmed her heart. If a tiny creature with so many predators seeking to destroy it could trust her, then shouldn't she trust more in God? Everything happened for a reason. Wasn't that what she had learned from her father? And who was she to question God's plan? Perhaps she was in the middle of the story, and the ending would be far better than she could ever dream possible.

But in the meantime, she knew she must do more than just trust; she must also obey.

Chapter Fourteen

By midmorning on Friday, Ella had to stop hoeing the weeds in the garden for the fourth time in order to wipe the sweat from her forehead. Despite the fact that it was not even ten o'clock in the morning and it was well into August, it was already overwhelmingly hot and humid. Indian summer was upon Echo Creek, that was for sure and certain. She wasn't certain how much longer she could stay out there working in this heat.

"Hello there, Ella!"

She froze at the sound of her name being called. Despite having her back turned toward the street, Ella didn't have to look to know who it was: Hannes.

With her hair covered only by a handkerchief and the old work dress that she was wearing already covered in dirt, Ella was horrified at the thought of Hannes seeing her in such a shabby condition. But her manners outweighed her vanity, and she turned to greet him.

"*Gut morgan,* Hannes."

He leaned against the white picket fence and glanced at the garden. "Hard at work, *ja*? Again?"

She tried to smile. "Idle hands are an open invitation for sin . . ." It was a saying that her mother and father had often used. Only now that Ella said it, she wondered if Hannes would agree. Perhaps he would remember that Linda had chastised her for being lazy when he had been at the store.

If she was worried about that, she soon learned otherwise.

"Well, I'm not surprised," Hannes said slowly. "You always seem to be hard at work."

The way he said it, enunciating the word "always," made Ella wonder if he meant it as a compliment or, perhaps, as a complaint.

Hannes glanced at the garden and then up at the sky. "It's a hot day for gardening, don't you think? Mayhaps you might take a break and sit in the shade for a spell. I don't think God would mind a few minutes of idleness to cool off."

The idea of doing just that both excited and terrified her. While she wanted to spend time with Hannes, she also knew that if her stepmother discovered that she had put aside her chores to visit with someone, *especially* Hannes, Ella would surely never hear the end of it.

"Oh, I . . . I don't know." Embarrassed, Ella tried to avoid making eye contact with him. "God might not mind, but my stepmother certainly would."

At the mention of Linda, Hannes frowned.

Ella felt as if she owed him an explanation for her comment. "She left me a long list of chores to do, and . . ." Ella bit her lower lip. "Well, you know how people talk. Surely someone would notice if I stopped working to sit with you. And that Amish grapevine would surely make its way to my stepmother's ears . . ."

"I see."

She wondered if he did, and if so, what exactly he saw. Did he think that she was putting him off, or did he see that she lived in fear of her stepmother's retribution? Not wanting him to think the former, and uncertain whether he would realize the latter, she quickly added in a soft voice, "I reckon she couldn't complain if you kept me company . . ."

He seemed to like her suggestion and, without being asked, jumped the fence and sat down on the grass near where she was working in the garden. He folded his knees and wrapped his arms around them, watching her as she continued plucking weeds.

"You continue to impress me, Ella, with what a right *gut* hard worker you are."

Relieved to hear that he felt that way, and had not put any stock in Linda's harsh words from the other day, she gave a slight laugh. "No more so than other Amish women, I reckon."

"Well, you seem to work harder than most people." He glanced toward her house. Reaching down, he plucked at a piece of grass and wrapped it around a finger. "Idle hands may invite sin, but everyone needs to take a break from time to time."

Ella wanted to quip that someone needed to share that expression with her stepmother. But she knew that saying such a thing would be disrespectful and show a lack of filial duty toward Linda. So even if she thought it, she remained silent instead.

"One of the things I've learned in my short life is that things aren't always what they seem, Ella."

She tugged at a weed and tossed it into the nearby bucket. "That's true, for sure and certain."

"I mean it, Ella." The serious undercurrent of his tone caused Ella to stop working and look at him.

Only then did he continue speaking. "I've learned that sometimes it's best to keep a cool head until I can figure out exactly what is what."

Ella pursed her lips, wondering what Hannes was getting at. Surely she couldn't agree more with his words. "That's right *gut* advice, Hannes. I sure wish more people followed it. The world would be a more peaceful place, don't you think?"

Despite his somber expression, he gave a little chuckle, his eyes still studying her every movement. "Indeed I do, Ella. Just remember that, though, Ella. Sometimes things might be going one way, and then, when you least expect it, they turn around in your favor."

She leaned against the end of the hoe, considering the serious nature of his words. Hannes barely blinked as he stared at her, his gaze steady and intent as if trying to tell her something without actually saying it. It was the Amish way, to speak cryptically when avoiding unpleasant topics. However, she couldn't help but wonder what the hidden message of his words might be.

"I'll . . . remember that," she said at last.

"*Gut*!" Satisfied, he tossed aside the piece of grass and wiped his hand on his pants. "I stopped by to let you know that I'm leaving Echo Creek."

Now it was Ella's turn to become solemn. "*Ja*, so I heard." What she didn't tell him was that she had barely slept at all since hearing the news about his abrupt departure. While she hadn't thought he'd stop by to bid her farewell, she was glad that he had, even if she was dirty and wearing an old, ragged dress. At least she could tell him goodbye in person—for she was certain she'd never see him again. What reason would he possibly have for returning to Echo Creek now?

"I'm not surprised you heard." He glanced up at the sky, squinting his eyes at the sun. "My meeting with Linda yesterday did not go as planned." With a sigh, he added, "It doesn't appear that we'll be partnering with your stepmother after all."

Nervously, she swallowed. "I heard that, too."

Hannes cleared his throat. "She's an interesting woman, that stepmother of yours," he said in a strained voice.

"Interesting" wasn't the exact word Ella would have chosen, but she respected Hannes's civility toward Linda.

"It's a shame, Ella, because I can see that there's a lot of potential at that store. It could certainly be run in a more efficient manner, which you already know." He exhaled, and Ella sensed that he felt frustrated. "When I first came here, my *daed* had asked me to look at the store for business opportunities, such as working with vendors to create distribution channels like those wedding clocks. Then he thought that, perhaps, we should outright partner with the owner. We had heard that she was in some financial trouble, with the unpaid taxes and all."

Ella's cheeks heated at the realization that Hannes and his father knew about Linda's financial situation. To think that others had learned the truth and the story had spread to other towns was humiliating enough. However, she was even more embarrassed at the graceless way Linda had treated him. Here she was, a woman in trouble, acting as if *she* was doing Hannes a favor and not the other way around.

If Hannes noticed her shame, he was kind enough

to pretend otherwise. "The truth, Ella, is that I don't think partnering with your stepmother is in my *daed*'s best interest."

"But I thought she turned you away."

Hannes gave a soft, short laugh. "*Ja*, I can see where she might say that."

Clearly Linda's version of the previous day's meeting differed from Hannes's, and that meant that Linda had, once again, lied. Now Hannes knew it, too. She could read between the lines of his carefully chosen words, and she knew exactly what he was hinting at. Despite her mortification, Ella appreciated the gracious way Hannes spoke.

To her surprise, Hannes continued sharing his thoughts with her. "In fact, I don't think partnering with *anyone* is in his best interest." He glanced at her. "Nor mine."

"Oh?"

He gave a simple nod of his head. "You see, my *daed* wanted to set me up in business, Ella. My older *bruder*'s already helping to run Daed's store."

She remembered him having mentioned something about that when they were skipping stones at the pond that Sunday evening.

"There's not much there for me—not long-term and if I want my own family, anyway," he added.

Ella held her breath, stunned that he would confide something so personal.

Hannes appeared unaware of her shock. "At first, Daed had arranged for me to distribute products, like working with that vendor who makes the clocks. That's all well and good, but what I really want to do is run my own store." He tossed a small stick into her bucket of weeds. "I enjoy interacting with people, helping to solve problems, finding ways to make others' lives more enjoyable and satisfying while saving them money. Dealing with someone else who has their own business goals, or even their own operational ideas that counter mine, well . . ." He scratched the back of his neck. "It seems a bit like a futile collaboration, don't you think?"

Now Ella understood his frustration. She also understood why his father had sent Hannes and not accompanied him. This was Hannes's opportunity to decide if he wanted to partner with Linda to run the store. And clearly he had realized that was not a sound business decision.

As if he read her mind, Hannes continued. "Partnering with someone is just like buying a cheap horse at an auction. What you see isn't always the truth. The horse might prance about well enough during the bidding, but once you bring it home, you realize that you've inherited a lot of existing problems, *ja*? Otherwise, why would the owner have gotten rid of the horse in the first place? Chances are, without a lot of hard work and aggravation, you aren't going to be able to fix what's broken."

Ella couldn't agree more.

"Whether it's your stepmother or someone else, I just don't want to partner with anyone."

"Mayhaps you could start your own store?" she offered.

For a moment, he stared into the distance as if contemplating her solution. "I reckon that might be something to consider." He turned to look at her. "But where?"

She wanted to suggest Echo Creek, but knew that doing so would be disloyal to not just Linda but her father's memory. He had worked so hard to start that store for the residents of Echo Creek. And everyone had appreciated his dedication to providing good products at fair prices.

If only Linda would realize all of her mistakes!

But that was an unlikely scenario.

Ella wondered if Hannes might come to recognize that there was enormous potential in opening his own store in Echo Creek. She knew that if it wasn't Hannes who recognized the prospective opportunities, it would certainly be someone else.

Still, Ella held her tongue, knowing that once spoken, she could never retrieve those words. Offering her thoughts about his opening a competitive store in Echo Creek would serve one, and only one, purpose: her interest in Hannes. And even if Hannes considered opening his own store in Echo Creek, there was no indication that his attention to her would continue. For all she knew, there might be a girl in Blue Springs who held his affections.

"Anyway," Hannes said as he stood up, "I wanted to say goodbye to you." Standing before her, he met her gaze. "For now, anyway."

Just those three words gave her a glimmer of hope. "For now? You'll be back, then?"

"Of course." He gave her a curious look while suppressing the hint of a smile. "Echo Creek is, after all, a rather interesting town, Ella."

"Interesting for business reasons or interesting for other reasons?"

He laughed and winked at her. "That's for me to know and you to find out." And with that, he tipped his hat and left.

Ella stood on the edge of the garden, gazing after him as he walked down the street. She noticed that he crossed the road and turned up a side street. A few moments later, she saw a horse and open-top buggy appear and, upon recognizing the breed of the horse as a Dutch Harness, she knew that it was Hannes, leaving Echo Creek.

Despite his claim that he'd return, Ella felt distressed. She had enjoyed spending what little time she could with Hannes Clemens. Whatever hope she may have secretly harbored that they could develop a special friendship, one that might bloom into something more, she realized that it was as fleeting as the flowers on the morning glory vines: they opened one day and gave the world a glimpse of their beauty, only to close, wither, and drop to the ground by nightfall.

Disheartened, Ella turned away from the road and headed back into the house. She didn't want any more reminders of what her stepmother had done, not just to the family and the store, but to Ella's dream that her relationship with Hannes could be more than just a fleeting break from what was, otherwise, her unhappy life.

Chapter Fifteen

On Tuesday, with the day of the charity event looming ever near, Ella was in a frenzy to finish all of her weekly housework in order to prepare the cakes and pie. She knew that she'd have to bake them on Saturday morning so that they'd be fresh for the evening's event. But Linda seemed determined to keep her busy, both at home and at the store.

One of her stepmother's new ideas was to reorganize the shelves—and not in the way that Hannes had recommended. Ella didn't agree with that decision. How on earth would people find things if Linda continually changed their locations? Linda, however, would not listen to reason.

Last night, after supper, Linda had sent Ella to the store to clean the shelving units. Again. By the time Ella returned home, she was exhausted and practically collapsed into her bed. Despite all of her hard work the previous night, Ella rose before the others to bake the bread and prepare the morning meal.

It didn't seem fair that Drusilla and Anna never chipped in to help. Not only that, but once again, Drusilla asked for the afternoon off, saying she wanted to console the despondent Rachel Whitaker. And Anna claimed she felt poorly, another headache plaguing her from the intense late August heat.

Linda had easily given in to their requests and instructed Ella to pick up their shifts at the store.

Unfortunately, it hadn't been busy.

Until now.

"Good day, Ella."

Ella looked up from where she sat on the floor of the store, reorganizing the items on the bottom shelf according to the list Linda had given her. What had once been an aisle full of fishing tackle was now lined with canned goods. Ella could only imagine the look on the men's faces when they went looking for hooks and bobbers only to find jellies and jams and pickled beets!

"Hello, Rachel." Ella scurried to her feet as she greeted Rachel Whitaker. "I hope all is well?"

Rachel nodded her head slowly. She was an older woman, but still very pretty for her age. With dark hair and a pale complexion, it was more than apparent that she rarely worked outside. When Sadie's father had first married her, the gossip in Echo Creek had been that he was besotted with her looks, not her personality or character. While Ella shied away from gossip, she couldn't help but wonder if those particular rumors might hold a kernel of truth. From what little Ella knew about Rachel, her handsome face was about the only thing righteous about the woman.

Oblivious to Ella's thought, Rachel forced a dramatic sigh. "As right as it can be, I reckon. Given the situation, anyway."

Ella wanted to inquire about Sadie, but she wasn't certain if she wanted to make that inquiry of Rachel. After all, Ella knew that Rachel had been about as kind to Sadie as Linda was to her. Ella wasn't surprised to see that the woman didn't look despondent or poorly at all. So instead of asking about Sadie, Ella settled on saying, "I keep your family in my prayers."

"*Danke*, Ella." Rachel's gray eyes scanned the aisle and frowned at the mess on the floor. "Moving things again, I see?"

Ella merely shrugged as she nodded her head.

"I understand that Linda's been talking about partnering with someone. Is that true?" There was something hopeful in the way Rachel asked the question.

Ah, Ella thought. *Now the truth comes out.* While Ella would have preferred to shoot down the gossip, to tell Rachel that no, Linda had chased away Hannes Clemens from wanting to partner with her, she knew it was not her story to tell. Besides, Ella wasn't one to attempt reading Linda's mind. Who knew what her stepmother was thinking about today?

So instead, Ella simply replied, "Linda's in the back if you'd like to ask her directly."

When Rachel wandered toward the back of the store, presumably to inquire of Linda about the rumors, the bell over the door jingled again. This time, Ella was already standing, so she greeted Miriam King with a broad smile.

"Well, hello, Miriam!"

"Oh, Ella! It's right *gut* to see you out of the *haus*!" Miriam shifted the basket on her arm and gave her a quick embrace, something that most Amish women did not do. The gesture surprised Ella, but she welcomed it nonetheless. It wasn't often that she received affection from anyone. "You spend far too much time alone. It's about time you start stepping out some more, *ja*?"

While the idea was appealing, it would have appealed to Ella even more if Hannes were still in Echo Creek.

"Now, I'm sure I needn't ask whether you'll be at the event on Saturday?" Miriam gave her a mischievous smile, her eyes turning into small half moons.

Before Ella could answer, Linda appeared and interrupted them. She must have heard Miriam's voice and deserted Rachel near the back counter. Clearly the wife of the deacon trumped the stepmother of a missing girl.

"Miriam! So glad you're here. What can we help you with? I've a mind to personally assist you, because as you can see"—she gestured toward the large boxes of goods still spread out upon the floor where Ella had just been seated—"we're rearranging the store to help serve you better."

"Is that so?" Miriam raised her eyebrows. "To help serve the town better?"

Rachel walked up behind them, a scowl on her face at the affront Linda had given to her by racing over to Miriam. "Mayhaps you could serve us better by lowering the prices, then."

Ella held her breath. She knew that Linda would not take kindly to Rachel's contemptuous comment. However, with Miriam standing there, Linda would be forced to calm her tongue.

So instead of retorting as she most likely wanted to, Linda merely shot Rachel a fierce look. "I can assure you," she replied pointedly to Rachel, "that the prices in my store are as low as I can possibly put them without losing the roof over my own head."

Rachel clicked her tongue. "I find that rather hard to

believe." And then she smirked. "On second thought, perhaps I don't, considering the word that's spreading around town."

"Now, now, Rachel," Miriam coaxed gently. "Just remember that 'bread of deceit is sweet to a man; but afterwards his mouth shall be filled with gravel.'"

Ella pressed her lips together, stifling a small giggle. She was uncertain to which woman Miriam was addressing that particular Scripture. Perhaps both of them. Regardless, Ella found Miriam's choice of Bible verse amusingly appropriate.

Neither Rachel nor Linda appeared fazed by it, however.

With great impudence, Rachel sniffed at Linda and stormed out of the store, her arms empty. Ella suspected that the only thing she had come shopping for was information.

"I daresay something must be troubling her," Miriam said, more to herself than to Ella or Linda.

Linda, however, responded, "She heard that I was in discussion with someone about the store."

Miriam raised an eyebrow. "Oh? Is that so?"

Her response did not indicate whether she was asking about the discussions or merely Rachel having heard about them.

Linda, however, heard it as an invitation to lament her woes. "*Ja*, a father and son from Blue Springs. But the young man was a bit too presumptuous for my taste," Linda boasted.

"In what way, if I might ask?"

Ella was just as curious as Miriam to hear Linda's response.

"Well, honestly, a man of just twenty-something years should defer to those who are more experienced, don't you think? Instead, he just marched in here, barking demands to rearrange shelves . . ."

Miriam cast a questioning glance at the box of goods on the floor near Ella's feet.

". . . and wanting to lower prices."

"Oh, my." That was all Miriam said. Once again, Ella was uncertain exactly how the deacon's wife meant that, for her tone expressed nothing that indicated whether she was shocked at Linda's dismay over a perfectly legitimate suggestion or shocked that Hannes had proposed it at all.

"My thoughts exactly!" Linda, however, clearly presumed Miriam was supporting her. "Such arrogance and overconfidence from someone who obviously has little to no experience running a business! Who could work with such a person?"

Miriam shook her head. "I agree, Linda. No one should consider conducting any business with someone like you've described, that's for sure and certain." Miriam shifted her basket on her arm.

Ella returned to her work, biting back the terse remark that lingered on her tongue. While she couldn't agree with Miriam more, the problem was that Linda had actually described herself, not Hannes! Hannes was anything but arrogant or overconfident. And it was clear that Linda had no idea about his background, or his father's, for that matter. Without doubt, they both knew more about running a store than Linda did. Besides, Linda had only been running Troyers' General Store for a short while, and look at the poor financial state it was in under *her* management!

It irritated Ella that Linda could speak so poorly of someone she barely knew at all. And to Miriam King, of all people! Why, Hannes Clemens had worshipped in Miriam's house just that past weekend. Certainly Miriam had met him. And her husband, too. What on earth must Miriam think of Hannes now?

"Anyway," Ella overheard Miriam say to Linda, "I've come on business today. John asked me to find out what baked goods your *dochders* will be donating for the auction."

Ella paused in her work, wondering what Linda would say. She had a small sense of satisfaction that she knew Linda had no idea, because Ella hadn't told Drusilla or Anna about the cakes she'd promised to make for them.

"Oh . . . I . . ." Linda stumbled over her words. "I'm not rightly sure." She peered around Miriam at Ella. "Do you know?"

Sitting on her heels, Ella gave an innocent look. "Me? Oh, I've not heard what they're baking."

Because Miriam stood before her, Linda couldn't rebuke her, or even demand more information from her, without giving away that it would be Ella, not Drusilla or Anna, baking those cakes. Linda's expression remained fixed, but there was something dark and threatening in her stepmother's eyes.

And then, just as quickly, Linda returned her attention to the deacon's wife. "Whatever they are baking, I'm sure it will be *wunderbarr gut.* You know that my *dochders* are the best bakers in this town!"

"Really?" Miriam widened her eyes and looked directly at Linda. She seemed genuinely surprised. "I hadn't heard that about Drusilla and Anna. Such a secret that you've kept from all of us! You must be rather proud."

Linda gloated at the compliment, although Ella wondered why. Pride was not something most Amish people would admit to having. After all, pride and worldliness went against the Ordnung, the unwritten rules of the Amish church. In every Amish church, regardless of the leadership, pride was viewed as being one of the most terrible of sins. Therefore, Ella was more than surprised when Linda didn't brush aside the flattery bestowed upon her by the deacon's wife.

Miriam, oblivious to what had just happened, continued prattling on about Linda's daughters. "Now I'll sure be looking forward to see what, exactly, they bake for the auction." She started to step away from Linda, but paused. "Speaking of baking, I sure would love some of that baked bread you always have. I've had company at the *haus* and haven't had time to bake any myself. I could use two loaves, I think."

Linda snapped her fingers at Ella. "Go fetch two of your loaves for Miriam, Ella."

"Oh? Is it Ella who bakes that bread? Why, I'm surprised your *dochders* don't make it," Miriam said before casually adding, "seeing that they're such *wunderbarr gut* bakers!"

"Oh, no. They're far too busy working to bake bread."

"Truly?" With a curious expression on her face, Miriam looked around the store. "And where are they today? I haven't seen them since the last worship service."

"Well, Anna's home sick, the poor dear. And Drusilla went visiting Rachel Whitaker today, because she's been feeling poorly," Linda said, her voice giving away her pride in her daughter for being so concerned about others. "Such a good girl, my Drusilla."

Miriam frowned and looked over her shoulder at the door. "The same Rachel Whitaker who was here . . . just a few minutes ago?"

Once again, Ella suppressed a giggle as she stood

up and hurried to the back room to fetch the bread for the deacon's wife, but not before hearing Miriam add, "I'm sure she looked more than fine. Still, I'll have to send John to check on her."

No response came from Linda as she evidently realized the error of her statement and the deceit in her daughter's declaration that she was going to visit Rachel.

Hurrying back, Ella handed the two loaves to Miriam, who promptly put them in her basket. She opened her purse and began riffling through her money. "Now that I know *you* are the baker behind this right *gut* bread, I'll be sure to buy more of it each week." She handed Ella a five-dollar bill and gave her a pleasant smile.

As soon as Miriam left the store, Linda pivoted and gave Ella a harsh glare. While she was clearly angry, she had no one to blame but herself. Still, she didn't waste any time in retaliating against Ella.

"What are you standing there for? You have more shelves to rearrange!" Then, an angry, twisted look on her face, Linda wheeled around and stormed to the back of the store, where she promptly disappeared into her office and slammed the door shut.

Oh, it didn't happen very often, but Ella felt a sense of satisfaction that both Drusilla and Linda had been caught telling falsehoods. There was nothing Linda could say to blame *her* for this one. And without Linda hanging around, barking orders at her, Ella found a small slice of contentment. Finally.

Chapter Sixteen

On Thursday evening, Ella walked through town, enjoying the cool breeze on her face. It had rained earlier, and now there was a welcome respite from the hot, humid weather that sometimes fell over Echo Creek during the late days of August.

After stopping at the feed store to order hay and grain for their cows and horse, Ella wandered over to spend a few minutes visiting with Elizabeth Grimm, who was still at the schoolhouse. Even though the students had gone home hours earlier, Elizabeth was tidying the building for Saturday night's charity event. Elizabeth had welcomed the visit, even though her cousin, Anna Rose, was already there.

"Might I help you, then?" Ella offered. "Mayhaps I could wash the windows and scrub the floor." Cleaning was, after all, her specialty. Besides, working alongside friends always made work seem more like a social visit anyway.

"You sure could, *ja,*" Elizabeth said. "Wash the windows, anyway. Those young students sure do like to press their noses against the windowpanes when they look outside."

While they worked, Ella inquired whether either of them had heard any news of Sadie.

"Not one word," Elizabeth admitted. "Odd that no one seems more distressed about it."

"It's been what? Two weeks now?" Anna Rose asked.

"Sounds about right, *ja*." Suddenly, Elizabeth stopped wiping down the baseboard and sat back on her heels. "Funny thing about that."

"What, cousin?" Anna Rose asked.

"Have you seen our other cousins since then?"

Ella had almost forgotten about their older cousins, the seven Grimm brothers, not one of them married, who lived in the woods south of Echo Creek. They rarely came to town and never attended worship. Ella wasn't even certain if they had ever been baptized into the church.

"I can't say that I have. Oh, I sure hope nothing has happened to them!" Anna Rose speculated. "I'll have to see if Daed might go visit to check on them. However, they sure do love my *maem*'s cooking. Why, I cannot recall a month that has gone by that those cousins haven't been by for supper! But you know how old *buwes* can be . . . set in their ways and often unsociable. I'm not too worried."

An hour later, as Ella made the short walk back to her house, she took a deep breath, feeling a bit more relaxed for once. Just spending a little bit of time with Elizabeth had improved her mood. Both Drusilla and Anna had been in terrible moods that morning, fussing about what they were going to wear to the charity event. And Linda had been bemoaning her financial woes for the past two days.

The sound of a buggy approaching from behind

caused Ella to step aside. However, the buggy did not pass her. Instead it pulled up alongside her.

"Ella! Ella Troyer!"

She turned at the sound of her name. Sure enough, a beautiful Dutch Harness horse trotted up behind her, its black mane fluttering in the breeze while it practically pranced as it pulled the buggy.

"Hannes!" Ella could hardly contain both her surprise and her delight. "You've returned so soon, then?"

He stopped the buggy and stepped on the brake with his foot. "*Ja,* can't seem to get enough of Echo Creek," he said joyfully, leaning out the open door as he greeted her, his blue eyes sparkling as he held her gaze. "Even if it's such a long drive."

Ella stepped forward toward the horse. She reached out and brushed her hand across the horse's neck. "Can't be too far. Your horse is barely winded."

"Oh, this gal could drive forever," he said cheerfully. "If she's not pulling a buggy, she's not happy, I can tell you that for sure and certain."

The horse nickered, as if knowing that Hannes was talking about her.

For a moment that felt like eternity, they stood there in silence. Ella wasn't certain what to say to him. She hadn't been expecting to see him again. At least not so soon. With her tongue tied and her heart happily racing, she could only stare at him, wondering why *he* didn't seem in a hurry to start another conversation. He had, after all, called out to her, not the other way around.

A few more seconds passed and, despite her discomfort, Ella finally asked the question that was on her mind. "What brings you back to Echo Creek so soon? More business?"

"Oh, *ja*, business indeed."

When he didn't offer any more information, Ella realized that she felt disappointed in his response. She didn't know why. Perhaps it was because he seemed to be keeping something secret from her. Or maybe it was knowing that his business was, most certainly, not with Linda.

Hannes must have sensed her feelings, for he leaned farther out the opened buggy door and, pretending to lower his voice as if confiding in her, he whispered, "Don't fret, Ella. It's nothing too secretive. You see, I heard there's a *wunderbarr* charity benefit on Saturday. Some of the finest cooks in town are going to be auctioning off baked goods, and I sure do love sweets."

Immediately her disappointment vanished, replaced with amazement. "You returned for the charity auction?" She couldn't help but smile, hardly believing that what he said was possible. Had he truly returned just for the auction?

He puffed up his chest in a teasingly prideful way. "That I did."

"And two days beforehand?"

With a playful lifting of his shoulders, he said, "Like I said, can't get enough of this pretty little town."

This time, she laughed with him.

When their laughter quieted, she patted the side of the horse once again. "Now seriously, Hannes, did you truly drive such a long distance for a charity benefit?"

He raised an eyebrow at her question.

Ella felt the heat rise to her cheeks. She heard her words echo in her ears, and she wondered if he had misunderstood her. Quickly, she corrected herself. "I meant, surely you must have business here, *ja*? That's an awful long way just to bid on baked goods."

Hannes jumped down from the buggy, one hand still holding on to the reins. He stood next to Ella and smiled down upon her. She liked the way he looked at her, his eyes always full of life and enthusiasm. "*Ja*, besides wanting to buy a certain young woman's pie, I do have business here."

"And what might that be?" she inquired, genuinely curious. She knew that he had no plans to partner with Linda, so what business could he possibly have?

"Oh, you see, there's this very stubborn store owner here in Echo Creek that my *daed*'s interested in doing business with, for some unknown reason."

Just the way he said it made Ella laugh, although she was surprised that Hannes, and his father, for that matter, had had a change of heart, especially after Linda had treated him so poorly. "I knew it wasn't just for the auction! But I am curious that you've reconsidered working with my stepmother so soon."

"Ah!" He held up a finger, pointing it toward the sky. "Things don't always look as they appear, remember? Besides, don't think I didn't time my return trip to coincide with the charity auction. Like I said, I have a hankering for some fresh-made pie . . ."

She blushed.

"Anyway," he said, taking a step backward. "I bought something for you."

She looked at him in surprise. "For me?" She couldn't remember the last time that someone had bought anything for her.

He reached into the buggy and opened the little door to the compartment in the dashboard. "*Ja*, you." With a closed hand, he turned and held it in the air before her. "Close your eyes."

Quickly, Ella scanned the street. The last thing she

needed was for anyone to witness this exchange. Gossip would fly quicker than bees to honey! "Oh, I . . ."

He tilted his head and gave her a sideways glance. "Close them . . ." he said in a low voice.

Obediently, she did as he said.

"Now hold out your hands."

"Both of them?"

He laughed. "*Ja*, both of them. And no peeking."

She knew that her hands trembled as she cupped them together and held them before her. For what seemed like minutes, instead of the few short seconds that it actually took, she waited. She felt silly, standing there in the street, her eyes closed and her hands outstretched.

Finally, Hannes placed something small and cool into her hands. "You can open them now."

Her eyelids fluttered open and she looked down at the tiny object that he had placed on her palm. She caught her breath when she realized that it was a small glass figurine. Upon closer inspection, she saw that it was the bloom of a morning glory. "Oh, Hannes!" She held it up so that she could see it better. "It's . . . beautiful."

"If you hold it to the sun, you'll see all of the colors of a rainbow."

She did as he instructed, and after shutting one eye, she stared through the crystal at the sun. "Look at that!" Sure enough, little rainbow colors could be seen in the figurine. "Wherever did you get this?"

"I saw it in a catalog and knew you should have it. So I ordered it and had it shipped to my *daed*'s store in Blue Springs."

Stunned, Ella stared at him with a look of incredulity. "You ordered this for me?"

Clutching his hands behind his back, he rocked on the soles of his feet. "*Ja*, I did."

"Oh my!" While she appreciated the gesture, she felt it was too dear a gift and was about to tell him so. But he seemed to sense her reservation.

"Now, now, don't make a fuss over it. It's just a small token of my affections, Ella Troyer." He reached up to remove his hat and ran his fingers through his hair. "I'd be honored if you'd keep it and, mayhaps, when you look at it, think of me." Taking a step backward, he reached up and touched the side of the buggy. "Reckon I best let you go." He climbed into the buggy and gave her one last smile. "See you on Saturday, *ja*?"

Ella stood there, the pretty glass flower in her hand, watching as he drove away. It was only when the buggy disappeared that she looked up and saw that her two stepsisters were standing on the other side of the street, having witnessed the entire exchange between her and Hannes. And they looked none too happy about it. With angry expressions on their faces, they turned and stormed back into the store.

She could only imagine what they were saying to Linda at that very minute.

Embarrassed, Ella closed her fingers around the figurine and turned away from the memory of their reproachful eyes. Oh, she knew that she'd hear about it later, probably over supper. She'd get quite the tongue-lashing and probably be given a dozen senseless new chores. But in the meantime, she didn't want anything to spoil the moment. Hannes had not only returned to Echo Creek, but he had done so with this very special gift just for her. While she didn't want to read too much into it, she could feel that small seed of hope beginning to grow, once again, inside of her.

Chapter Seventeen

"Now, Ella," Linda said in a feigned tone of sweetness. It was a tone that, unfortunately, Ella had grown far too familiar with. Especially recently. It was the tone of voice that usually came with some unreasonable demands. "I have a few special things for you to do."

Ella looked up from the sink, where she stood washing the dishes from their Friday supper. Linda stood by the table, already dressed for the day in a dark brown dress, with her white prayer *kapp* neatly pinned to her head. There was a smug look about her stepmother.

"Special things?"

It wasn't that Ella was surprised; she had expected to be given a long list of chores. No, she had expected that. It was Linda's favorite thing to do: bombard Ella with long lists of useless chores in order to punish her or, in some cases, just to keep her busy.

This time, however, what surprised Ella was how Linda appeared to be making the effort to be nice about it—if such a thing was actually possible.

The previous evening, Ella had been surprised when no one had mentioned Hannes's return to Echo Creek and, therefore, no one reprimanded her for having spoken to him in the center of town. Supper had been a normal affair, with Drusilla and Anna talking about nothing other than the charity auction on Saturday. No one had thought to include Ella in that particular conversation.

While Ella didn't care, she had found it hard to believe that her stepsisters hadn't wasted one minute tattling to their mother. Surely they would not have wasted the opportunity to make Ella look bad. After all, if she had time to talk with Hannes, she was not spending time on chores. That was when Ella realized that Linda didn't seem to care.

For once.

Now, however, Ella wondered if she had been mistaken.

"*Ja*, indeed. Special things."

Bracing herself, Ella slowly reached over and shut off the faucet, her eyes falling upon the pretty glass flower Hannes had given her. She had placed it on the windowsill over the sink so that, when the sun rose in the mornings, she could see the rainbow colors shining through the glass. And, just as Hannes had requested, every time she looked at it, she thought of him. Those moments gave her a secret sense of joy that not even her stepmother could steal from her.

Facing Linda, Ella watched as her stepmother took a deep breath and straightened her shoulders. "Both of the girls need new dresses." Linda pointed toward the other side of the kitchen. "I've left the fabric on the mudroom counter."

Ella wanted to ask why Drusilla and Anna never made their own dresses, but she didn't. She already knew the answer: they simply couldn't. Neither girl could sew if her life depended on it. They had never made a quilt, didn't know how to knit, and certainly couldn't crochet. Whenever their dresses were torn, it was Ella who repaired them. And to make their own dresses? No, they would sooner wear torn and tattered clothing than learn how to cut a pattern and sew it.

Not for the first time, Ella wondered what Drusilla and Anna would do when they finally *did* marry. They never cooked or baked, cleaned or washed, and they certainly could not manage a household! How on earth would they ever survive? An Amish husband would never accept a wife who merely sat around and expected others to do everything for her.

Glancing over her shoulder toward the open door of the mudroom, Ella saw the fabric and caught her breath.

The fabric was the very bolts of material she had seen at the store! In fact, when Ella had unpacked it, she remembered having admired the fresh, new colors. But she had not admired the cost on the receipt from the vendor. At seventeen dollars a yard, the price was far too dear for anyone in the community to actually purchase the fabric, even before Linda marked it up for resale.

Now that the fabric was staring at her from the mudroom, it dawned on Ella that Linda had known that no one could buy it when she originally purchased it and displayed it for everyone to see at her store.

While the price was too expensive for the regular young women of Echo Creek, nothing was too exorbitant for Drusilla and Anna.

"I . . . I suppose I can work on them next week," Ella replied, a pit forming in her stomach. When was the last time *she* had had a new dress? Linda never bought her any fabric, and Ella knew better than to complain.

Linda would tell her to spend her own money, knowing full well that Ella had few, if any, opportunities to earn spending money.

Instead, Ella was given hand-me-downs, the old, worn-out dresses of her stepsisters. Fortunately, she always managed to fix them, sometimes patching them so that they did not look so threadbare. Still, it sure would have been nice if for once she, too, could have a new dress.

While new clothing was too good for Ella, nothing was too good for her stepsisters. But that fabric was very fancy. Where on earth would Drusilla and Anna wear those dresses?

She quickly found out.

"Oh, no." Linda shook her head and clicked her tongue. "Next week won't do, I'm afraid." She leveled her gaze at Ella. "The girls must have them for tomorrow's event."

Immediately, Ella's mouth opened in surprise. Had Linda actually said she wanted both dresses made by *tomorrow*? With all of the chores that Ella already had been assigned to do, sewing new dresses for a charity auction that was less than twenty-four hours away was simply not realistic.

"That might be a little difficult," Ella said slowly. When she saw Linda's expression darken, Ella continued, "I mean, what with baking the cakes in the morning for the charity event, along with my other chores, and then getting ready to help at the auction . . ."

Linda interrupted her. "Help at the auction?" she echoed with an incredulous tone in her voice.

That pit in Ella's stomach felt as though it grew even bigger. "I . . . I told Elizabeth Grimm that I'd help her and Anna Rose with preparations for the auction.

You know, setting up the tables and placing the baked goods out for display. And, of course, I offered to help collect the money afterward."

Lifting her chin just enough so that she could stare down her nose in a haughty manner, Linda gave her a condescending look. "I'm afraid that might be a little difficult . . ." she said, borrowing Ella's words from a few moments earlier.

Her mouth suddenly dry, Ella swallowed. "And I . . . I was planning on baking a pie for the event."

"But you already are." Linda's mouth twitched as if suppressing a smile. "For your *schwesters, ja*?"

"*Ja*, of course. I promised them I would bake their items for donation." She wanted to add that it was unfair that neither Drusilla nor Anna had not even offered to help her when she baked their cakes. Instead, they were apparently more concerned with what they were to wear while Ella was being forced to make their new dresses.

"So there you have it, Ella. You are already donating to the cause."

"But I thought I would bake and donate my *own* pie, too."

Linda's masquerade of kindness evaporated before Ella's eyes. She watched as her stepmother's jaw tensed and her lips tightened. Gone was the facade of calm. In its place was a look of complete hostility and anger. For a moment, Ella was frightened. While she had witnessed Linda's fierce temper in the past, this was a new level of fury.

Ella's fear only increased as Linda leaned forward, her face just inches from Ella's, and she glared at her. "Then you thought wrong!" Linda snapped, her voice filled with venom as she enunciated each word. "You have enough to do here. We have enough pies to auction off, anyway. And you will *not* be going to that auction."

Ella felt light-headed, wondering if she had imagined her stepmother's harsh words. After all, how on earth could her stepmother think that there could *ever* be enough items to auction for charity? And, to make matters worse, Linda had basically outright forbade Ella to attend the event. What Ella couldn't understand was why. Why wouldn't her stepmother want her to attend? Surely there was something else going on that Linda was not telling her.

"I . . . I'm sure I don't understand," Ella stammered.

Linda leaned her hip against the table and raised her hands. She began to count on her fingers. "First, you need to finish making the dresses for Drusilla and Anna." A second finger pointed upward. "Next, you need to clean that basement." A third finger joined the rest. "You have to weed that garden." Finally a fourth finger was raised. "Lastly, you have all of your regular chores to do, including baking the bread for the store, tending the animals in the barn, and cleaning the house."

Ella took a deep breath, willing herself to not cry. But her throat constricted, and she felt a stinging in the corners of her eyes. Why would her stepmother do this to her? Give her so many chores for one day? And why were Drusilla and Anna excused from helping? It was a question that Ella asked herself not for the first time.

"That's so much work," she mumbled.

Linda feigned concern. "Unfortunately, those things

must be finished, Ella. Work before play. Isn't that the way the expression goes?"

Something stirred inside of Ella. It was as if a little voice had whispered in her ear that nothing was impossible, including finishing all of her stepmother's seemingly endless list of chores. All she had to do was believe in God, that he would not let her down. Hadn't her mother told her so?

Straightening her shoulders, Ella lifted her chin and decided to listen to that little inner voice. Determined to not let Linda get the best of her—not this time!—Ella met her stepmother's superior gaze with one of her own, one that was filled with defiance and determination.

"But if I finish all of those chores?" Ella asked, an unusual sense of resolve in her voice. "Then may I go?"

To Ella's surprise, Linda laughed. It wasn't a happy or cheerful laugh. No. It was a laugh full of malice. The sound of it sent a chill down Ella's spine. "Oh, Ella. You always were such a foolish child. Optimistic, perhaps, but foolish."

Her stepmother's words stung. What was wrong with always trying to make the best of even the worst situations? And she had encountered the worst situations possible, especially after her father had passed away.

Feeling a sense of defiance, Ella stood her ground, stoically waiting for a response to her very reasonable question.

"Why, Ella, of course you may attend the event if you complete *all* of those chores." But the tone of Linda's voice made it clear she did not believe it was possible. Without another word, Linda turned her back to Ella and left the kitchen.

Standing there, alone, Ella made a silent vow that she would do everything Linda wanted and more. Not even Linda and her outrageous, never-ending demands would stop Ella from attending the charity event. She would bake the bread, the cakes, and her own pie while somehow finding a way to do all of the cleaning so that the house sparkled, even if it meant that she stayed up all night and worked all the next day. And somehow she would make those dresses for her ungrateful and undeserving stepsisters. She would ensure that Linda couldn't find one thing to complain about, and she would go to the event after all.

For once, Ella would not give her stepmother the satisfaction of ruining *this* fun event that was being held in Echo Creek.

Chapter Eighteen

The wall clock chimed twelve times, each chime reverberating in the empty house. Ella waited until it stopped, as if the twelfth chime were some magical cue. When the last chime finished resonating, she packaged up the cakes and pie in a basket, placing a horizontal wooden divider between each item so that not one of them would get damaged in transit. First went the poor man's cake, then the lazy-daisy oatmeal cake, and finally, on the top, she carefully placed her own apple crisp pie.

Pushing aside the feelings of guilt for disobeying her stepmother, Ella covered the basket and hurried out the door so that she could drop off the treats at the schoolhouse and quickly return home before she was even missed.

The previous night, while trying to sleep, Ella had tossed and turned, debating with herself whether or not she should disobey her stepmother's orders. And yet, every time she almost convinced herself to forget the whole thing, that defying Linda was certainly not worth the inevitable mistreatment that would ensue,

Ella's mother's words echoed in her ears: *Be kind and good, no matter what happens, for God has a plan for you.*

And that was when Ella made up her mind.

Baking a pie for charity was a *good* thing. Her stepmother had no right telling anyone—never mind her own stepdaughter!—not to participate. Even if Linda insisted that she couldn't attend the event—something else that was ridiculous!—Ella had every right to donate a pie, especially since she had already agreed to bake Drusilla's and Anna's cakes.

So she had arisen extra early and finished baking the bread for the store long before the others had woken. Then, when everyone had left the house for the day, Ella had quickly baked not just the cake for Drusilla's donation and the cake for Anna's donation, but also her favorite pie from her mother's secret recipe.

No one would stop Ella from doing the right thing, and donating the pie was just that: the right thing to do.

However, the entire time that she had been baking the pie, her heart beat rapidly and her nerves were on edge. Oh, how she felt deceitful and underhanded, as if she were doing something terrible and not merely disobeying her stepmother! The only way that Ella had managed to follow through with finishing the pie was that she continued to remind herself that she *was* an adult and Linda was *not* her mother. Just like every other baptized woman in the church, Ella had the right to make up her own mind over something as simple as baking a pie for a charity auction.

And yet, Ella had still felt anxious and skittish. When the wall clock had begun chiming at noon, she had nearly jumped out of her skin, as if she expected her stepmother to magically appear, catching her in the act of packing up the baked goods.

But no one had returned to the house.

Relieved, Ella secured the lid on the basket and hurried to the door.

Even if Linda or one of her daughters saw her walking through town with the basket, they wouldn't question why she was in town. After all, someone had to deliver the baked goods to the teacher for the auction. If she bumped into either of her stepsisters on the main street of town, Ella knew that neither one of them would bother checking to see how many items were in the basket. They were more concerned with who might buy their cakes.

Ella's secret was safe at last!

She was halfway to the schoolhouse when she caught sight of Hannes, leaning against a tree and carving the bark off of a stick. He seemed to be waiting for something . . . or, perhaps, someone.

Ella shifted the basket to her other hand, hiding it behind her skirt.

"Ella Troyer!" He flung the stick to the ground and shut his small knife blade. "I thought I might run into you today." Shoving the knife into his back pocket, he jogged over to walk alongside her.

"Oh, *ja*?" She smiled back at him. "And why's that, Hannes?"

He gestured toward the school. "All the young women are bringing their baked goods for tonight's event. I figured I'd be seeing you around sooner or later."

She laughed. "So you've been standing out here all morning, then?"

"Oh, Ella." He gave her a soft smile. "I'd have waited all day if that's what it took to get a moment alone with you."

His confession caught her off guard, and she blushed. He must have sensed her discomfort, as he quickly resumed his teasing tone. "After all, I wanted to find out which pie I should bid on tonight."

"Which pie?" She gave him a sideways glance. "Why, I reckon you'd buy the one that you fancy the most!"

"Or the one made by the baker I fancy the most, since I'm supposed to share the first piece with her!"

Ella had forgotten about that. "Oh help," she muttered, more to herself than to him. How could she have forgotten the evening when Linda was ranting and raving about this new twist to the auction?

"Is something the matter?"

Quickly, she shook her head. "*Nee, nee.*" She tried to compose herself. "It's just that . . ." Think fast, she told herself. ". . . I couldn't tell you which pie I baked."

He stopped walking and faced her. "Why ever not?"

A smile formed on her lips. "That would be cheating."

"Cheating?" He placed his hand on his chest in mock horror. "Me? Why, I'd never stoop so low as to sneak a peek at your pie!"

Ella felt her heart skip a beat. And, from the way her cheeks grew warm, she knew that she was blushing. What was it about Hannes that made her constantly flush pink?

"Besides," he said in a tone that suggested he was telling her a big secret, "I'm not the only fellow lingering around the schoolhouse trying to catch a glimpse of his girl bringing in her treat."

Ella blinked. Had she heard him correctly? Had

Hannes just called her *his* girl? Her heart quickened at the thought. Surely she had misheard him! Still, her mind reeled at the possibility that she hadn't. Did Hannes actually consider her to be walking out with him? They'd only had a few interactions, and nothing that remotely bordered on a formal courtship. While the idea of courting Hannes—seriously courting him!—was certainly not unpleasant to her, she also knew that he would return to Blue Springs soon enough, and she'd probably never see him again.

Hannes interrupted her whirlwind of thoughts.

"See?" Hannes gestured with this head toward the far side of the schoolhouse, where, along the road that led into town from the south, two young men were leaning against their buggies, talking to each other as casually as could be. And yet, the one kept glancing over his shoulder toward the road as if waiting for someone to appear.

Ella recognized the man as Paul Hostetler, and he was most likely waiting for Martha Esh. It was common knowledge that he fancied her, even though Martha hadn't been too quick to reciprocate his affections. At least not openly.

"Now," Hannes said lightly, "if you won't tell me what pie you made, let me at least carry the basket and walk with you the rest of the way to the school."

Relinquishing the basket to his care, Ella gave him a feigned stern look and wagged her finger at him. "No peeking."

"It's heavy." He felt the basket, raising and lowering it several times. "Let me guess." He scrunched up his eyes as if thinking hard. "I'm supposing there are three pies in here." He pretended to feel the basket once again. "No. Make that two cakes and one pie."

Ella gasped. "However did you know?"

Nudging her arm with his own, he started walking again. "I am a man who knows his desserts."

As they walked to the schoolhouse, Ella glanced at the general store. To her surprise, her stepmother was standing outside the doors, her arms crossed over her chest. There was an angry look upon her face, and Ella realized that Linda had certainly witnessed her talking with Hannes. Now her stepmother was watching as Hannes carried the basket and accompanied her to the schoolhouse.

Oh help, she thought. *Surely this will not end well at home.*

Ella lowered her head and wished she knew why, exactly, her stepmother looked so very angry.

Inside the schoolhouse, Ella greeted the teacher, Elizabeth Grimm. Today she wore a pretty, light green dress, and with her blond hair pulled back, neatly tucked under her prayer *kapp,* she looked every bit the proper Amish woman.

"*Gut morgan,* Ella." She stood up and hurried around the desk to greet Ella. Her eyes glanced over Hannes. "And you are . . . ?"

He set the basket on the edge of the desk. ". . . Buying the desserts in this basket later tonight."

Elizabeth tried not to laugh. "Oh? Is that so?"

With a wink at Ella, Hannes patted the top of the basket with all of the confidence in the world. "That's for sure and certain."

"You haven't peeked, have you?" Elizabeth asked.

Hannes shook his head. "I'd never stoop so low."

Elizabeth tried to hide her amusement at Hannes's serious declaration. She lifted the lid of the basket and peered inside. "Oh Ella! You made your *maem*'s special . . ." She stopped short before giving away what it was and glanced at Hannes as she added, ". . . dessert."

"Special dessert? What makes it so special?" Hannes asked.

Ella feigned a look of secrecy. "She always made it with a secret ingredient."

Hannes rubbed his hands together. "And the plot thickens!"

Smiling, Elizabeth placed her hands on the basket handle. "Now, you know you're supposed to eat the first piece of dessert with the young woman who baked it, *ja*?" She lifted the basket. "And this feels like it's holding more than one. I hope you bring your appetite as well as your money to bid."

"I shall bring both, Teacher." He dipped his head in a charmingly exaggerated manner that caused Elizabeth to laugh and Ella to blush. "Now, we'd best leave you to sort out the pie . . ." He glanced at Ella. ". . . and cakes."

Once outside, Ella glanced toward the general store. Sure enough, Linda was still standing there. Only now, her two daughters stood on either side of her. Both of them glowered in her direction.

Hannes must have seen Ella look toward the store, for he did the same, and upon seeing the unwelcome—and clearly unhappy—audience, he exhaled sharply. He reached for Ella's arm and began to guide her down the street.

"Let me walk you home, Ella," he said in a low voice. "Seems a bit crowded in town for us to talk any more here."

Any sort of response was trapped in her throat. Simply put, Ella couldn't speak. She had seen that look once before on Linda's face, and that was just the previous week when Ella had left the Scrabble game early. What was it about Hannes Clemens that Linda did not like? From what Ella had observed, he was a good Christian man with fair business practices—and a lot of patience, considering he was still apparently dealing with Linda!

Suddenly, it dawned on Ella that her stepmother might not have a problem with Hannes, but with the attention he was bestowing on *her*.

The day of the Scrabble game, both Drusilla and Anna had appeared particularly pleased when their mother told Ella she couldn't go to the youth singing. And when they had witnessed Hannes talking with Ella in the street earlier that week, both of them had looked especially irritated. Was it possible that Drusilla and Anna were complaining to their mother? After all, both girls had made it quite clear that they were interested in Henry "Hannes" Clemens, and Ella knew that Linda would stop at nothing to get her daughters anything they wanted.

"Are you feeling okay?"

Startled from her thoughts, Ella realized she had forgotten that Hannes was still walking beside her. Absentmindedly, she nodded.

But he clearly didn't believe her.

"I trust I didn't get you into any sort of"—he paused as if struggling for the correct word—"strife with your stepmother."

Too quickly, Ella shook her head. "*Nee*, of course not." But even she knew that the words were not believable.

"Ella?" He prodded gently. "That doesn't sound convincing."

She forced a smile. "She'll just be wondering why I wasn't home finishing my chores."

For a moment, Hannes was silent, as if contemplating what she had said. They continued walking toward the white house near the edge of town, Ella deep in thought and Hannes remaining quiet. It was only when they stopped at the white gate that he spoke at last.

"Ella, I certainly hope that I see you later this evening." There was something amiss about the way he said that. "I would be disappointed if you were not there."

Ella stared at the ground. She couldn't meet his gaze, too afraid that he might see the truth in her expression.

He took a deep breath and sighed. "It's been rather difficult to get to spend any time with you."

She swallowed, her pulse quickening. What was he trying to say? That if she did not attend, his disappointment would hinder him from pursuing a courtship? Had she misread him all along? Or did he simply think she wasn't interested in him and was, perhaps, avoiding him?

"I'm sorry," she whispered, this time avoiding his gaze for fear that he would see the tears that now welled in her eyes. She simply *had* to get to the charity event. She couldn't disappoint him one more time. "I . . . I had best get inside to finish my chores."

She started to turn when he reached out and touched her arm, holding her back. She had no choice but to look at him. His blue eyes studied her face, and she saw him frown. Oh! How could she blame him for not wanting to walk out with someone like her? Her situation at home was far too complicated, thanks to Linda and her daughters.

"I'll see you later?" The way he asked was more than just a question. It was almost as if there was a warning in his tone.

God willing, I'll be there, she thought, but her heart remained heavy. Instead of saying what she was thinking, she merely nodded her head and hurried off, the tears quickly falling from her eyes as soon as she was a safe distance away. How could she have thought Hannes was enamored with her if he would give up so easily?

Chapter Nineteen

"Knock, knock?"

Ella looked up, her eyes blurry from having spent so much time working on Drusilla's dress. Her neck ached and her shoulders were sore from being bent over the fabric. It was almost two o'clock, and she still had so much work to complete, including Anna's dress and weeding the garden.

"Ella?" a voice called from the doorway.

"In here."

She looked up and, to her surprise, saw that Miriam entered. She wore a light gray dress—an unusual color for an elderly Amish woman, but one that Ella found rather flattering for her.

"Miriam King!" Forcing a smile on her face, Ella tried to appear pleasant. While she was always glad to see Miriam, the stress of having to finish the dresses before Drusilla and Anna returned was hindering what otherwise would have been a fine surprise visit. "What a nice surprise!" she said, setting down the fabric. "What brings you here?"

Miriam glanced around the kitchen, her eyes widening as she saw the dishes that needed washing and the fabric spread across the table. "Seems like you're elbows-deep in chores, Ella." She set a bag onto the counter and walked over to the table. "Hmm. What a pretty fabric," she said as she peered over Ella's shoulder. "What are you making?"

Ella tried to swallow her contempt for her stepsisters as she answered with a simple, "Dresses for Drusilla and Anna."

Miriam raised an eyebrow. "Shouldn't you be getting yourself ready for the event tonight?"

Ella couldn't help but sigh. "I doubt that I'll be attending, Miriam."

Miriam gasped. "Why ever not?"

There were far too many ways Ella could answer that question, but she didn't want to disrespect Linda. Even though her stepmother might deserve a little disdain from time to time, Ella knew that a good Christian should not speak ill of another. And she certainly wasn't about to complain to the deacon's wife!

"I . . . I just haven't finished my chores," she admitted.

Dismissively, Miriam waved her hand. "Oh, stuff and nonsense! Chores, indeed." She let her fingers drift to the fabric. "Making your stepsisters' dresses can surely wait."

Ella shook her head. "*Nee*, it cannot. The girls want to wear new dresses tonight."

A dark cloud passed over Miriam's face. "It's high time those two girls made their own dresses . . ." She leveled her gaze at Ella. "And baked their own treats, *ja*?" She didn't wait for an answer. Instead, she pulled out a chair and sat down. "I'll tell you what, my dear child. You let me handle these dresses. After having ten children—and six of those *dochders*!—I know a thing or two about dressmaking."

Just the thought of allowing Miriam to assist her mortified Ella. What would Linda say if she found out? "Oh, I couldn't!"

Miriam frowned at her and wagged her finger. "Oh, you can and you will, indeed!" She reached for the fabric.

Reluctantly, Ella released it.

Satisfied, Miriam walked over to the sofa near the windows along the back of the kitchen. She settled down and examined the dress. "You stitch well, Ella."

Ella flushed at the compliment. No one ever noticed her work, never mind recognizing it with kind words.

"Why! I'll have them done in less than an hour!" She lifted her gaze and smiled at Ella. "Now, you go finish whatever else needs to be done and leave this to me."

Still, Ella hesitated. If Linda came home and saw Miriam there, sewing dresses for Drusilla and Anna, she would be more than displeased. She'd be downright humiliated and angry.

As if reading her mind, Miriam said, "Your stepmother's busy at the store. She won't be home for at least two hours, so don't you fret none." And then she smiled. "Now, go on and finish whatever else needs to be done to satisfy that stepmother of yours. I'm more than happy to help out." Once again, she studied the fabric. "I can't remember the last time I made a dress with such fine material as this is!"

"It's a new material that Linda ordered."

Miriam pursed her lips and furrowed her brow. "I imagine it's rather dear." Clearly she held an unfavorable opinion, and she shook her head in disapproval. "Seems a bit prideful to use it for her own *dochders*."

Ella couldn't agree more, but she said nothing in response.

With nothing left to say, Miriam bent her head over the dress and began to finish stitching the hem. Under her breath she began to hum a hymn, a smile on her lips as she sewed. Her hands moved so quickly that Ella watched her for a moment, fascinated at the woman's ability to focus so intently on the unexpected task she had undertaken.

Satisfied that Miriam was indeed content, Ella got up from the table and headed toward the door. With Miriam helping her, Ella could finish weeding the garden and clean the kitchen. Everything else had been taken care of, since she had arisen so early to tackle baking the bread and cleaning the basement before making the cakes and pie.

At the door, Ella paused and glanced over her shoulder. "*Danke*, Miriam."

Another wave of her hand. "Never you mind, child. After all you do for everyone else, it's high time someone help you. Now go on and let me finish this dress."

Outside, the sun was still high overhead, and the air remained fresh.

Suddenly, it dawned on her that she had been remiss in inquiring about the reason behind Miriam's unexpected visit. It wasn't like Miriam, or anyone else, for that matter, to stop by the house. Belle and Sadie had been the only two people who ever did visit unannounced. But Belle was married now, and Sadie had run off.

Why *had* Miriam stopped by?

For whatever reason, God had known exactly what Ella needed: help.

Miriam *was* right. When was the last time someone

had helped her? Ella was so used to being the caretaker that she had forgotten it was fair to accept the assistance of someone else from time to time. Otherwise, her efforts were far too one-sided, and *that* was not the way God intended life to be.

Long ago, Ella had learned that there were givers and takers. While she tried to not keep score, she didn't need a scorecard to realize that some takers never gave. Instead, they merely took advantage of the givers, who, being so used to giving, never saw reason to be on the reciprocating end.

Having someone actually help *her* for a change felt strange. But Ella had known that the only way she'd get to the charity event that evening was with God's help. Somehow he had found a way, and that way included Miriam's unexpected visit and her experienced hands for sewing.

He had, indeed, provided for her.

Ella took a deep breath and walked down the porch steps. With summer ending, the garden had almost finished its productive cycle, but the weeds continued to grow. Still, there were pumpkins beginning to form, as well as butternut squash, two staples in the Troyer household for autumn meals.

Kneeling by the pumpkin vine, Ella began plucking the weeds and pinching back the leaves on the vine. Underneath the green growth, her fingers touched a large pumpkin, and she paused to look at it.

It was round and orange, which surprised her. It was far too early for the pumpkins to be ripe, but this one was, indeed, ready to be plucked.

When she finished with the garden, Ella carried the pumpkin to the porch and set it near the steps. She still needed to finish her barn chores: feeding and watering the animals before milking the dairy cows. Fortunately, since the cows and horse had been outside for most of the day, the stalls did not require cleaning, and to Ella's delight, she was back inside the house before an hour had passed.

To her amazement, Miriam stood at the sink, washing dishes. The kitchen sparkled, and there were neatly folded dresses on the kitchen table.

"My word, Miriam!" Ella hurried over to the table and pressed her hand on top of the pile of clothes. "You weren't teasing about being an amazing seamstress!"

Turning off the faucet and then shaking the excess water from her hands, Miriam exhaled. "You already had the patterns cut, Ella. With wider stitches, it wasn't that time-consuming," she said, wiping her hands on a dish towel, "as you can see."

Ella unfolded the first dress and held it up so that she could look at it. The bright blue fabric with tiny dark navy stripes, barely noticeable to the eye, was expertly sewn in such a manner that even Ella could not tell that Miriam had used wider stitches. She draped the dress over her arm and had started to reach for the second dress, which was similar, but in green, when she noticed a third dress.

"Miriam, what is this?" Picking up the pink dress at the bottom, Ella looked at the elderly woman.

"That? Oh, that's nothing." But Miriam smiled in a mischievous way.

It didn't look like "nothing." In fact, it appeared to be a third new dress. And the material was twice as beautiful as the blue and green fabrics used to make Drusilla and Anna's dresses. The brightness of the pink contrasted with a faint shimmering color, just barely visible to the eye. As Ella tilted her head, the colors changed in the light, just a little, giving it an almost iridescent look.

Surely the bishop would not approve of such material!

"Where did this come from?" Ella asked.

Miriam shrugged. "Just a little something I made."

"For . . . ?"

The older woman leaned against the counter. "For you, Ella. I made it for you."

For a moment, Ella didn't know how to respond. No one had ever made anything for her. That wasn't the way of the Amish. Gift giving was only on special occasions and was usually just something small—a token gift, perhaps, on special birthdays. When young girls turned sixteen, they might receive a new cookbook or devotional, but never something as grand as this.

"But why?" she asked at last.

Miriam pushed away from the counter and walked over to where Ella stood. She placed her hands on Ella's shoulders and, with a smile on her lips, stared into her eyes. "Now, Ella, there are some questions that cannot be answered so easily. Let's just leave it at that."

With those words, Miriam took the dress from her and placed it back into the basket. After covering it with a cloth, Miriam handed it to her. "You'd best set that aside somewhere so that no one sees it. I reckon Drusilla and Anna won't take kindly to being outshone by their stepsister." She paused before adding a soft, "Again."

It dawned on Ella that Miriam had made that special trip just to give her the dress. Miriam had actually made it for her before coming to visit.

The clock on the wall chimed, and Miriam glanced at it. "Oh help! It's almost four thirty. I'd best get going now, *ja*? Have to feed my own brood before we meet at the schoolhouse for the charity auction." She gave Ella a brief hug—another unexpected surprise!—before she headed toward the door.

"I'll be anxious to see who you sit with after the auction," she said with a wink. "I'm sure there's one very lucky young man who will be enjoying the most delicious pie in Echo Creek tonight."

As Miriam disappeared outside, Ella stood transfixed in the middle of the kitchen. Something tightened inside of her chest. Not since her mother had passed away had anyone done something so kind for her. While her father had always tried, Linda had somehow managed to turn things around so that her daughters, not Ella, benefited. And Ella's father was never one to engage in conflict, especially with a woman.

Finally, someone had taken an interest in Ella and her needs. That realization struck her like a thunderbolt, and Ella found herself fighting the urge to shed tears of joy. What had she done to deserve such an amazing angel in her life?

Chapter Twenty

"And where, exactly, do you think you are going, Ella?"

She had just hurried down the stairs, having heard Drusilla and Anna chattering happily in the kitchen. The new dresses that Ella had made for them were the main topic of conversation. Linda had been standing near the door appraising her daughters when Ella had joined them.

And at that moment, the room had fallen silent.

If Drusilla and Anna had been excited by their new dresses, one look at Ella had robbed them of any joy.

For she, too, wore a new dress—the very one that Miriam had made for her.

"Maem!" Drusilla cried out.

Anna pointed furiously at her stepsister. "Where did you get that dress?"

Even Linda looked stunned. "Indeed, Ella, where did you get that dress?" She stepped over to Ella and touched the skirt that hung to her stepdaughter's mid-calves.

Ella bit her lower lip. Perhaps wearing Miriam's dress was a mistake after all. For the past half hour, Ella had contemplated whether or not she should wear something so beautiful. But after listening to Drusilla and Anna giggling and laughing from the other bedroom, Ella had taken one final look in the mirror and told herself that, for once, she, too, deserved something special. With a new sense of determination, she had donned the dress and made her way downstairs.

Now, however, she knew she had made a mistake.

"It . . . it was a gift," Ella responded at last.

Linda frowned. "A gift? From whom?"

Ella's gaze darted from Linda to the two girls standing behind her, their eyes clearly coveting the dress. The envy in their facial expressions stunned Ella. Never had she seen anyone so desirous of a material object! At that moment, Ella realized why the church leaders spoke so vehemently against worldliness. When people had nice things, others did not share in their joy. Instead, they longed to possess those items. Such longing was nothing short of sinful.

"I asked you a question, Ella." Linda's loud voice broke Ella's concentration. "Who gifted you that dress?"

If Ella told Linda, Miriam would get in trouble. Yet Ella also knew that she couldn't lie. "I . . . I do not want to answer that," she finally said.

Linda inhaled sharply. "Very well, Ella."

Behind her, both Drusilla and Anna started to speak. Linda, however, merely held up her hand to silence them. "It doesn't matter, for I daresay you cannot wear that dress. Surely the bishop would not approve."

"But . . ."

"No buts. As the head of this household, my word is the final word. Besides, where, exactly, do you think you are going?"

Ella felt her heart begin to pound. With the three of

them staring at her, she could hardly think of how to respond. Surely they knew the answer, so why were they asking the question? "The . . . the charity auction."

There was a long moment of silence—a silence that was deafening. Ella waited, holding her breath in the hope that Linda would respond positively. Did her stepmother truly think that she would miss the event? Everyone in the community planned on attending!

At last, Linda broke her gaze and stared down at her own dark purple dress. She leaned over and brushed some imaginary dirt from her black apron. "I'm afraid not, Ella."

Ella could hardly believe she'd heard her stepmother properly. "Afraid not what?"

"Afraid you will not attend the event."

Drusilla and Anna snickered, their envy turning to vengeful spite. Ella glanced at them, realizing that no matter how beautiful their dresses, their contemptuous smiles showed their true ugliness.

Returning her attention to Linda, Ella took a deep breath. "And why not?"

"Because," Linda started in a slow, measured tone, "you did not complete your chores." She lifted her head and stared directly into Ella's face. "I told you that I needed the basement cleaned . . ."

Immediately, Ella breathed a sigh of relief. She *had* cleaned the basement, just as her stepmother had insisted. Right after she had baked the bread that morning, she had set about the unpleasant chore. In fact, she had reorganized the shelves, scrubbed the floor, and even refilled the kerosene lanterns that hung from the thick wooden rafters. There was not one thing out of order.

"Oh, Maem," she said, relieved that her stepmother

was, once again, incorrect. "I did finish cleaning the basement. Have you taken a look at it?"

Linda raised an eyebrow. "Have *you*?"

The expression on her stepmother's face caught Ella off guard. It was almost as if Linda was savoring a secret—knowledge of something sinister that, not surprisingly, delighted her.

And Ella had a sinking suspicion of what it was.

The silence in the kitchen hung heavy between them. Without saying a word, Ella crossed the floor and opened the basement door. The stairwell was dark. Reaching inside for a flashlight, she clicked it on. One sweep of the brilliant beam showed Ella exactly why Linda appeared so smug: the basement was a mess.

Turning around, Ella turned toward her stepmother and, with tears in her eyes, whispered, "Why?"

Just one word, but it asked so many questions. Why did her stepmother dislike her so much? Why had Linda done such a thing? Why didn't she want Ella to go to the charity auction?

But Linda did not respond. She merely took the flashlight and pointed toward the open doorway. "Finish your chores!" she snapped. "And forget about going tonight."

There was no sense arguing with her. Ella pressed her lips together and started down the staircase. Tears stung at her eyes, but she tried her best to resist outright crying. She would not give them the satisfaction of realizing how much her heart hurt.

At the bottom of the steps, Ella paused and assessed the damage. Someone had knocked over the bin of flour and, from the looks of it, thrown handfuls of it all over the room. Everything was coated in a fine white dust: the shelves, the jars, even the walls. Nothing had escaped the flour. It would take hours to clean it.

Oh! She fought the sob that threatened to escape her throat. Why on earth would Linda have done this?

From the top of the stairwell, the basement door shut. Footsteps on the overhead floor made it clear that Linda had stormed outside, not taking a moment to gloat over her victory. Drusilla and Anna, however, could be heard giggling to each other, and after a moment, Ella heard the distinct sound of a clicking noise.

Had one of them just locked the basement door?

She managed to find her way up the stairs, and she reached out to turn the knob. Her efforts were met with resistance, and she knew that, indeed, she was locked in.

In all of the years that Linda and her stepdaughters had been a part of Ella's life, there had been far too many incidents of unfairness toward her. But never had they behaved so maliciously as they had tonight. Ella knew that she would have to pray very hard in order to find a way to forgive them.

Ella wiped a final tear from her eye.

What's done is done, she told herself, trying to have faith that she was strong enough to deal with this terrible turn of events.

Still smarting and feeling aggrieved, Ella forced herself to descend once again to the bottom of the staircase. In the darkness, she felt her way along the wall to the place where she knew the kerosene lantern hung overhead. Nearby was a metal box of matches hanging on the wall. She pulled one out, and after hitting the strike pad, she carefully lit the lantern.

Grabbing a broom, she began to sweep up the flour.

If only they hadn't locked the basement door, perhaps Ella could still have made it to the charity event. Although the beautiful dress Miriam had given her was now covered in flour, Ella knew that she could always change into her Sunday dress. But if she showed up, Linda would see her, and if she was so ungodly as to have sabotaged Ella's hard work, what might she do if Ella openly defied her?

And that thought led to another demanding question. *How am I supposed to forgive this?* Ella wondered. *Is it even possible?*

For as long as Linda and her two daughters had been a part of the Troyer family, Ella had known that she held no favor with them. However, she was shocked by this blatant expression of what she could only consider to be loathing. What had she done to deserve such terrible treatment? For her entire life, Ella had tried to follow her mother's advice to be good and kind. Now, however, Ella wondered if her mother would still want her to follow that advice after she'd been treated so badly by her stepmother.

From the other side of the basement, Ella heard the sound of scurrying. She started at the noise, but upon turning, saw that it was only a small mouse. Ella managed to smile, and lifting the lantern, she walked toward the back of the basement. In the corner, she saw a small gray mouse cowering, as if afraid of the light.

"Oh, come now," Ella cooed. "I'm the one who always saves you! Remember me? You've nothing to fear from me, little one."

The mouse gave a squeak and jumped in the air, spinning as it did so. Then it scurried along the wall and into the shadows. Ella followed it, her lantern held high. But the mouse had disappeared. There was only a stack of boxes there, but the mouse did not come out the other side.

"Where'd you go?" Ella asked into the darkness.

Curiosity got the best of her, and after setting the lantern down on the floor, careful to keep it a safe distance away from the boxes, she began to push them aside. There were no signs of the mouse; however, the flame from the lantern flickered ever so slightly.

Ella retrieved it and stared at the flame. The closer she brought it to the place where the boxes had been, the more the flame danced.

A breeze. There was a breeze in the basement.

Ella frowned. She lifted the lantern and held it closer to the wall. To her amazement, she noticed a small hole on the floor, which had been hidden by the boxes. Certainly the mouse had scurried in there. But what was more interesting to Ella was that it appeared the hole had been chewed into the bottom corner of a door . . . a door she had never seen before.

"What on earth . . . ?" she muttered to herself. With her free hand, she felt along the wall, just barely able to make out the edge of the door. There was no doorknob, but she could feel the hinges. All she needed was something to pry it open.

A feeling of fear flooded over her. A secret door in the basement? How many times had she been down here, not once noticing it? Of course, those boxes had been stacked there for years, and she hadn't many reasons to walk this far back into the basement. But still. The thought of opening that door frightened her.

Have faith.

The two words popped into her head as if someone had whispered them to her. The voice seemed familiar, but Ella could not place it. Soft. Gentle. Kind. The voice was all of those things. And yet the voice was just imaginary, something in her own mind. Even so, it soothed her, and Ella felt more at ease.

She looked around the basement until she found a metal pipe. Fitting it into the hole where the mouse had disappeared, Ella jiggled it enough so that the old door swung open. A burst of cool air hit her face, and she recoiled, for it was damp and musty. But when she held the lantern into the doorway, she caught her breath.

There was a cedar trunk inside, and judging by the carving on its top, it was a very special trunk, indeed. Ella started to move it, pulling it out of the secret room, when the light from the lantern illuminated something else that surprised her: stairs.

"Oh help!" she whispered.

There was a second entrance into the basement from the outside. How could she have never known about its existence? For a moment, she forgot about the trunk and focused on the stairs. At the top of the stairs was a flat door. A sliver of light filtered through the edge. Cautiously, Ella climbed the stairs and put her hand against the door. It took her three tries to shove it open. And when she poked out her head, she realized that she was under the front porch.

Stunned, Ella stood there for a moment, half in the basement and half out. She'd have to crawl over the dirt and push aside some of the lattice in order to be free of the basement. But she could attend the charity event after all.

With a new sense of determination, Ella made up her mind. She would not be held hostage in her own home, even if she *was* frightened of Linda's reaction.

Chapter Twenty-One

By the time Ella made her way to the schoolhouse, almost an hour had passed. The sun was slowly sinking in the sky behind her, a blessing in itself, as it would hinder anyone from seeing her approach.

The auction was being held outdoors, which, based upon the size of the crowd, was probably out of necessity, especially since the evening air was still warm. Seeing all of those people gathered, seated upon the pine benches usually reserved for worship, was surprising to Ella. With the exception of Sundays, weddings, and funerals, Ella couldn't recall ever seeing the entire community—and far too many guests to count!—meeting together.

And that was a good thing to see!

Near the school entrance were several long tables covered in a variety of tablecloths: red and white checkered, green and yellow striped, and even a few floral ones. Displayed on top of them were pies and cakes and other baked goods. There were so many items that Ella wondered if everyone in the entire town must have contributed one, if not two, items for the auction.

Ella couldn't help but wonder why she had never

found out where the money was being donated. Surely it was an important cause, for the entire town seemed more than willing to contribute.

Standing behind a large oak tree, she peeked around it to watch. She had missed the very beginning of the auction, but from the looks of it, the deacon had only just begun selling the treats from the unmarried women's table.

Miriam stood near a table. Next to it were two benches, and as Ella leaned forward, squinting her eyes, she saw that seated upon them were all of the unmarried Amish women in Echo Creek. Each woman wore her best Sunday dress, and of course, Drusilla and Anna wore their new dresses in the fancy fabric that made them stand out among the others.

Surely that was what Linda had planned all along.

"Now, who will bid on this pie?" the deacon called out. Behind him, Miriam held up the pie so that everyone could see it. "Looks like a delicious peach pie! And we all know how sweet the Echo Creek peaches are at this time of year!"

Several young men began bidding on the pie, and the deacon reminded everyone that this was for charity, encouraging them to bid even higher.

When it was finished, Abram Riehl won the prize for fifteen dollars.

"And that pie was made by . . ." The deacon paused, his eyes scanning the crowd.

Ella suspected that Rose Grimm had made that pie, and she found herself breathlessly waiting for the deacon to announce the baker.

". . . Johanna Miller!"

Ella smiled to herself. Timothy Miller's younger sister. *Of course,* she thought. They had quite the orchard of peach trees on their property. At just sixteen, this was Johanna's first year on *rumschpringe*. Now she'd have something fun to remember: sitting with Abram Riehl as he ate a piece of her peach pie.

The next item was a buttermilk pound cake, and that fetched eleven dollars. While the auction was exciting, Ella found herself enjoying trying to guess who had baked which item and laughing whenever she was wrong.

What fun! she thought, only wishing that she, too, could have participated. But Linda would be furious if she knew that Ella was watching. And Ella wasn't about to chance stoking her wrath, not after what had happened that evening. She had never known her to be so spiteful. Thankfully, Ella had escaped, but if her stepmother would go to such an extreme to keep her away from the charity auction, Ella was worried about what else she was capable of doing.

For the next hour, pie after pie was auctioned off. Slowly, the line of young women seated upon the pine bench dwindled until there were only two women remaining: Drusilla and Anna.

Miriam reached for something on the table that Ella couldn't see. When the deacon's wife turned back around, Ella saw it was her basket.

Ella almost gasped at the realization that Hannes would know that one of the desserts in the basket was hers. And yet, she wasn't there to share it with him if he won the bid.

Removing the two cakes and one pie, Miriam set them on the table. Then, she grabbed the first cake and handed a slip of paper to her husband.

"Ah, a lazy-daisy oatmeal cake!" The deacon glanced over at the almost-empty bench where just Drusilla and Anna sat. "I suspect we know which household baked this cake, but not *which* of these fine, upstanding young women!"

Drusilla lowered her eyes, attempting to look coy, while Anna stared at the ground, clearly indicating that it was not she who had baked it. Neither one of them was aware that several people chuckled at the name of the cake.

"For the last bids, we won't tell who baked them until the auction is over!"

Several people in the audience laughed and nodded, clearly agreeing with the deacon's decision.

"Now, who will start the bid on this lazy-daisy oatmeal cake? Shall we start with five dollars? Five dollars? Anyone?"

Timothy Miller raised his hand. "Five dollars. Right here, Deacon!"

"That's a *wunderbarr* start!" The deacon looked pleased. "Anyone for six dollars? Six? Do I hear six?"

There was a long moment of silence. And then a hand raised.

"I'll bid six."

Ella glanced over and tried to make out who had bid. But all she saw was the back of a straw hat.

"Seven!" cried out Timothy.

"Eight!"

"Ten!" Timothy countered.

"Twenty! I'll bid twenty dollars!"

There was a collective gasp among the rest of those seated, and even Ella felt dismayed for the young man. She knew that the Millers were not a wealthy family. They raised sheep, and the mother spun it into wool. But selling that wool was their primary source of income.

Timothy Miller couldn't afford to bid more than twenty dollars.

Standing up, he faced his opponent. "You can't jump that high!" Timothy looked back at the deacon with a desperate expression on his face. "Right, Deacon?"

The deacon shrugged. "No rules stating otherwise."

"That's not fair!"

But the deacon gave him a stern look. "It's for charity, son. It's not a marriage proposal."

The people laughed and, red-faced, Timothy Miller sat down.

Drusilla, however, looked extremely pleased. It was clear to everyone it was the cake she had donated.

The deacon set down the cake and picked up the poor man's cake. "Well, look at this! A poor man's cake. Why, I haven't had one of these since I was a boy!" He made a noise of approval. "Mmm-mmm! I'd reckon to bid on this myself if my *fraa* wouldn't be upset."

"I'll make you a poor man's cake, John, but you leave that one to the young men out there!" Miriam countered.

More laughter.

"Let's start the bidding on this, the last cake, at ten dollars."

A collective gasp could be heard from the spectators. None of the other items had started that high. Anna straightened her shoulders and lifted her chin proudly.

"Ten dollars? Anyone? It's our last cake of the evening." The deacon scanned the crowd. "Charity, people. Ten dollars?"

A hand raised. Joshua Esh. "I'll bid ten dollars."

Anna looked crestfallen. Joshua Esh was known to be slow-witted, sometimes stuttering for up to a minute before speaking a full sentence. Whenever Ella was at the store and Joshua came in, whoever else was working quickly disappeared. But Ella didn't mind waiting patiently for Joshua to find his words. Everyone had their own individual quirks. Who was she to judge?

"Twelve dollars," another voice called out. Immediately, a look of relief swept over Anna's face.

Joshua looked nervous. "Th-th-thirteen!"

The color drained from Anna's face.

"Fifteen."

Ella's heart ached for Joshua, who reached up and tugged at his collar. She hadn't realized that Joshua was sweet on Anna, and that, too, made her heart heavy.

"S-s-s-sixt-t-t-een?" Joshua swallowed.

"Twenty-five dollars!"

The crowd turned around to see who had bid so high. They all stared in the same direction as before.

The deacon raised his eyebrows in surprise and looked back at Joshua. "You gonna go higher?"

He appeared defeated, his shoulders slumping and his eyes downcast, as he shook his head no.

Anna, however, had brightened at this unexpected turn of events. Not only had she dodged having to sit with Joshua Esh, but her cake had outbid her sister's.

"There you have it, folks. The end of our auction—"

"Hold on there, John," Miriam interrupted him. "There's one more pie here."

Surprised, John turned around as if he didn't believe his wife. "Well, I'll be!" He took the pie from his wife and looked at the piece of paper. "An apple crisp pie." He flipped over the slip of paper. "And no name attached to it." Confused, he stared into the crowd. "A mystery pie! How exciting."

Ella pressed her lips together and clenched her fist.

That was her pie, and she should have been seated up there on the pine bench. She should have been given the same opportunity as all of the other young women in Echo Creek. But Linda had stolen that special moment from her.

Several people in the audience looked around, their heads turning this way and that as they tried to figure out who had baked that pie.

"I reckon we'll start the bid for this at five dollars."

Several hands raised and the bidding quickly went to fifteen dollars. Just as the auction appeared to end, a voice interrupted the noise generated by the excited crowd.

"Fifty dollars!"

A moment of stunned silence was followed by a low murmuring. Suddenly, Ella realized who had bid on that dessert. And Anna's and Drusilla's.

Hannes.

She smiled to herself, a bittersweet kind of smile, for she understood what he had done. When he saw the basket that he had carried earlier in the day, he had bid on all three items, figuring that one of them was Ella's. He had spent over one hundred dollars in order to sit with Ella and enjoy her pie. Unfortunately, he would also have to sit with Drusilla *and* Anna—a sacrifice he had made in order to have time with Ella.

But Ella wasn't seated on the bench. Who, exactly, did he think he'd enjoy the pie with?

"Now, who made this mystery pie?" The deacon looked into the audience, his eyes crinkled up as he tried to identify the person. "Anyone?"

There was a brief pause, and then the unthinkable happened. Simultaneously, Drusilla and Anna stood up.

Drusilla's "I did!" blended with Anna's "Me."

They both glared at each other. No one spoke; all eyes were on the two young women. The silence continued until, at last, Linda stood up, clasping her hands and giving a skittish laugh. "Now girls," she said, walking toward them. "Let's give credit where credit is due."

A low murmur began to spread through the crowd, everyone talking about the strange turn of events. As Linda reached her daughters and turned to face the rest of the people gathered, Ella's ears perked, eager to hear what her stepmother would say.

Placing her hands on her daughters' shoulders, Linda stood between them. "You *both* made the pie, isn't that right?"

Ella caught her breath. Once again, her stepmother had outright lied. And to everyone in the congregation, including the deacon and other church leaders. Her heart raced and she clenched her fists, wishing that she could shout out the truth. But she was too fearful of what would happen. Surely Linda would retaliate and behave in an even more awful way than she already had.

Meanwhile, both Drusilla and Anna continued arguing, each claiming that she was the sole baker of that pie.

Suddenly, a hush fell over the crowd as the man who'd bought the desserts stepped out of the shadows. As Ella had suspected, it was Hannes. He walked forward and took the pie before looking Linda directly in the eye.

"I'll be anxious to try this one," he said in a voice loud enough for Ella to hear even from where she stood behind the crowd. "It's my favorite type of pie. Why, if it's as good as it looks, I might just be inclined to marry the woman who baked it!"

Ella's mouth dropped open as the rest of the people gasped. Linda's eyes narrowed for a minute, and then, as if she had realized something important, they widened. "What a peculiar thing to say," Linda replied lightly as she smiled at him. "But how fortunate for my *dochders* that they are both amazing bakers."

Ella turned away and leaned against the tree. How on earth could this be happening? How could Hannes not realize the truth? Tears stung at the corners of her eyes, and she brushed them away with her fingers. She couldn't stay there anymore. She needed to return home. Her heart broken, she ran down the dusty lane toward the small white house on the edge of town. The last thing Ella could stand was seeing Hannes seated between Drusilla and Anna, eating the treats that they claimed to have baked—but did not!—while they tried to win his heart and hand.

Chapter Twenty-Two

"Good news at last!" Linda sang as she burst into the kitchen on Thursday evening. She practically floated across the floor, a smile on her face.

Unfortunately, the fact that Linda's mood was joyous did nothing to improve Ella's own mood.

Seated on the sofa—the very one where, just the week before, Miriam King had finished the two dresses worn by Drusilla and Anna to the charity event—Ella barely looked up. Instead, she kept her attention on the blanket that she was crocheting. Though it was too warm to crochet, Ella didn't care. It kept her mind focused on anything other than the disastrous charity auction and how horrible her stepmother had been to her.

She knew that she had to forgive Linda and her stepdaughters. The Bible told her so. But Ella found it increasingly hard to do.

That previous Saturday night, Ella had slipped back into the house and disappeared into her bedroom. She had thrown herself onto the bed and cried into her pillow. Fortunately, Linda was so ecstatic over the events of the evening that she had forgotten all about

Ella and the basement. So had Drusilla and Anna, who spent the next two days gushing about Hannes and their cakes. Each time either of the girls mentioned his name, Ella cringed and turned away, her heart aching with disappointment.

On more than one occasion, Ella was forced to listen in excruciating detail about Hannes sitting with the two sisters, tasting their cakes and the contested apple crisp pie. Drusilla repeatedly claimed victory over Anna, asserting that Hannes favored *her* over her sister. But, not to be outdone, Anna practically swooned when she remembered how complimentary he had been about her poor man's cake.

Both of them were convinced that Hannes was the most handsome of men, and each of them bragged that he most certainly had eyes only for her.

Ella could hardly bear listening to them.

At night, Ella had cried herself to sleep, emotionally wounded to think that Hannes could possibly shift his attention so easily. During the day, she stayed inside the house, not even caring if the garden grew weeds or the bird feeder was empty. She went about her chores, her head down and her shoulders feeling heavy. Whenever she felt depressed and disheartened, she tried to tell herself that anyone who was so shallow, so fickle with his affections, was not the right person for her.

But she still had a hard time believing it could possibly be true.

Even when she cleaned the kitchen, Ella tried to avoid thinking of him. The windowsill no longer held the crystal trinket that he had given her, having been removed by someone, probably one of her stepsisters.

It had been a bittersweet moment when she had realized it was missing. But she counted it as a small blessing, for now she wouldn't have to look at it and be reminded, yet again, of Hannes's capricious behavior.

While she had never heard of anyone dying from a broken heart, she couldn't help but wonder if she might be the first.

And still, she persevered.

Today, however, Drusilla and Anna were making life particularly hard for her. They had been sitting at the table, talking yet again about the past Saturday evening, when their mother had burst into the room.

"Did you hear me, Ella?"

Despite her feelings toward her stepmother, Ella remembered that she needed to show respect. God commanded it, even if her stepmother was not a kind person. She looked up at Linda with weary eyes that were puffy and red from all of the past sleepless nights that she had spent crying.

Irritated, Linda stood there, her hands on her hips, glowering at her. "You aren't still brooding about last weekend, are you? After all, the basement *did* need cleaning! And you were not locked down there on purpose! Drusilla said it was an accident!"

Ella couldn't believe her stepmother's audacity. Ella knew Linda was more than aware that someone had sabotaged the basement by knocking over that bin of flour and throwing it all over the place. And they both knew that the door had been locked on purpose. Ella had witnessed too much cruelty and dishonesty from her stepmother over the course of the past few weeks to doubt that for a moment.

Setting down her crocheting, she forced herself to

meet her stepmother's gaze, too aware that both Drusilla and Anna were snickering about their mother's comments. "What is it?" she asked.

"Oh, good!" Linda looked delighted that Ella had spoken at last. "Perhaps now you can finish with your sulking!"

"Sulking" wasn't exactly how Ella would have put it. She was broken, perhaps, but not sulking. And who wouldn't be broken after being locked in a basement and having her stepsisters claim *her* own pie as theirs when it had been purchased by the kindest man she'd ever known? To have sat there and pretended they had baked it while he ate it? No, she wasn't sulking at all.

"What's the good news?" Drusilla finally asked, which earned her a special smile from her mother.

Linda walked over to the table. "Those Clemens men sent word that they'll be coming to town and wish to have supper here on Saturday evening." Linda cast a smug look in Ella's direction.

"Whatever for?" Anna asked, an eagerness about her that irritated Ella.

"Oh, Anna! Please." Drusilla sniffed at her sister. "You know that Henry loved that pie. I'm sure he intends to court me, and that's the reason they invited themselves over for supper!"

"Or me!" Anna puffed her chest and gave her sister a defiant look. "He thinks that I made the pie, too!"

Ella felt a lump form in her throat. It had been almost one week since the charity auction, and no one had seen hide nor hair of Hannes Clemens. She was certain that he had returned to Blue Springs and that would be the end of seeing him in Echo Creek. So she was both surprised and dismayed to hear that he would be returning. Even worse, he'd be having supper at their house. Ella would be forced to see him. If it was true that he had shifted his affections from her to Drusilla or Anna, she wasn't certain she could sit in the same room with him!

"It doesn't matter *which* one of you he courts, just that he court *one* of you!" Linda sounded irritated. "After all, he said that the pie was so good, he'd consider marrying the woman who baked it."

Ella caught her breath. Surely Linda didn't believe that he had spoken such words in anything other than jest!

But evidently, Linda had taken his words at face value. "And, if that is the case, I wouldn't be surprised if the older Clemens is coming to make an offer on the store. We can be rid of it at last, pay off our debt, and still live comfortably if that Clemens boy marries one of you."

At Linda's announcement, Ella felt as if her heart had fallen to the depths of her stomach. She cried out in disbelief. "Sell the store?"

With an exasperated sigh, Linda dropped her hands to her sides and shook her head. "Dear Ella," she said, although Ella suspected that the "dear" was thrown in only as window dressing, "you can't imagine that I would want to keep working like this, day in and day out, at that store. For what? A continued loss in profits?" She clucked her tongue and shook her head. "*Nee*, child, I've decided that selling the store is the *only* thing that makes sense. And if the Clemens boy marries one of my girls—why!—not only would my financial woes be resolved, my future would be set, too. We'll be able to stay here." She held out her hands, palms up, as she gestured around the kitchen.

But then, just as suddenly, she paused. "At least, some of us."

Ella turned away, blinking her eyes rapidly in the hope of preventing her tears from falling. She didn't need to ask what Linda meant. The meaning was clear: if the Clemens family purchased the store and Henry married either Drusilla or Anna, both properties would become his.

Even more distressing, however, was that Linda had clearly indicated Ella would no longer be welcome in the family home.

Her family's home, not Linda's.

But Ella knew that was not the way it worked. When her father had died, everything had passed to Linda. If only he had expressed his wishes to the bishop, or even in a letter, things might have been better. But his death had been unexpected. Who knew that he would die so young and so suddenly?

Ella tried her best to avoid crying. She knew it was terrible to feel sorry for oneself, but she couldn't help it. When had everything gone so wrong?

"Girls, we must have a *wunderbarr gut* supper for the Clemens men."

Drusilla looked horrified. "Surely you don't expect us to cook, Maem."

Scoffing, Linda shook her head. "Don't be daft, child. Of course not! We want to tempt these men, not terrify them!"

A moment of silence fell over the room as all three pairs of eyes simultaneously turned and stared at Ella.

Stunned, Ella couldn't even respond. They didn't need to say what they were all thinking. Ella could read their minds. Did they truly expect her to cook a supper for Hannes and his father? A meal that was intended to entice him to marry one of Linda's daughters? And after Linda had just all but informed Ella that she would be forced out of the house?

For once, Ella knew that she needed to speak up, to stand up for her rights. After so many years of abuse and mistreatment, God would definitely understand if she refused to obey this final unspoken request. Surely he would not fault her for denying this one thing.

Just as she was about to rebel at last and put voice to the endless stream of slights and abuse that they continually threw at her, she heard that all-too-familiar voice whispering in the dark recesses of her mind.

Be kind and good, no matter what happens, for God has a plan for you.

Ella shut her eyes and inhaled, wishing that, for just once, she could ignore those words from her mother. Surely her mother would allow her to stand up for herself . . . just once?

But the words seemed to repeat themselves, over and over again.

Be kind.

And good.

God has a plan . . .

Inwardly, Ella groaned. She wanted to press her hands to her ears and shake her head, forcing those words to disappear forever. She was tired of living by that promise. She was tired of always being kind and doing good. She was growing tired of waiting for the big reveal of what God's plan for her actually was!

Ever since her mother had died, that's exactly what she had done: lived by those words. And what had it gotten her? Nothing but misery that begot more misery. Maybe, just maybe, her mother had been wrong. Maybe this was God's plan for her.

Still, Ella knew that a promise was a promise. Breaking her promise would be tantamount to lying, and that was a grave sin indeed. Besides, even if she wanted to deny Linda and her daughters this one request, how could she possibly ignore her mother's final wish? Her mother, one of two people who had truly loved her from the moment she was born. No, Ella knew that she could never live with herself if she broke her promise to her mother.

"I'd . . . be happy to cook the meal," Ella forced herself to say, even though she spoke in a strained voice. She knew that she was doing this for her mother, not because she wanted to do it. After all these years abiding by that promise, Ella knew she couldn't break her word now.

When they realized what Ella had offered to do, Drusilla and Anna cheered, and even Linda gave her a surprised smile that was filled with genuine regard.

"That's very kind of you, Ella," Linda managed to say, and Ella suspected that her stepmother meant it. Without Ella's help, the supper would be a disaster. They all knew it and, for once, seemed grateful for her offer.

For the rest of the evening, Ella was forced to listen to Drusilla and Anna argue about which one of them would marry Hannes while Linda sat at the table, poring over some paperwork and scribbling her thoughts on a pad of paper. When she could take it no more, Ella quietly removed herself from the kitchen and headed upstairs to the safety and security of her bedroom, wondering how much longer she might actually be able to find solace there before she was forced to find a new place to live.

Chapter Twenty-Three

Ella could hardly believe her eyes and ears. On Friday evening, Hannes and his father appeared at the gate to the Troyers' house. It was close to seven o'clock, and Linda was sitting outside, her feet resting on a wooden box as she fanned her face from the extreme heat.

Drusilla and Anna were sitting with her, the two of them arguing over who would work the morning shift the next day, since they both wanted to be home early in order to get dressed for the Clemens' visit.

But lo and behold! Hannes and his father had appeared a day early.

"Hello there!"

Linda turned her head, and upon seeing Hannes at the gate, gasped and sat up, quickly reaching to touch her hair. "Why, Henry! I . . . I thought you and your father were coming tomorrow?" She appeared caught completely off guard by this surprise visit.

If he noticed, Hannes did not let on. Instead, he laughed good-naturedly, glancing at Ella for just a brief second before he turned to greet Drusilla and Anna, both of whom were straightening their dresses and smiling at him with such forced cheer that Ella feared they might shatter their teeth.

"We've arrived in town early," Hannes said and gestured toward his father. "I wanted to introduce you to my *daed*, Johannes Clemens."

The older man nodded his head once in Linda's direction and then turned his attention on Drusilla and Anna. He appeared to be studying them, his eyes narrowed and his lips pressed together. While his attention was on the girls, Ella took advantage of his distraction and studied him.

He was a distinguished-looking man with graying hair and a long gray beard that hung past his second shirt button. Like Hannes, he was lean in his build, but he also appeared strong. His face was free from the deep wrinkles that often plagued aging Amish men. And his blue eyes, so similar to Hannes's, twinkled just enough to appear lively.

Certainly Johannes Clemens was not a dull man.

"I've heard so much about your *dochders*," Johannes said, his voice strong and clear. "Let me guess. You must be Drusilla." He correctly held out his hand to shake Drusilla's. "And that means that you must be Anna."

Anna flushed and gave a girlish giggle as she shook his hand.

And then Johannes turned and saw Ella, standing near the doorway, out of the way but still close enough to greet.

Johannes nodded his head at her but said nothing, leaving Ella to wonder what, if anything, Hannes had told his father about her. Perhaps he had shared that she didn't attend the youth gatherings and had not appeared for the charity auction.

Turning to face Linda, Johannes cleared his throat before he spoke. "Linda Troyer," the elderly Clemens said cheerfully, "my son and I . . . we're looking forward to supper tomorrow evening and wanted to confirm the time."

Linda smiled at him, as pleasant as pleasant could be. "Why, five o'clock should be just fine." She glanced at Drusilla, who sat primly on the edge of her seat, her bare feet tucked underneath her as she batted her eyes at Hannes. "Don't you think, Dru?"

"Oh, *ja*, Maem. Five o'clock is right *gut*."

Anna cleared her throat as if to draw attention to herself. "Enough time for visiting before supper, I should think."

Ella felt invisible. Neither Hannes nor his father had acknowledged her presence.

And that hurt.

"Now, Linda," Hannes's father started, "there's something I'd like to talk about with you." He paused before adding, "In private."

It was only after Linda and Johannes had stepped inside that Ella spoke up. "Would you care for some meadow tea? I made it fresh this afternoon."

Hannes turned his head, his gaze focused on her at last. There was a coolness in his eyes as he responded, "How kind. *Ja*, Ella, I would like that."

She stood up and hurried into the kitchen. Outside the window, she could hear Drusilla and Anna fighting for Hannes's attention. Their voices grew loud and shrill as each one tried to be heard over the other. Ella stole a glance out the window and caught sight of Hannes trying to listen attentively, first to one and then to the other. It looked as if he were watching a volleyball game.

If it hadn't been so comical, Ella might have felt sorry for him. But she quickly reminded herself that he had put himself into this very position with no help from anyone else.

After pouring the tea into a glass with two cubes of ice, Ella walked back onto the porch and handed it to him. For the briefest of moments, he hesitated before taking it from her. When she looked at him, he gave her a smile that caught her off guard.

"*Danke*, Ella."

"You're welcome, Hannes," she managed to say, still surprised that he had directed any attention to her at all.

"Hannes?" Drusilla made a funny face, as if mocking her. "His name is *Henry*, Ella." Her laugh sounded as cruel as it felt to Ella.

To his credit, Hannes leaned forward, resting his elbows on his knees. "Actually, Drusilla, my father calls me Hannes."

The smile evaporated from Drusilla's face.

"All of my good friends call me that." He took a sip from the glass and set it down on the table. "Now, why don't you tell me more about those wonderful cakes you both made, hmm?"

Anna glanced at her sister. "Why . . . of course, *ja*."

Ella waited long enough to listen to Anna begin describing her poor man's cake, not once talking about the recipe but her own satisfaction that Hannes had enjoyed it.

Shaking her head, Ella made her way back to the kitchen. She simply couldn't listen to another deceitful word out of either girl's mouth. If Hannes couldn't see through their dishonesty, then perhaps he actually deserved to marry one of her stepsisters!

Not even five minutes later, Ella heard Linda's voice as she rejoined her daughters and Hannes on the porch. Ella saw that the two men were preparing to leave, so she slipped outside once again, knowing she couldn't be discourteous, even if she felt it was warranted.

"Then we shall see you tomorrow, *ja*?"

Johannes nodded and gestured for his son to join him on the steps. "Enjoy the rest of the evening."

As the two men descended the steps and began to cross the walkway toward the gate, Linda waved her hand in the air. They paused, smiling briefly, before they disappeared down the street.

Immediately, Linda spun on her heels to face her daughters.

"Maem! Tell us what Johannes said!" Drusilla insisted.

Anna clapped her hands before her chest. "*Ja*, tell us. Does he want to court one of us?" She shut her eyes and smiled to herself. "Oh, I do so hope it's me!"

Drusilla nudged her. "Oh, hush, Anna. There are more important things, like whether they want to buy the store. Do they, Maem?"

Linda licked her lips as she contemplated her daughters. There was something edgy about her expression, and Ella leaned forward in order to better hear Linda's response.

"Court you? Buy the store?" Her words were drawn out in a dramatic fashion. "Oh, *ja*. *Ja*, indeed."

Both girls screamed in delight and reached to hug each other. And then, as if realizing that they were embracing their competition, they quickly split apart and scowled for a moment.

Linda returned to her seat. She sighed and shut her eyes as she put her feet atop a wooden box.

Ella couldn't help but wonder what was bothering her stepmother. After all, this was what she had wanted—to marry off a daughter and sell the store. But from the look on her face, something else weighed heavily on her mind.

"What is it, Maem?" Anna asked.

Drusilla made a face at her sister before she asked her own impatient question. "Which one of us has he chosen?"

"He *hasn't* chosen yet," Linda said with a hint of irritation in her voice. "Which makes tomorrow's supper even more important."

"Oh, Ella, please say you'll work at the store tomorrow!" Anna cried out. "I'll need to get ready so that I can look my best!"

"Have you forgotten that she's going to cook the meal? Besides, she's going to work in the morning for *me*, Anna, not *you*!" Drusilla declared.

Anna crossed her arms over her chest. "And what makes you so certain of that?"

"Because that Henry Clemens is going to choose me!"

"That's not fair!" Anna looked at her mother. "Tell her that's not fair, Maem! She already has Timothy Miller wanting to court her!"

"Oh, *pshaw*!" Drusilla waved her hand in the air dismissively. "Timothy Miller is a farmer, not a businessman."

As their voices continued to rise, each one pressing her case loud enough for half of the town to hear, Linda raised her hand. "Enough!" She rubbed her temples and began pacing the floor. "Neither of you will work tomorrow at all."

Silence.

"In fact," Linda continued, now that she had their attention, "the store will be closed early."

In all the years that Ella could remember, the store had never closed early unless for a wedding or funeral.

"Why's that, Maem?" Drusilla asked.

"Because we need to prepare for the dinner with Johannes and his son. The results of that dinner will affect their business proposition with me." Despite what should have been joyous news, Linda did not appear happy. It was more than apparent that their proposition was not entirely to Linda's satisfaction.

"What type of business proposition?" Anna prodded, having picked up on the pall of seriousness in her mother's voice.

Linda lifted her chin and stared down her nose at her daughters. "The fact is that the father will buy the business for more than enough money to pay my debts and take care of me for years to come, but only if his son marries one of my daughters." She narrowed her eyes. "And Henry insists that he will only consider wedding the one who baked that pie from Saturday night."

Ella couldn't help but avert her eyes, but not before she caught sight of Linda, who was standing there, her arms crossed over her chest, scowling. She looked none too pleased.

Clearing her throat, Linda continued. "That's right, Drusilla and Anna. Since there was such confusion over which one of you, exactly, made that pie, he wants you each to make it after supper tomorrow," she said and paused until both of her daughters looked at her. "By yourself."

Simultaneously, Drusilla and Anna turned their heads to look, wide-eyed, at Ella.

"You have to make it for me!" Drusilla cried out as Anna mirrored her sister's sentiment. Drusilla gasped and turned toward Anna. "Henry favors me, Anna, not you!"

Anna looked taken aback. "He said no such thing!" She looked at her mother. "Ain't so, Maem?"

While the two young women bickered, Ella felt a heaviness in her heart. How could it be that Hannes would base the commitment of a lifetime on a pie? Crestfallen, she looked down at the ground and shook her head. Whatever God's plan was for her, she had never expected this.

Linda held up her hand to stop her quarreling daughters. "Unfortunately, that won't be possible. There's a stipulation," she said slowly. Immediately Drusilla and Anna quieted, their attention riveted on their mother. "He wishes the pie to be fresh—so fresh that he'd like you to make it while he's here."

Both Drusilla and Anna gasped, and Ella looked up in surprise. Such an odd request.

"Maem!" Drusilla flung her hands into the air. "You know that's impossible! I can't bake!"

Linda raised an eyebrow. "Then I suggest you start practicing!" she snapped. "One of you must bake that pie and win his affections. It's the only way to save us from financial ruin and ensure that we have a future!"

Quickly, Ella stood up and excused herself. She could not possibly listen to one more word. Her sisters were bartering with each other over a man of whom they knew practically nothing. They were basing their affection on two things: his handsome looks and his father's money. There was no discussion about Hannes's commitment to the community, his devotion to his family, or, most importantly, his dedication to serving God.

And on a more personal level, neither Drusilla nor Anna knew anything about his personality, his depth of character, or his charming sense of humor.

All of those were the things that Ella knew created a strong foundation for friendship, and only with that foundation could love ever develop.

Hannes Clemens was not an object to be bartered for. He was a man. And yet Ella couldn't help but feel disappointed in his decision to select a bride in such a manner. Her mother had always teased that the way to a man's heart was through his stomach. Clearly she hadn't been jesting.

The only good news, Ella thought, was that Drusilla also hadn't been joking. Neither one of them knew how to bake, never mind cook or clean or sew. If winning a man's heart was done through a meal, there was little chance of either Drusilla or Anna claiming much of a victory. The only thing they would achieve was to give Hannes Clemens a good case of indigestion.

Chapter Twenty-Four

On Saturday morning, Ella watched with bittersweet amusement as Drusilla and Anna practiced making the apple crisp pie. Several times, they asked Ella for help, but each request was met with a firm refusal. She merely shrugged her shoulders and pointed toward the cookbook on the counter.

"Ella!" Anna whined.

"*Ja*, Ella! You simply must help me!" Drusilla demanded.

But Linda was at the store, busy preparing her records for Johannes to review. She couldn't come to the rescue of her daughters.

And so, for the first time, Ella stood her ground. "How many times have I offered to give you baking lessons? Now you wish to learn in one day? To claim a pie that wasn't baked by your hand to begin with?" She shook her head and clicked her tongue. "For shame."

"Oh, Ella! Don't be such a spoilsport!" Drusilla glared at her. "Just because he's no longer interested in *you*!"

Rather than continue listening to them alternate between arguing with each other and berating her, Ella walked out of the kitchen and headed toward the flower garden on the far side of the property. She sank down to her knees near the bluish-purple morning glories and said a silent prayer, begging God to forgive her for not being more willing to help her stepsisters.

She just couldn't.

While she knew better than to question God, she couldn't help but feel that all of this was unfair. After so many years of hardship and sorrow, Ella had hoped that everything was changing when Hannes had first appeared in her life. But her hope had quickly unraveled over the past week. First with Linda's determination to keep her away from the charity event. Then with Hannes appearing so suddenly enthralled by Drusilla and Anna. Now with Linda having sold away the store and the house. In just seven days, her entire world had gone topsy-turvy.

But none of that compared to the disappointment she felt that Hannes was not the man she'd thought he was. She couldn't believe that he would throw away their special friendship to marry a woman—especially Drusilla or Anna!—based only on a pie that satisfied his taste buds.

She could hardly make heads or tails of any of this.

By the time the sun reached well overhead, Ella knew she had no choice but to return to the kitchen. She needed to begin preparing the evening meal. A promise was a promise, after all. But oh, how she dreaded having to do this!

When she entered the room, she caught her breath at the mess that greeted her. Both Drusilla and Anna were covered in flour, a bitter reminder of the previous weekend, when Ella had been forced to clean up the basement. The counter was littered with bowls and pie pans, spoons and hand mixers.

What on earth were they baking?

As comical as the scene was, Ella could only sigh. One more thing for her to do: clean the kitchen before the Clemens men arrived.

"Well, this recipe makes hardly any sense!" Anna complained as she squinted at the cookbook. "White sugar *and* brown sugar?" Exasperated, she looked up at her sister. "Is there a difference? Why can't I just use one or the other? And where are my glasses? I can hardly read the tiny print in this book!"

Ella bit her lower lip to stop herself from laughing.

"Let me see that recipe!" Drusilla demanded, and snatched the cookbook from her sister. "My recipe calls for oats and only white sugar!"

"Oats!" Anna pushed her way past Drusilla and stared at the open book on the counter. "I've never heard of oats in an apple crisp."

"Clearly there're different variations of the recipe."

Wide-eyed, Anna stared at her sister.

Suddenly, both of them turned toward Ella.

"You must help us, Ella. Which recipe did you use?"

Adamantly, Ella shook her head. Her mother had said to do good and be kind, but she hadn't said to help other people cheat, and if she helped them, that would be what she was doing: cheating.

"I'm afraid you must figure this out on your own," Ella said, her voice firm.

"Oh, Ella!" Anna wailed, tossing her hands in the air and casting a piece of dough onto the floor. "I can't do this."

To her surprise, Ella found the courage to reprimand Anna. "Maybe that'll teach you not to take credit for other people's work."

Drusilla narrowed her eyes and glared at Ella as she

repeated her earlier insult. "Don't listen to her, Anna. She's just sore because Henry isn't paying any attention to her anymore." She smirked, her mouth twisting into an ugly mockery of a smile. "How easily his affection shifted . . ."

Her words stung, but Ella refused to give Drusilla the satisfaction of knowing it. Instead, she merely gave Drusilla a cool look as she reminded her of the truth. "Mayhaps his affections shifted, but don't forget that his change of heart is over a pie that neither of you baked. How satisfying that must be for both of you, knowing that you must resort to tricking a man in order to find one willing to marry you."

Upon hearing Ella's surprisingly harsh rebuke, Drusilla gasped and Anna had started to respond when the kitchen door opened and Linda walked into the house. She quickly assessed the disaster.

"Heaven help me! What happened in here?"

Ella stood quietly, watching as Linda waited for an answer.

"It was Ella!" Drusilla pointed at her.

"*Ja*, Ella!" Anna chimed in. "She wouldn't help us make the pie, and then"—Anna turned and looked around herself—"this happened."

"Well, this is unacceptable! We've guests arriving in a few hours and I don't even smell supper cooking yet." Slowly, Linda turned in a circle, her hawkish gaze taking in the disaster of the kitchen. "I want this kitchen cleaned and the table set immediately!"

When no one made a move, Linda pressed her lips together. "Didn't you hear me, Ella?"

Stunned, Ella stood there, her hands at her sides. "Me? I didn't make this mess!"

"I don't care *who* made it, but I've asked *you* to clean

it." Her voice boomed in the kitchen. Even Drusilla and Anna appeared taken aback by their mother's forcefulness. As if sensing the rising tension in the air, Linda took a deep breath. "Besides, Drusilla and Anna need to get ready for tonight. I want no more arguing in here. I've been reviewing the proposal from the Clemenses all day, and frankly all of this excitement has given me quite a headache."

"And what happened, Maem?" Drusilla asked eagerly. "Are they going to buy the store?"

"It's already done, Drusilla. The only thing left is for Hannes to determine which of you he wants to marry."

Drusilla and Anna jumped up and down, squealing in delight.

"Oh, tell us, Maem! What's happened?" Anna begged.

Ella felt her shoulders sag as she listened to Linda explain everything.

"Henry's father is more agreeable than I had hoped," she said. "He was rather generous in his offer to buy everything—the store, the inventory, and this *haus.* I had him figured all wrong." She gave a weary sigh of satisfaction. "And Hannes insisted that he will follow through with his promise. We even wrote that into the contract I signed."

Ella shut her eyes, hardly able to listen to one more word.

"So it's all settled?" Drusilla's voice pierced Ella's ears.

"It's all settled, indeed. We'll be quite comfortable, I can assure you. Now, if you don't have any other questions, I need to lie down. We've much work ahead of us, preparing for a wedding and all." Linda started to cross the floor. But before she opened the door, she paused and looked back at Ella. "And use your mother's china. It's a quaint little pattern. I daresay that Henry will be rather charmed by how provincial it is."

After she disappeared into her bedroom, Drusilla and Anna cast a last look at the mess on the counter. The despair etched onto their faces made Ella feel a momentary wave of compassion for them. After all, it wasn't *their* fault they were so self-centered, for their mother had trained them to be preoccupied with their own needs over everyone else's.

"Mayhaps you might want to peel the apples before Hannes comes," Ella offered.

Anna's eyes widened at the suggestion, and she started to reach for the peeler on the counter.

Drusilla, however, quickly stopped her. "Wait!" She narrowed her eyes and gave Ella a long, hard stare, evidently not trusting her advice. "It could be a trick," she whispered to her sister.

"Oh, please, Drusilla!" Ella almost laughed. Perhaps if she hadn't so much work ahead of her to prepare for the supper—and with no help from her stepsisters—she would have found the energy to do just that! "If you prep your ingredients beforehand, you simply have to mix them and bake them. Why, it won't even take much more than an hour in the oven if you listen to me."

Clearly, Drusilla was not quite convinced.

"Just make certain you put the apples in water so they don't brown."

Anna leaned over and whispered, "It's true, Drusilla. I think I remember Maem doing that once."

"Really?" Drusilla looked as surprised as Ella felt. "I don't remember her ever making apple crisp pie," she whispered back to her sister.

"*Ja,* once when we first moved here." Anna freed her

arm from Drusilla's grasp and grabbed the peeler. Immediately, she began attacking a bag of apples, scraping the peels off the fruit and dunking the apples into a bowl.

Not to be outdone, Drusilla tried to wrestle the peeler away from her sister. "Give me that!"

Within seconds, the two sisters were fighting over the peeler, their feet sliding on the linoleum floor and making an even bigger mess for Ella to clean.

Knowing that this argument would not end well, Ella took a deep breath and tried to separate the two of them. "Stop it. Both of you!" She managed to separate the two women and gave them each a stern look. "One at a time, *ja*? It only takes a few minutes to peel an apple anyway."

For the next few minutes, the kitchen remained quiet as Anna focused on peeling her apples and Drusilla stood nearby, drumming her fingers against the counter as she waited for her turn. While the *tap-tap-tap* was grating on Ella's nerves, it was far better than the earlier fighting.

She took advantage of the momentary peace to begin cleaning the kitchen. Whenever she cooked, she needed organization and cleanliness in her surroundings. She couldn't understand how women cooked when their kitchens were already messy.

"Finished!" Anna said triumphantly.

Drusilla didn't waste a minute before snatching the peeler out of her sister's hand and beginning on her own apples.

"Ouch! You cut me!"

Taking a deep breath, Ella counted to ten. Quickly.

Twenty minutes later, both girls had finished peeling their apples. Taking advantage of their momentary joy in having accomplished something in the kitchen with nothing more than a cut finger and bruised egos, Ella suggested that they both start getting ready.

While there were still three hours until the Clemens arrived, Ella needed that time without her stepsisters in her way. After all, she had to wash the floor, set the table, and prepare the food . . . all so that Drusilla and Anna could attempt to ensnare Hannes into proposing to one of them.

Narrish, she thought. The whole situation seemed crazy to her indeed. When she had first met Hannes, she had harbored hope that she might develop a special friendship with him. Clearly that was not going to happen. While it distressed her to think that she had misjudged him so, she knew better than to question God's will.

Simply put, she knew that it was the Amish way to forgive, forget, and move on.

And that's what she intended to do.

Chapter Twenty-Five

When Johannes and Hannes arrived at the house, promptly at five o'clock, the kitchen smelled as if it were a holiday meal. Linda had spared no expense on the food for that evening. And Ella had somehow found the fortitude to actually cook it—with no help from anyone else, of course.

"How good to see you," Linda said as she welcomed the two gentlemen into the kitchen. She gestured toward the table, which was set with a brand-new white linen cloth and the china from Ella's mother.

Johannes removed his straw hat and set it on the counter. Hannes, however, kept ahold of his.

"Why, it smells *wunderbarr gut* in here!" Johannes gave Linda an approving look.

Linda clasped her hands together before her. "It isn't very often we have visitors for supper."

Fussing with his hat, Hannes looked at the table and frowned.

Blinking her eyes, Linda leaned forward to catch his attention. "Is something wrong, Hannes?"

He made a point of using his finger to count each

of the plates. And then he frowned. "I see only five place settings."

His observation practically bounced off of Linda. But Ella felt a moment of excitement. Hannes had noticed that there were not enough place settings. Did he realize that Linda had not included her in the evening's meal?

To her surprise, Johannes also studied the table. "Ah, dear me. I must have been remiss." He raised his hand and playfully knocked at his head. "The old thinker must not have been working properly. Did I fail to mention that I invited my sister and her husband?"

Dumbfounded, Ella's mouth dropped. Not only at the fact that Hannes and his father had invited two more people, but that Hannes had *not* remembered her at all.

For once, Linda appeared equally stunned. "Your sister?"

"*Ach*! I did forget." Johannes made an apologetic face and sighed. "How terrible. I do apologize."

Hannes rolled his eyes and shook his head. He leaned toward Linda as if conspiring with her as he said, "Daed's grown a bit forgetful in his old age, I fear." Then Hannes bestowed a charming smile on Linda. "Fortunately, I see from all of the food you've prepared that it shouldn't be a hardship to include them, *ja*? Perhaps if Drusilla or Anna would just add two . . ." He paused, quickly counting the plates and chairs. "No, wait, three more settings."

"Three?" Linda practically choked. "Have you invited *another* family member, then?"

"Oh, no." Hannes laughed politely. "I believe one blunder is enough for an evening, *ja*? But I do believe you forgot to include a spot for yourself." He pointed at the table. ". . . Unless, of course, you forgot to include Ella?"

For the first time since he entered the kitchen, Hannes looked directly at her. He wore a look of triumph as he stared at her, just for a split second. But it was enough. If moments earlier Ella had been crestfallen, believing that Hannes had completely forgotten about her, Ella suddenly realized that she had, indeed, been mistaken.

Delightfully mistaken.

And she had to press her lips together to suppress a smile.

Linda had just opened her mouth to respond to Hannes, most likely to defend herself, when their conversation was interrupted by the opening of the kitchen door. Everyone turned, and before anyone could speak, Johannes spread his arms to greet the newcomers. "Ah, there you are!"

With wide eyes, a startled Ella found herself staring as John and Miriam King walked into the kitchen.

Apparently Ella wasn't the only stunned person in the house. "What on earth . . . ?" Linda couldn't even finish her sentence.

Miriam gave Johannes a quick embrace before greeting Linda. "How kind of you to invite us for supper! It's not often we get to spend time with my *bruder*. Blue Springs is too far for frequent visits, so this is such a delightful treat." She glanced around the kitchen. "Good friends, good food, and good family. That's the recipe for a *wunderbarr* evening, don't you think?"

Her husband nodded. "For sure and certain, Miriam."

Miriam crossed the room and eyed the platters on the counter. "Oh help! Look at all this food." She looked up at Linda, who had not moved from where she stood. "I can scarce believe this feast, Linda! And everything looks most delicious."

Since Drusilla and Anna had not moved, either, Ella slipped away from the shadows and made her way to the cabinet where her mother's old china was stored. She carried three more plates and set them on the table.

"Why, there you are!" Miriam gave her a big smile. "You were missed last weekend at the charity event. I hope you weren't ill, Ella."

Ella didn't have a chance to respond.

Somehow Linda found her voice and addressed her daughters. "Girls, go fetch more chairs."

Drusilla and Anna started to move, each in a different direction. And then, realizing their mistake, they turned to look at Linda. It was Anna who asked the question.

"Uh . . ." She lowered her voice. "Where do we keep them, Maem?"

Linda paused, the color draining from her cheeks. "Oh . . ." She turned to look at Ella and, with a strained look in her eyes, silently implored her for help.

"The basement," Ella said quietly. "The extra chairs are kept in the basement."

While Drusilla and Anna disappeared downstairs, Johannes and John sat down at the table, each taking one end. Hannes joined them by sitting in the middle on the side facing the kitchen counter.

"Now, Linda," Miriam said. "It's not like me to come empty-handed, but when Hannes told me about the apple crisp pies and how your *dochders* were making them tonight for dessert, I knew I couldn't compete. Why, Hannes has done nothing but rave about that apple crisp pie since last week! And to think, both of your *dochders* baked it together? I simply cannot wait to see who wins this contest tonight!"

Linda tried to respond, but no words passed her lips.

Miriam bustled over to the kitchen counter. "Now, let me help serve the meal, *ja*?" She glanced up at Ella and smiled. "Just put me to work, Ella."

By the time the platters adorned the table, Drusilla and Anna had returned to the kitchen with the chairs. Hannes made certain that they sat on either side of him. Ella sat next to Hannes's father, with Miriam seated beside her. And Linda was placed just to the right of John King.

After the silent prayer, everyone began filling their plates. Roast chicken, herb-crusted potatoes, carrots cooked in maple syrup, fresh pumpkin bread, cinnamon applesauce, and chow chow. The food seemed endless, and everyone took a few minutes to sample everything before Linda managed to ask the question that was lingering in Ella's mind.

"I'm quite surprised to learn that you're family to the Kings. I would have thought you might have told us that," Linda said, addressing Hannes directly. Her voice was filled with trepidation, and Ella could understand why. She recalled only too clearly how Linda had spoken about Hannes to Miriam at the store that one day.

But Hannes didn't hear her question, or perhaps he was merely more focused on the food. As he sampled the potatoes, Hannes shut his eyes, a look of sheer pleasure on his face. "Why, these are so delicious." He looked at Anna. "What are the herbs you used? Are they from your garden?"

"I . . . uh . . ." Anna stumbled over words as she tried to respond but couldn't.

"And these carrots." Once again, Hannes shut his eyes as if savoring them. "Which one of you cooked them? They're absolutely perfect."

Both Drusilla and Anna stared at him, although Hannes had moved on to the next item on his plate.

"And the chicken. Such flavoring. What is it?" This time, he turned to look at Anna and then Drusilla, clearly waiting for a response.

Neither Drusilla nor Anna answered, and an uncomfortable silence fell over the table.

Finally, Ella cleared her throat. "Paprika and rosemary," she said. "And a healthy salt rub on the skin with a fresh butter and garlic mixture under it."

No one spoke except Hannes, who lifted his eyebrows and took another bite. "How kind of you to help your stepsisters, Ella."

Linda leaned forward and gave Ella a stern look of reproach. Then, just as quickly, she plastered another smile onto her face and addressed Johannes directly. "I'm so curious, Johannes, to learn more about this surprise that you're related to our dear Miriam."

This time, it was Miriam who responded. "Oh, Linda, surely you remember my *maem* talking about my older *bruder* when we played Scrabble, *ja*?" She laughed good-naturedly and waved her hand in the air dismissively. "In fact, I thought for sure that I had mentioned that my nephew was staying at my *haus*." She pressed a finger against her cheek as if thinking. "Oh help. Mayhaps I didn't. I was too interested in the game, I reckon." She gave a little laugh. "I must have forgotten."

Ella was stunned by this new information. All those trips to Echo Creek, Hannes had been staying at the Kings' house? She had never once thought to inquire about where he was staying when he visited their town. It was too far to go back and forth to Blue Springs. But she hadn't thought to ask.

Suddenly things began to make sense. After all, how else would Hannes and his father have heard about the store to begin with? If Linda had spoken to the deacon, certainly one of them might have reached out to Miriam's brother in the hope that an arrangement could be made to help the Troyers.

And then, something else dawned on her.

Miriam.

Stunned, Ella looked first at Hannes and then at his aunt. Both of them avoided looking at her, but there was a hint of a smile on each of their faces.

Things aren't always what they seem, Ella, Hannes had said to her before he'd left Echo Creek after determining that he couldn't partner with Linda. *Sometimes things might be going one way and then, when you least expect it, they turn around in your favor.*

He had been giving her a hint of things yet to come. Had he known even then?

"Oh help!" she whispered and looked once more at Hannes, his words echoing in her head.

And suddenly all of this made sense. The sudden interest in Drusilla and Anna. The surprise request to dine at their house. The strange desire for Drusilla and Anna to bake the pie in front of them. And then the inclusion of John and Miriam King at the supper.

Her mind reeled with all of this newly discovered information, which only made more questions for her, rather than answers. While she didn't quite understand *why* this was happening, she certainly knew *what* was happening. She suspected, however, that she wouldn't have to wait very long to find out more.

Johannes clapped his hands together and pushed back his plate. "I've had my fill of supper. That was quite a fine meal, Linda. Why don't we say the after prayer now and retire to the porch while your *dochders* make this famous apple crisp pie? A bit of fresh air and some coffee sounds just about right, *ja*?"

A few minutes later, everyone but Drusilla and Anna sat on the porch. Ella had carried out a tray with a pot of coffee and empty mugs, and she began serving the guests. It was Johannes who frowned as she did so.

"*Danke*, Ella," he said. "But I must ask, why aren't you in there baking one of the pies?"

Linda's cheeks drained of color. "Oh, but . . ."

John King saved her from her humiliation. "*Nee*, Johannes. The pie was made by Linda's two girls. They said as much at the event."

It was Miriam who chimed in. "That's right. I remember it clear as if it were yesterday. I must have told John a dozen times if I told him once how impressed I was that Linda Troyers' *dochders* baked a pie together for the auction, especially knowing that a young man would bid on it." She leaned over and placed her hand on her husband's arm. "Didn't I, John?"

"A dozen?" He gave a single, hearty laugh. "Two dozen times."

But Johannes scratched at the back of his neck. "Well now, that does create quite a predicament. After all, what we discussed today was that Linda's *dochders* would each make a pie. Doesn't seem right that Ella shouldn't be included." He looked at his brother-in-law. "Don't you think?"

John shrugged his shoulders. "Don't matter none to me who bakes the pies."

Johannes turned toward Hannes. "Seems you might want to decide. After all, you're the one interested in marrying the baker of that pie."

At this, John raised an eyebrow. "Say now, what is this about?"

Once again, Miriam placed her hand on her husband's arm. "Oh, John, didn't I tell you?" She gave a nervous laugh. "Silly me. I must have forgotten to mention that Johannes has agreed to buy Troyers' General Store and the *haus*, as Hannes says he will marry one of the *dochders*."

John's expression changed from curiosity to disbelief. He turned toward Hannes and simply stared at him.

Miriam, however, seemed oblivious to her husband's reaction. "*Ja*, Hannes said he would do just that, but he wants only to consider the one who baked that pie."

The shock in John's face intensified as he looked from Hannes to Johannes and then to Linda. "Is this true?"

Johannes gave a little shrug. "The boy's insistent."

Hannes nodded. "Indeed I am."

"As for the store and *haus*, Linda and I signed all the paperwork this morning, didn't we now?" Johannes glanced at Linda who didn't respond. She stood there as if still shell-shocked at how the evening was transpiring.

John King appeared stunned. "To marry someone because of a pie? Sure seems like a strange arrangement."

Miriam clucked her tongue. "I reckon people have married for even more peculiar reasons, John. Of all people, you should know that. Why, you counsel most of the married folk in this town!"

But John was appearing increasingly unsettled. "A pie as a reason to marry? Why, I've never heard of such a thing!"

Miriam, however, was undeterred. Quickly, she stood up and approached Ella, reaching for her arm. "*Kum*, Ella. Let me go with you into the kitchen. I have a curiosity about this famous apple crisp pie, anyway. Mayhaps I might keep you girls company, *ja*? I'd love to watch how it's made."

Without waiting for anyone to argue otherwise, Miriam guided Ella away from the others on the porch and into the kitchen, but not before Ella caught the suggestion of a smile on Hannes's face as he watched her leave.

Chapter Twenty-Six

Ninety minutes later, two of the pies were on the table, and Drusilla and Anna each stood behind one of them. Neither of Ella's stepsisters looked as confident as they had at the charity auction. Ella, however, felt more nervous than either of them looked. What on earth was going to happen when Hannes tasted the two pies made by Drusilla and Anna?

As Hannes walked into the room, his father and uncle following close behind, Ella noticed that Linda lingered near the doorway. For the first time in Ella's memory, her stepmother remained unusually quiet.

Hannes kept a pleasant smile on his face as he approached the table. Everyone watched him as his eyes scanned the pies, and to his credit, his expression never wavered.

Ella imagined that was no easy task.

John King, however, did not mask his thoughts. One look at the pies, and he was obviously taken aback. He made a face as he said, "What on earth . . . ?" He left the sentence unfinished, his manners catching up to his surprise.

The first pie had an uneven crust, the edges broken in some places, while in others they were burned. Some of the filling had dribbled down the side of the glass pie plate and left black marks, making the entire dessert look amateurish and inedible. John King didn't need to be a master baker to see that!

The second pie was grossly shaped, with large and bulbous chunks of apple peeking through the broken, crumbly topping. Unlike the first pie, this one barely looked like it had a crust at all. It was so thin that the filling had bubbled over the edges, burying it in a sea of dark, sticky goop.

"Oh!" The deacon's eyes flew to look first at Drusilla and then at Anna. "Are these your pies?"

They both nodded their heads, clearly proud of their creations.

"Oh, my." John looked at his wife in disbelief. "And they just baked these pies? Tonight?"

As if immune to the dreadful-looking pies on the table, Miriam gave a delighted smile. "Oh, *ja,* John. I was in here just gabbing away and watching the whole pie-making process. How interesting," she said cheerfully, "to see the different ways one can make an apple crisp pie!"

From the doorway, Linda groaned.

"And this is this same pie you both claim you made for the charity auction?" John asked the two girls, his tone displaying his disbelief.

Neither Drusilla nor Anna answered. Instead, they looked to their mother for guidance. None came.

"Of course it is!" Miriam said cheerfully in response

to her husband's question. "What do you think? That they would *lie* to the entire congregation?" She gave him a disapproving look. "Honestly, John, whatever are you suggesting?"

John frowned and directed his next question to Ella. "And your pie?"

She gestured toward the oven. "It's still baking. There wasn't enough room for all three at once," she explained.

"I see."

Miriam clapped her hands together. "Now, isn't this exciting? Such suspense!"

Ella noticed that Johannes remained silent, watching the whole scene unfold with an amused expression on his face. John looked confused, and Linda, who hadn't moved from the doorway, appeared beyond miserable.

Miriam, however, remained in a buoyant mood. She took ahold of Hannes's arm and gave him a gentle push in the direction of the pies. "Why don't you go on, Henry? Get started on tasting these *wunderbarr gut* pies, *ja*?"

Slowly, Hannes approached the table. He stood in front of the first pie and leaned down, inhaling deeply. Ella could hardly imagine how awful it smelled. Burned pie crust was never a pleasant scent. "Why, this smells almost identical to the pie from last weekend," he declared.

Ella frowned. Surely he was jesting! However, Drusilla suddenly became much more confident in her baked creation. Puffing out her chest, Drusilla gave Anna a smug look, as if to say, *I told you he liked me better.*

Patiently, Hannes waited for Drusilla to cut the pie and put a piece onto a plate. It fell apart on the plate, some of the apple mixture trickling down the side and plopping onto the tabletop. She didn't seem to notice that she had made a mess. Instead, with great fanfare, Drusilla handed the plate to Hannes, a foolish smile plastered upon her face.

"*Danke*, Drusilla. This looks quite"—he paused—"appealing."

Once again, Drusilla beamed with pride.

With his fork, Hannes cut through the pie. Or, rather, he attempted to cut through the pie. "What's this?" he asked as he tried again, forcing the fork into the pastry.

But the fork met with resistance.

He glanced at Drusilla and gave a short, bewildered laugh. "Seems to be . . . something wrong here." Using the fork, he pushed aside the top layer of crumbs and exposed the problem: apple peels were mixed in with the apples.

With his fingers, he lifted one up and held it before his eyes. "How interesting."

Drusilla gave him a pleased smile. "I thought it would add some extra flavoring."

Without commenting, Hannes placed the peel onto the side of the plate and managed to find an apple to taste. But as soon as he put it in his mouth, he began coughing and turned his back to the table. Ella thought she saw him spit out the contents of his mouth.

"What's wrong?" Miriam asked.

Ella quickly moved to the sink and fetched the still-coughing Hannes a glass of water. She hurried to his side, handing him the glass.

Still coughing, Hannes drank the water and took a moment to compose himself. Finally, he managed to say one word that explained Drusilla's fatal mistake. "Salt."

Taking a step backward, Ella pressed her lips together

and shut her eyes. She almost giggled but managed to suppress it. *The poor man,* she thought. She didn't know what, exactly, Hannes was up to with this little contest, but she certainly hoped he survived long enough to taste her pie.

Behind Hannes, John King's brow furrowed, and he began to pay closer attention to what was happening, the horrified expression on his face changing into one of comprehension that something was definitely amiss.

Next it was Anna's turn. Now that Drusilla had clearly lost the baking contest, Anna appeared much more confident. Eagerly, she cut a piece of her lumpy-looking pie for Hannes and placed it on the plate. The apples dripped away from the crust as she handed it to him.

Apprehensively, he glanced at it. "No peels?"

Smiling, Anna shook her head. "No peels."

"No salt?"

For once, Anna seemed to have triumphed over her sister. "No salt."

Hannes looked relieved.

As he had done with Drusilla's, Hannes made a big display of smelling the pie and commented that this, too, smelled almost exactly like the pie from the contest. He reached for a fresh fork and hesitated for a brief moment before he took a piece. Ella held her breath as she waited for him to taste it.

The first thing that went wrong was that the apple slices were far too big. He withdrew a large chunk of apple that stuck to the fork. Holding it up, he stared at it. Then, in an attempt to be gracious, he put it back on the plate and sliced through it with his fork so that it was smaller. It slid across the plate a few times before he managed to cut it.

Slowly, he lifted it to his mouth.

In even less time than he had with Drusilla's, Hannes promptly spit the apple back onto the plate, not even bothering to turn his back this time. He also didn't wait for his aunt to inquire as to what he thought of the pie. Instead, he ran directly to the sink, turned on the faucet, and quickly guzzled not one but two glasses of water.

"What on earth . . . ?" John King put his hands on his hips and stared at his nephew.

Hannes held his hand over his mouth. His cheeks were flushed brilliant red, and his eyes watered. "Hot." He looked up, a tear falling from one eye. "Too hot."

"How could it possibly be so hot?" John asked, reaching for a fork to taste it himself.

"No!" Hannes crossed the floor in two steps and snatched the fork from his uncle's hand. Then he turned to Anna. "Did you put cayenne pepper in that pie?"

Anna's eyes widened, and she looked at Drusilla, who, despite her own cooking error, seemed satisfied that her sister had made one, too. "I thought I was supposed to," she said in a hushed voice.

"Oh, Anna," Miriam said, shaking her head. "Cinnamon, not cayenne. How could you make such a mistake?"

"I . . . I . . ." She stared wildly at her mother, and then at Ella. "I . . . misplaced the cookbook. I couldn't find it."

Miriam walked over to the bookshelves by the sofa. "You mean this cookbook?" She withdrew a book and lifted it so that everyone could see it. "Or this one?" She held up a second one. "Where else would a cookbook be, Anna, but on the bookshelves?"

Angrily, John turned to face Hannes. "I don't know what's going on here, but it's quite clear that you are not obligated to go through with any agreement you made. It appears you've been misled, Hannes." He shifted his eyes to look at Linda. "I'm beginning to question all of the Troyers' behavior—yours and your daughters'—and you can be quite certain that this will be discussed with the church leaders—"

"Wait, John," Miriam interrupted him, and she pointed to Ella. "You forgot that there's one more pie to taste!"

"Oh, nonsense!" He waved his hand at her. "Hasn't our nephew already suffered enough?"

But Hannes was adamant.

"A deal is a deal, right, Deacon?" he asked his uncle. "Why, Linda and Daed worked awfully hard on the paperwork this morning, going over numbers and drawing up a contract. Doesn't seem right to just toss away all of that hard work—and opportunity—without finishing my end of the bargain. That would be akin to lying, and we all know how lying is a sin, right?"

All eyes watched as Ella made her way to the oven and opened the door. Delicious cinnamon and apple smells filled the room. She reached for a hot pad and bent down to remove the pie. As she lifted it, she waved her free hand over the top.

"Be careful. It's hot," she said as she set the pie upon a pot holder before Hannes. "And not from cayenne," she whispered to him.

His lips twitched as if stifling a laugh.

Carefully, Ella cut into the pie. Compared to the other two pies, hers was a vision of pie perfection. The top was golden brown, and not one drop of the filling had burned the pan.

Ella glanced at the deacon, who, once again, looked mystified. She followed his gaze as he looked at Drusilla and Anna, both of whom had backed away from the table and appeared miserable. And then John

King looked at Linda, and his scowl deepened. She, too, looked miserable, as if she wanted to escape her own house.

Only it wasn't her house any longer, Ella remembered. She had signed it over to Johannes, along with the store, earlier that very morning.

Hannes cleared his throat, and she returned her attention to him.

"I'm eager to try your apple crisp pie," he said softly, as if he had read her mind and wanted to bring her back to the task at hand.

Carefully, she cut a piece and, once again, took a moment to wave her hand over the top. When she finally handed the plate to Hannes, she saw him smile. A real smile. She had almost forgotten what it was like to be swept into his blue eyes, as if diving into the crystal clear waters of a pond on a hot summer's day. It dawned on her that Hannes Clemens knew exactly what he was doing, and she suddenly began to realize that she never should have doubted him.

Lifting the pie to his nose, he made a great show of inhaling the apple scent. "Ah. Perfection. Just like the one last week." He cut into the pie and took a short piece. Before he brought it to his lips, he blew on it, heeding Ella's warning about the temperature.

At last, he pursed his lips and made eye contact with Ella as he took the first bite. The room was quiet as he chewed, and everyone waited to see what would happen.

Setting down the plate, Hannes nodded his head. "It's perfect. Just like the pie I bought at the auction. Exactly as I suspected," he whispered to her. "*Nee*, as I *knew*." He winked at her. "And now *they* know, too."

"Well?"

Hannes turned around and looked directly at his uncle. "It *is* the same pie as last weekend."

John King scratched the back of his neck. "Surely that can't be! Ella wasn't even there!"

"*Nee*, she wasn't." Miriam spoke up and walked over to Ella's side. She slipped her arm around Ella's shoulders and turned a stern eye to Linda. "And I suspect I know why. But perhaps we ought to hear from Linda exactly why Ella was not at the charity auction."

The color drained from Linda's face. "She . . . she didn't want to go."

Miriam's eyes narrowed. "Then why would she have made a pie, Linda? And why would your *dochders* claim to have made it when my nephew bought it?"

Hannes pursed his lips. "I seem to recall that Linda herself claimed the same thing."

The deacon frowned. "I must say that I'm a bit confused by whatever is happening here." John King was a fair man—one of the reasons he had been nominated for the deacon position. "I am, however, curious to learn more." He turned around to look at Linda. "Perhaps you'd care to enlighten me?"

"I . . . I have no idea what happened," Linda stammered. She glanced at her daughters. Their faces were almost as pale as her own. "Surely there must be some trickery here."

Hannes moved over to stand beside Ella and for the first time spoke rather sharply. "If there is trickery here, it was made by your hand."

Linda's mouth opened as if she was about to argue with him, and then she shut it tight. After what had just transpired, even Linda must know that there was no way to avoid disclosing her role in the deception played upon Hannes and his father.

"Henry?" John King gave him a warning look. "That's quite an accusation."

Quickly, Miriam intervened. She walked forward and placed her arm on her husband's arm. "John, mayhaps we should move outside, where Linda and her *dochders* can explain exactly what has happened." She gave a stern look of warning to Linda. "And I'd be happy to fill in some details, should anything be omitted."

Johannes cleared his throat. "*Ja*, that might be a right *gut* idea. Especially since the store and this very *haus* are now my property, I'd like to find out what duplicity there may have been in Linda's business dealings." He gestured with his head toward Hannes and Ella. "However, from what my son has told me, I suspect these two young folk might want a private moment to discuss a few things."

Stunned by the turn of events, Ella could only watch as, reluctantly, everyone cleared out of the kitchen, Linda and her daughters with their heads hanging down and Miriam with hers held high. She could hardly believe that she had just witnessed the ruination of her stepmother, but as the door shut behind them, she knew that Linda and her daughters had only themselves to blame for their undoing.

Chapter Twenty-Seven

Only when the door shut and she was standing alone in the kitchen with Hannes did Ella find the courage to turn and face him.

"How . . . how did you know that I had baked that particular pie for the auction?" she whispered as he reached for her hands. Gently he held them, his thumb caressing her skin, as he stood before her. She felt a shiver run along her arms. No one had ever held her hand before, and while it felt strange at first, she also realized that it felt wonderful at the same time.

Hannes gave her a warm smile, his blue eyes meeting hers. He stared at her with so much emotion that she felt her insides warm. "How did I know?" he repeated in a soft, tender tone. "Perhaps the question should be 'How *couldn't* I have known?'"

She gave him a questioning look.

"Oh, Ella, it wasn't that hard."

But she persisted.

"*Ja, vell,* then . . ." Gently, he released her hands and ran his fingers through his hair. His dark curls drooped over his forehead. "Remember that I saw the basket you were carrying that day to the charity event."

"You carried it yourself," she pointed out.

"*Ja*, I did, didn't I?" Another smile. "Obviously, I knew that one of the items inside *must* be yours. And when I told Miriam that I saw you carrying a basket to deliver the baked goods for the event, she asked me to describe the basket. It wasn't hard, for yours was the only one that contained three baked goods for the auction. She set aside your basket and made certain that those items were the last to be auctioned off."

Ella placed her hands over her eyes, embarrassed that she hadn't figured that out. "Of course! She was the one giving the pies to John for auctioning." What didn't make sense, however, was why Miriam would do such a thing in the first place.

Once again, Hannes reached up to take hold of her hands and remove them from her eyes. There was a glow on his face. Clearly he was delighted with the unraveling of this mystery, which had finally exposed the perpetual wrongdoing of Linda and her daughters.

"But there's more," he said. "You know that I bought all three items. I figured that I would rather buy all three than miss out on yours. It was clear from your sisters' reactions which item each had donated. Drusilla claimed her lazy-daisy oatmeal cake, and Anna claimed her poor man's cake. Appropriate naming of them; I must commend you. But the third item . . . At first, no one claimed the apple crisp pie, but both of your sisters—"

"Stepsisters," she corrected gently.

"*Ja*, stepsisters. They *both* claimed that pie."

"So you knew?"

He nodded. "I suspected, *ja*. And when I didn't see you at the auction, I had a hunch that something had gone awry at home with Linda. I suspected that she had kept you at home so that you would have no chance to compete with her own daughters."

Ella bit her lip, wanting to tell him about what had actually happened that night. Instead, she chose to remain respectful of her stepmother. After all, Hannes already knew the most important thing: she *had* wanted to go to the auction, but hadn't been permitted to attend.

"That's when I suspected that her *dochders* would do something dishonorable and claim that they, not you, had baked that last pie." He raised an eyebrow and gave her a sideways glance. "Although, after tonight's baking contest, I can only surmise that you baked all three desserts. Is that true?"

Reluctantly, Ella nodded.

"Your kindness certainly knows no boundaries, Ella Troyer," he said sternly but kindly. "But in the future, I will hope that you will know that doing good and being kind should never come at such a high price that you sacrifice so much of yourself." He gave her a look of reproach. "Especially when it benefits those who are not only unappreciative but too selfish and lazy to help themselves."

"I never thought of it that way," she whispered. "My mother told me to always do good and be kind." She gazed at him, fighting the tears that threatened to fill her eyes. "It was the last thing she told me, her dying wish, and, ever since then, I've done everything in my power to honor it."

Hannes digested her words and then, as if coming to a realization, he raised his eyebrows. "Now it makes sense," he said softly. "No wonder they took such advantage of you." Slowly, he pulled her into his arms, embracing her tightly. "Oh, my dear Ella, such a life you have lived with those women. How unkind and unfair they have been to you."

With her cheek pressed against his shoulder, Ella shut her eyes. She wished this moment would never end. When was the last time anyone had comforted her? For the first time in years, she felt a sense of joy that filled her entire body.

When he finally loosened his hold on her, he pulled back and looked into her face. "Ella, I wasn't surprised that Drusilla and Anna claimed the pie, nor was I surprised when Linda supported their deception. In fact, I had hoped they would do just that."

Startled by his confession, Ella couldn't help asking, "Why is that?"

"Because they did it in front of the entire congregation and the church leaders." Hannes's expression sobered. "Lying to everyone is one thing, bad enough in its own right. But to mislead and cheat makes the first sin even worse. If I had called them out on it, spoken up to defend your efforts and expose their dishonesty, it would have given Linda a chance to shield herself and her *dochders* from answering to the church leaders. Miriam and I came up with this plan to expose them in a way that could not be denied or argued."

Ella frowned. "I don't understand."

"Don't you?" He took a step away from her and put his hands behind his back. Slowly he began pacing the floor. "When you didn't show up, I spoke quietly to Miriam. We suspected that something like this would happen . . . I wasn't certain to what extent they would go to lie to everyone. But I had to pretend interest in the two *dochders*. Oh, Ella, that evening when my *daed* and I visited and I had to focus on Drusilla and Anna, how my heart ached. I could only pray that you would remember my words." Abruptly, he stopped and turned toward her. "Did you?"

"Your words?"

"*Ja*, the ones that I said to you before I left Echo Creek that one day. Did you remember that I had told you that sometimes things weren't what they seemed?"

Ella's mouth opened, just a little, as she remembered. Earlier that very evening she had recalled those words, but she had not thought of them when Hannes and his father had visited earlier in the week.

As if he realized that she had, indeed, remembered, Hannes nodded. "That's right. I could only pray that you knew that everything would sort itself out. Paying attention to them was increasingly hard to do, especially with all that I knew and when I only wanted to take you in my arms and tell you the truth." He paused and looked toward the ceiling. "Perhaps that, too, was deceitful, and I will pray to God for forgiveness."

"I'm sure he will pardon you for such a slight," Ella whispered.

"But I couldn't tell you the truth, not then. For we had to wait and expose your stepmother and her *dochders* here, in your own kitchen, in front of the deacon, where they could not manipulate or lie their way out of it." Hannes took a small intake of breath. "I had to wait until given the opportunity for their actions to contribute to their own demise in front of the deacon himself."

Suddenly, it dawned on Ella that, right now, as she was speaking in private with Hannes, Deacon King was learning the truth . . . the awful reality of what had been going on in the Troyers' home. The Amish church did not take kindly to such sinful behavior. "What will happen to them?" she asked.

"Surely they will face the *Meidung*."

Shunning? Ella found herself breathing hard as she began to panic. How could she live in the house of a shunned family? She wouldn't be able to talk to them, eat with them, have any interactions with them. And how would Linda react? Certainly she would blame *her* rather than reflect on her own role in her fall from grace.

Hannes seemed to read her mind. "Never you mind, Ella. It was her own doing. With the store already sold to my *daed*, and the house along with it, you will never have to deal with Linda Troyer and her awful *dochders* again."

"Where will they go?" Ella suddenly exclaimed. "They'll be homeless!"

"*Nee*, Ella." Solemnly, he shook his head. "That is not our way. But, once again, I'm impressed by your willingness to overlook the abuse you have suffered at their hands and show concern for their well-being. My *daed* will permit them to remain in the house. He will give them a week, maybe two, to find alternate housing. Hopefully in another town, far away from Echo Creek, so that you will not have to be reminded of their mistreatment of you."

Ella could hardly believe what she was hearing. "And your *daed* knows about all of this?"

"Indeed he does. I shared your story with him. It didn't take much to convince him to go along with our plans to liberate you. Besides, when I found the secret message you gave to me . . ."

His voice trailed off, and Ella stared at him, bewildered. "What secret message?"

"The one you put into the pie."

She had no idea what he was talking about.

Chuckling, Hannes reached into his pocket and withdrew something that he promptly placed into her hand. "I found this in the pie."

Ella frowned and looked down at her hand. The glass figurine! She caught her breath and looked up at him. "What on earth . . . ?"

A laugh escaped his lips. "When I went home with the pies, I found it baked inside, near one of the edges."

Horrified, Ella covered her face with her hands. "I'm so terribly sorry," she whispered, wondering what he must think of her carelessness. He had been so thoughtful to purchase such a pretty gift for her, and she had lost it! And in such a foolish way. "I'm so embarrassed."

He sounded genuinely bewildered by her statement. "Whatever for?"

Removing her hands, she gave him an apologetic look. "It must have fallen off the window ledge! How irresponsible of me. And here I thought that, mayhaps, one of my stepsisters had taken it."

Hannes sighed in an overly dramatic way, a mischievous twinkle in his blue eyes. "And here I thought you were sending me a secret message! Or perhaps it was the secret ingredient."

"The secret ingredient?"

"You mentioned that you baked your mother's recipe, one that had a secret ingredient."

"Oh, Hannes, I'm terribly sorry. It was truly an accident."

With a look of seriousness, he tilted his head and studied her. Despite his somber expression, there was something soft and compassionate about the way he looked into her face. "Mayhaps I was mistaken and you aren't interested in running that general store with me after all."

Speechless, Ella could only stand before him, her mouth slightly open in surprise. Run the store? What, exactly, was he trying to say?

"Ella," he said as he reached out for her hands. He held them as he gazed into her face, his blue eyes moving ever so slightly as he spoke. "Surely you don't think that all of this was orchestrated for any other reason than getting the store back into the hands of its rightful owner?"

"Orchestrated?"

He nodded his head. "My *aendi* . . . she helped me plan this whole thing."

At this news, Ella frowned. What could Miriam have to do with all of this? While she had known Miriam all of her life, she had very infrequent interactions with the deacon's wife, except on church Sundays. "Miriam?"

Hannes gave a little laugh. "*Ja,* isn't that amazing? A month or so ago, she told me about the problems at the store. She had known that Daed and I were looking for such an opportunity. At first, we arranged for our vendor, the clock maker, to come to talk with Linda. But you and I both know how that went."

Oh, Ella remembered that. The whole consignment issue and Linda's fussing over the product placement in a strange aisle and then arguing with Hannes when he made the suggestion to move them near the other household goods.

"When the clock maker first came, he, too, encountered difficulties with Linda. When he reported the situation to me, Daed sent me right away to find out what type of Amish person was running such an operation. On my first trip to Echo Creek, I stayed with the Kings and went to worship with them. I heard the most beautiful voice singing 'Das Loblieb,' and when I looked over and saw this beautiful young woman singing with all of her heart, lifting her voice to God, I knew that she was the woman for me."

His words caught her off guard. *Oh please,* she silently prayed, *let this not be a dream, and if it is, may I never wake up.*

"I returned home that afternoon and spoke with my *daed.* He sent me back later that next week. And wouldn't you know it? As I was walking through town, I heard that same voice singing from the banks of a hidden pond. Later, when I returned to Miriam's *haus,* I mentioned running into a lovely young Amish woman named Ella. Miriam didn't tell me that you were Linda's stepdaughter. But she did speak highly of your character. I took that as her approval for me to pursue you. She never mentioned you again, at least not right away. I suspect she wanted us to find each other, if that was God's will."

Suddenly, everything became clear. Miriam asking Ella to help serve the food to the men's table at church when Hannes was there that second time. Miriam showing up for Scrabble that same evening and insisting that Ella be allowed to leave to go socialize. Miriam arriving unannounced to help her finish her chores on the day of the charity auction.

"I never suspected a thing . . ." Ella's voice was barely audible.

"Neither did I," Hannes admitted. "That day when I learned you were a Troyer, I told Miriam how horribly Linda treated you and yet that, when given the chance, you refused to say one harsh word against her. If you felt bitterness or anger, you hid it behind hard and humble work. And, unlike so many others, you certainly never tried to beguile or impress me."

A blush covered Ella's cheeks.

"When I told all of this to Miriam, she came clean and confessed that she had suspected we were well suited for each other. She had hoped we'd find each other." He chuckled as if remembering that conversation. "She's a piece of work, that woman."

Ella wasn't certain how to respond. She was still too stunned to process everything that Hannes had just confided to her.

"So the question remains, Ella," Hannes continued, his eyes meeting hers once again.

"The question?"

"*Ja*, the question of whether or not you will help me run the store that your *daed* started. You know that my *daed* already signed the paperwork to buy it, Ella, and I can think of no other woman I'd like by my side, both for business and for life."

Ella blinked as she digested his words. Was it possible that he was truly asking her to marry him? Suddenly, she felt light-headed and feared that she had misunderstood him. "Are you . . . ?"

Once again, Hannes laughed. "Oh, sweet Ella, *ja*! I'm asking you to marry me, and I don't intend to wait until November! If you say that you will, John King will announce the banns tomorrow at worship, and Miriam is prepared to host the wedding at her *haus* a week from Thursday!"

"A week from Thursday?" She could hardly believe all of this was happening, and so quickly.

He bent down so that he was on eye-level with her. "But only if you will be my *fraa*. What do you say, Ella?"

What *could* she possibly say? Who would deny the opportunity to marry such a man, one who was righteous and kind, good-hearted and lively, mysterious and perceptive, all at the same time? In the short while she had come to know Hannes, she recognized that he was different from any other man in Echo Creek. Today he had proven her to be more than correct.

"All my life," she began slowly, avoiding his penetrating gaze, "I've tried to live by the final words my *maem* said to me. 'Be kind and good, no matter what happens, for God has a plan for you.' There were times when it was so very hard to obey her final request, especially after my *daed* passed away. At times, I doubted God had a plan for me. But now I see the truth." She lifted her eyes, and through the tears that began filling them, she stared at him. "My trials and suffering have done more than make me stronger. They've led me to you."

Hannes started to smile.

"You, Hannes Clemens, are part of God's plan for me."

"So," he said slowly, drawing out the word. "Does that mean you will marry me?"

A single tear slipped from her eye. "*Ja*, Hannes Clemens." She gave a joyful laugh and raised her arms, wrapping them around his neck as she embraced him. "I'd love nothing more than to marry you!"

Epilogue

Two weeks later, Ella sat on the front porch of the house, sipping a glass of fresh meadow tea. It was the last of the mint, and there was a hint of bitterness to it. Still, she found it refreshing in the waning heat of the September evening.

"There you are!"

Hannes walked through the door and sat next to her.

Ella greeted her husband with a broad smile. "Home so soon?"

"*Ja*, indeed." He leaned over and kissed the side of her head near the edge of her prayer *kapp*. His lips lingered there, pressed against her skin, and Ella felt as if she could have stayed like that forever. When he finally pulled away, Hannes brushed his finger against her cheek. "Our first Saturday evening as a married couple. How could I possibly work late at the store?"

Sad that the brief moment of intimacy had ended too soon, she handed him her glass of tea and watched as he sipped it. A strange feeling of electricity coursed through her body. Despite the newness of everything, their marriage and now living in the house, Ella felt strangely at peace. She wondered if Hannes felt the same way.

"Is it strange for you?" she asked.

"Your tea?"

One look and she knew that he was teasing her. With a little laugh, she leaned over and nudged him. "*Nee*, goose. Being here in Echo Creek, running the store, living here . . ." She gestured at the house. "Does it seem real to you yet?"

Hannes set the glass on the side table. "I hadn't looked at it that way."

For a moment, he remained quiet, as if considering her question. That was another thing that she loved about him. He never rushed to respond, but always gave proper thought and reflection to his answers.

"*Nee*, Ella Clemens, it doesn't seem strange at all. In fact, it feels like the most real thing in the world." He reached for her hand and held it. His touch felt warm and wonderful, something that she knew she could never get enough of. He gave her hand a gentle squeeze. "Sitting here with you on your parents' porch." He paused before correcting himself. "I mean *our* porch, for this is *our* home now. *Ja*, this is more than real." Gently, he squeezed her hand. "It's *right*."

Ella looked down at his hand, loving the sight of their entwined fingers. Just being near him made her feel alive. For too long, she had been alone, untouched and unloved. In all of her years, she had never dreamed that she would be loved by anyone the way that Hannes loved her. Even more importantly, she had never thought that she could love someone as much as she loved this wonderful man seated beside her.

"And what about for you?" he asked. "Does this seem odd?"

Leave it to Hannes to always think about her feelings, too. Ella wondered if she'd ever get used to someone caring about what she thought and felt. "*Nee*, it does not." She shook her head. "Everything feels so perfect."

"Everything?"

She didn't want to admit that she tried to *not* think about Linda and her daughters. Whenever she did, Ella felt a bittersweet sense of fulfillment. Despite the sense of pity over her stepfamily's fall from grace, Ella was surrounded with so much joy that she rarely thought about them. She didn't want to ruin the happiness that filled her heart. Instead, she wanted to just focus on the positive—especially the fact that, just two days before, she had married the most wonderful of men.

"Oh *ja*, everything. Especially our wedding." She sighed dreamily. "It was just perfect."

The three-hour-long service, held in Miriam's house, had been followed by a whole afternoon of feasting and singing. The day had passed far too quickly for Ella. Even when she had sat at the *eck* table to sample the different desserts that people had brought for the celebration, with Hannes by her side, she had hardly been able to believe that he was now her husband.

And, of course, the fact that they were living in the only house she had ever known just added to the fairy-tale ending.

He lifted her hand to his lips and kissed it. "A more perfect day never existed."

For a long moment, they sat in silence.

"But, Ella, my question was how are *you* doing? With everything that's happened . . ."

It was true. So much had happened over the past few weeks. Ella's life had completely changed—and for the better. But that wasn't the case for her stepmother and stepsisters. Even though Ella tried not to think about them, she couldn't help but feel some sorrow for their plight. "I'm still trying to digest that the church leaders moved so quickly to shun Linda."

"And her daughters," Hannes reminded her.

A momentary look of sorrow crossed her face. "*Ja*, Drusilla and Anna, too. I'm grateful that Miriam let me stay with her while Linda and her daughters moved out."

The Saturday night when Hannes had proposed, Miriam had insisted that Ella stay in their home. John King had readily agreed, for which Ella was filled with gratitude. After the events of that evening, she could hardly imagine what life would have been like in the house with Linda and her daughters, knowing they were undoubtedly to be shunned.

And they had been shunned, indeed.

The very next day at worship, after the bishop had announced that Ella would marry Hannes, the congregation had gathered for an emergency meeting at which the fate of Linda, Drusilla, and Anna was decided. With the store and house sold, there had been no reason for them to stay in Echo Creek.

As soon as they had moved out, Hannes had insisted on having the entire house repainted so that everything would be fresh when he brought home his new bride. Several people even donated new quilts and furniture for the master bedroom, removing the old items so that the house was devoid of any lingering reminders of Linda.

She felt him reach up and touch her chin, forcing her to look him in the eyes. "Don't forget that they tried to deceive everyone. And once everything was exposed, what else could the church leaders do?"

Ella nodded. "*Ja*, they did deceive a lot of people for

a long time, didn't they?" She gave a soft sigh. "I wonder where they have gone. Where they are living."

"Miriam heard tell that they're staying with a Mennonite family outside of Liberty Falls. Exchanging housecleaning and cooking for room and board."

Linda cleaning a house? Drusilla and Anna cooking? Ella couldn't help but laugh at such an idea. "Oh help!"

Even Hannes smiled. "Sometimes God has a sense of humor, too, *ja*?"

"I'm just happy that John King was here to witness the whole pie-baking disaster. That was rather clever of you, Hannes Clemens."

He dipped his head at her. "*Danke, fraa.*"

"I still don't understand how you and Miriam came up with such an elaborate scheme." Teasingly, she gave him a sideways glance. "Very sneaky, I must say."

"Ah." Hannes lifted his finger as if to indicate he was making a point. "Sneaky, but necessary, I'm afraid. You know that simply telling the church leaders would've served no purpose. The three of them had proven repeatedly that they'd lie over insignificant things such as who baked a pie. Without doubt, if someone can lie over a small thing, they will certainly be capable of lying about more important things, especially if lying might save them from being shunned."

She hadn't looked at it that way. "I reckon that's true."

"And Miriam worried that they would point the finger of blame at you." He squeezed her hand. "And neither one of us wanted that to happen, for we knew that you, in your obedience to God and his commandments, would never say a harsh word about your stepmother."

"Well, all's well that ends well, I suppose."

"'Woe unto the wicked! it shall be ill with him: for the reward of his hands shall be given him,'" Hannes quoted as he stood up and gently pulled her to her feet. "And while they may have gotten their just reward, I'm much more interested in getting *my* just reward for having worked hard all day!"

Ella gave him a quizzical look. "*Your* just reward?"

He led her to the kitchen door and opened it to let her pass through first. "Why, sampling whatever you have cooking in the kitchen, of course!" he exclaimed. "Everything smells delicious, Ella. I could hardly force myself to bypass the kitchen to find you on the porch."

She blushed at the compliment. "I've even made you a surprise for dessert."

He raised an eyebrow. "Let me guess? Apple crisp pie?" When she nodded, he laughed. "And did you make it with your *maem*'s secret ingredient? The one that you've never shared with me before?"

Ella nodded just once. "I most certainly did, Hannes Clemens. "

"And are you going to tell me what it is?" Before she could answer, Hannes whispered, "If you do, mayhaps I have a special surprise for *you,* too."

"What kind of surprise?"

"First you tell me."

She gave him a long look, studying him as if deciding whether or not to tell him. Then, after a few long seconds, she leaned over and whispered in his ear. "It's love, Hannes. The secret ingredient is to make it with love for the person who will be eating it. And I most certainly used that ingredient when I baked it for the charity auction, for the supper with your father and the Kings, and tonight. I will always bake that pie, and everything else for you, with that one special and very secret ingredient."

For once, Hannes appeared speechless.

Delighted, Ella couldn't help but give a little laugh. "And you thought it was my leaving the figurine in the pie."

"Why, you!" He wrapped his arms around her and pulled her close, giving her a soft kiss. "I like that special, secret ingredient, Ella Clemens. And I'll never tell a soul, I promise."

"Now, you have a surprise for me, *ja*? What is it, my dear husband?"

Gently he released her. "Indeed I do. After supper, my dear *fraa*, I am taking you for a buggy ride. You promised that you'd ride with me, did you not? That night after the singing you didn't go to. Well, you've yet to make good on that promise."

Ella tried to hide her smile. "Are you asking me to ride with you in your buggy?" she teased playfully.

"Today, tomorrow . . ." Hannes said, then leaned over and pressed his lips gently against hers. "And every day for the rest of our lives."

Ella's Special Recipes

Ella's Bread

1½ tablespoons active dry yeast
2 cups warm water (110°)
1 tablespoon brewer's yeast
½ cup organic sugar
1 tablespoon salt
2 tablespoons vegetable oil
6 cups all-purpose flour

In a large bowl, dissolve the active dry yeast in warm water. Let sit until it bubbles.

Add the brewer's yeast, sugar, salt, and oil and mix together.

Add 3 cups flour, one at a time, and beat until smooth. Stir in more flour to form a soft dough.

Turn the dough onto a floured surface and knead until the dough is smooth and elastic.

Place the dough ball into a bowl greased with oil. Turn the dough one time in order to coat the top with grease.

Cover with a clean, dry cloth and set in a warm place to rise.

After 90 minutes, the dough should double in size.

Punch dough down before turning it onto a lightly floured surface.

Divide the dough into two equal balls and shape into a loaf.

Place each loaf into a greased bread pan.

Cover and let rise 30–45 minutes until the loaf is doubled in size.

Bake at 350° for 30 minutes or until golden brown and bread sounds hollow when tapped. Remove from pans to wire racks to cool.

Apple Crisp Pie

FOR THE CRUST:

1⅓ cups all-purpose flour
½ teaspoon sugar
½ teaspoon salt
¼ cup unsalted butter, cut into ½-inch cubes
¼ cup frozen solid vegetable shortening, cut into ½-inch cubes
¼ cup (or more) ice water
½ teaspoon apple cider vinegar

Put cubed butter and shortening into freezer for 15 minutes.

Mix the flour, sugar, and salt together in a large bowl.

Add the butter and shortening and, using a pastry cutter, mix until it becomes crumbly.

Sprinkle the mixture with ¼ cup of water (remove ice cubes).

Add the apple cider vinegar before adding more ice water and mixing until the dough just barely begins to hold together.

Press into a pie pan and refrigerate until ready to use.

FOR THE FILLING:

5 to 6 cups thinly sliced peeled apples (Granny Smith preferred, but other types of apples work, too)
1 lemon
¼ cup butter
½ cup white sugar
¼ cup brown sugar
⅛ teaspoon nutmeg
3 tablespoons flour
2 teaspoons ground cinnamon

Squeeze the juice from the lemon and mix with the apples.

Melt the butter.

Mix both the white and brown sugar, nutmeg, flour, and cinnamon in a bowl with the butter.

Toss apples with sugar mixture to coat.

Pour into pastry.

FOR THE TOPPING:

1 cup all-purpose flour
½ cup sugar
¼ cup (packed) golden brown sugar
¼ cup rolled oats
1½ teaspoons ground cinnamon
½ teaspoon salt
6 tablespoons chilled unsalted butter, cut into ½-inch cubes

Mix flour, white sugar, brown sugar, oats, cinnamon, and salt in a separate bowl.

Use a pastry cutter to mash cold butter into the mixture until it becomes the texture of crumbs.

Spread evenly across the apples.

Bake at 350° for 40 minutes or until top is golden brown and sides are bubbling.

Poor Man's Cake

2 cups water
2 cups brown sugar
2 tablespoons solid vegetable shortening
1½ cups raisins (regular, golden, or a mixture of both)
½ teaspoon salt
½ teaspoon allspice
½ teaspoon nutmeg
1 teaspoon ground cinnamon
1 teaspoon baking soda
2 teaspoons hot tap water
3 cups all-purpose white flour

In a large saucepan, combine the brown sugar, shortening, raisins, salt, and spices in the water.

Bring to a boil and immediately remove from the heat, allowing it to cool to room temperature.

Dissolve the baking soda in 2 teaspoons of hot water.

Sift together the flour and baking soda.

Add to the batter, and mix well.

Pour into greased baking pan (9" x 13").

Bake at 350° for about 30 minutes or until a tester inserted near the center comes out clean.

Cool in the pan.

Lazy-Daisy Oatmeal Cake

Cake

1¼ cups water
1 cup rolled oats
5 tablespoons butter
1 cup white sugar
1 cup brown sugar
1 egg
1 teaspoon vanilla
1¾ cup flour
1 teaspoon baking soda
1 teaspoon ground cinnamon
¼ teaspoon ground nutmeg
¼ teaspoon salt

Heat water until boiling and then remove from heat and mix in the oats. Set aside.

In large bowl, beat butter and sugars until blended. Add the egg and vanilla and beat well.

Mix the flour, baking soda, cinnamon, nutmeg, and salt with the oat mixture. Combine with the butter, sugar, and egg mixture.

Pour the batter into an 8-inch pan.

Bake at 350° for 55 minutes or until a toothpick inserted near the center comes out clean.

Set aside while making the topping.

Topping

2 tablespoons butter
½ cup shredded coconut
½ cup brown sugar
½ cup rolled oats
3 tablespoons milk

Melt the butter.

Combine all ingredients in small bowl and mix well.

Sprinkle the mixture evenly on the top of warm cake.

Broil about 4 inches from heat for no more than two minutes or until topping is bubbly.

Cool cake in pan on wire rack.

Read on for an excerpt of
Sarah Price's next Amish romance,

Sadie: An Amish Retelling of Snow White.

Outside the window of the sitting room, the snow fell like tiny pieces of wispy cotton, covering the fields in a blanket of white. The dusty lane that led to the farmhouse slowly disappeared as Sarah Whitaker stared outside, one hand on her enlarged belly and the other holding the pieces of a baby blanket. She knew that she should be focusing on the quilt. It was *almost* finished. But the beauty of the winter's first snowfall kept her mesmerized.

Perhaps it was the pregnancy that made her so emotional. Or maybe it was the good fortune that had befallen her in the past twelve months. Regardless, she felt the sting of happy tears in her eyes, and she lifted her hand to wipe them with her fingers.

"Sarah?"

At the sound of her name, she turned from the window and smiled as her husband walked toward her. He was a large man, taller than most men in Echo Creek. And his beard was finally filling in. Gone was the patchiness of his newly married facial hair, replaced with a nice, full set of dark whiskers that covered his jawline.

He crossed the room, passing through the small kitchen and into the open sitting room, which still smelled like fresh paint and new wood. Kneeling before her, he reached for her hand and searched her face.

Sarah shivered at the warmth of his touch.

"You cold?" he asked, his bright blue eyes filled with concern.

"*Nee*," she whispered, and she gave his hand a gentle squeeze. "The fire's keeping the room warm enough, but *danke*, Jacob."

He didn't look convinced. "I can fetch more wood."

Sarah laughed softly. "I'm fine. I promise."

Such a fine husband, she thought. How had she ever managed to win his heart and hand? During her *rumschpringe*, many of the young women in Echo Creek had been eager to ride home in Jacob Whitaker's buggy. Somehow, however, Sarah had caught his eye, probably at worship service prior to her turning sixteen, for at only the second youth singing she had attended, he had laid claim to her.

During one of the breaks when the songs were put on hold so that the young people could talk with their friends or get a cool drink of lemonade, Jacob had sent his older brother, John, to where Sarah was standing with her friends in the barn. A nervous John shuffled his feet when he asked Sarah if she'd consider riding home with Jacob.

That was just the way things were done in Echo Creek.

And, with a blush on her cheeks and her eyes focused on the hay beneath her shoes, Sarah had said yes.

"How's the baby?" Jacob asked. He hesitated before he reached out and placed his hand on her stomach.

Sarah covered his hand with her own. There were so many things about Jacob that she loved. The gentle way in which he handled her was just one of them. He treated her like a precious figurine, always so gentle, as if she might break under his strong touch. And he was a strong man. Most farmers were.

"She's doing just fine," Sarah teased.

He raised an eyebrow. "She?"

Sarah nodded her head. "*Ja*, she."

Jacob tried to hide his smile. She could see that by the way the corners of his lips twitched. "Might be nice to start off with a boy, don't you think?"

"There'll be plenty of time for boys, Jacob," Sarah said in a soft voice. "But I long so much for a *dochder*, someone who can help me raise our sons and keep me company when I bake bread and can vegetables. A little girl who I can teach to sew and quilt." She glanced down at the baby blanket.

He leaned forward and kissed her hand. But as he did so, he shifted the blanket, and Sarah felt the pinch of a needle in her finger.

"Ouch!" Instinctively, she dropped the blanket and jerked her hand toward her mouth so that she could suck on the top of her thumb.

A look of horror crossed his face. "Did I do that?"

But Sarah merely shook her head. "It's one of the many dangers a woman faces when she quilts a blanket, I'm afraid," she teased. "Bound to happen again, too, so don't you fret none, Jacob."

Jacob, however, barely heard a word. Or, if he had heard, he didn't listen. Immediately, he was on his feet and hurrying to the sink. With amused eyes, Sarah watched as he took a clean dishcloth from the drawer, ran water over it, and hurried back to her side.

"You're bleeding," he said as he pulled her hand away from her mouth. Pressing the cloth to her finger, he shook his head. "I'm so clumsy sometimes," he lamented under his breath.

Sarah responded by placing her free hand on his cheek and gently guiding him to look her in the eyes. "*Nee*, Jacob. You are the kindest of men. And I can only hope that our *dochder* is just like you."

Despite the worried look on his face, he gave her a soft smile.

"She'll have your dark hair and lively blue eyes," Sarah continued in a wistful manner, her eyes slowly returning to gaze out the window. "And pretty porcelain skin the color of freshly fallen snow."

At this comment, Jacob chuckled, his fears at having hurt his wife slowly abating. "Then you'd best give me some sons soon after so that your little princess won't have to help me when it comes to harvesting the fields."

Sarah shook her head. "Oh, no! No field work for her. We can't have her skin getting all tanned and freckled, can we, now?"

This time, Jacob laughed. "A spoiled Amish girl for you? I don't think that would sit well with many people in Echo Creek. Nor will it help her land her own husband."

"*Nee*, not spoiled!" Sarah made a face at him. "That would never do, Jacob Whitaker!" Her expression softened. "*Nee*, our *dochder* will be hardworking, all right, but she'll help me in the house while your sons help you in the fields."

Jacob glanced down at her hand, which he had

wrapped in the towel. "Looks like it's stopped bleeding." His eyes traveled to the window and Sarah followed his gaze. "And the snow's sure falling harder." He gave a reluctant sigh. "Reckon I'd best be settling the livestock down for the evening, then."

He leaned over and placed a soft kiss upon her forehead. Sarah shut her eyes, savoring the moment. When he finally pulled away and left the kitchen, Sarah took a deep breath and prayed her thankfulness to God for having seen fit to grant her a place in Jacob's heart. She prayed her gratitude to God for allowing her to conceive so soon after her and Jacob's spring wedding just ten months earlier. And she prayed her hope to God for the health of her unborn child.

"One *dochder*," she whispered as she finally opened her eyes. "Just one, God. And then a whole houseful of boys for Jacob."

Oh yes. Sarah could envision her daughter, a smaller and more petite version of Jacob. She pictured the baby as she'd described her to Jacob—she'd have dark hair like his and skin the color of freshly fallen snow. Sarah glanced at her thumb and noticed a small bead of red blood at the place where the needle had pierced her skin. Ah, of course. Ruby red lips that, when she smiled, would light up every heart in the room.

Outside the window, Sarah saw Jacob's tall, lean figure, hunched over from the blowing snow, as he crossed the front yard and headed toward the barn. The snow was falling faster now, just as Jacob had said. Without a radio or television, they had no way of knowing how much snow was expected. But Sarah didn't care. There was enough food in the pantry to last them days, even weeks. They had no need to leave the small farm outside of Echo Creek, and with the baby not due for another six weeks, Sarah had no fears or worries. Jacob would take care of her and their child, regardless of whether it was a son or a daughter. Of that, Sarah was sure and certain.